Chasing Ashes

Chris,
I hope you enjoy this mystery about student journalists, then and now!
Joanne

Chasing Ashes

Joanne McLaughlin

CELESTIAL ECHO PRESS

ROSLYN, PA, U.S.A.

2023

ISBN: 978-1-951967-86-4

Cover art and design: Don Dyen

Editing: Gemini Wordsmiths, LLC

Published by
Celestial Echo Press
An imprint of Gemini Wordsmiths, LLC
P.O. Box 1191
Roslyn, PA 19001
celestialechopress.com

For Josie and Sadie,

the lights of my life.

Praise for *Chasing Ashes*

"Author Joanne McLaughlin's *Chasing Ashes* will draw readers in with a swirling tale that is as layered as its protagonist. The desperation and determination of the cast of characters burns brighter with every step as they draw closer to the truth behind a decades-old mystery."

-Benjamin Spada, author of The Black Spear series
-benspada.com

"From seasoned journalist Joanne McLaughlin, comes a novel that hits the ground running and never stops—a gripping mystery about an intriguing world, complex relationships, and the quest to reveal the secrets of the past."

-Jane Kelly, author of the award-winning Meg Daniels Mysteries
-janekelly.net

"*Chasing Ashes* is a one-sitting book, and for lovers of mystery, a story that will induce insomnia. Author Joanne McLaughlin's real-world journalism chops shine in this stylish and smoothly unfolding mystery and its characters. Her portrayal of investigative journalism, and cop methods and argot spice the story, yielding a true crime flavor. Nor are characters sacrificed on the altar of plot; rather love and loss, and, yes, subtle sex, make them all too human instead of the puzzle-solving automatons common in the mystery genre."

-Lanny Larcinese, author of *Get Bek* and *Fire in the Belly*
-lannylarcinese.com

Acknowledgments

Writing this book felt a bit like riding a bus along a route with dozens of stops. So many friends and colleagues rode with me over the years, including those who read random pieces of some version or another in critique group sessions. I owe a debt of gratitude to each of them. And now that this story has reached its destination, I must single out the individuals whose advice, expertise, patience, and very blunt criticism helped get it there.

Enormous thanks to my publishers, Ann Stolinsky and Ruth Littner of Celestial Echo Press, for seeing in this novel what I did, and to the cover artist, Don Dyen, for helping transform it from theoretical to tangible.

My earliest Beta readers, Kevin M. Smith and Rhonda Dickey, helped me find the strengths of this story and identify its flaws. Editor Lynn M. Ross smoothed the rough patches in early versions and kept me true to my vision. Amy Junod Placentra revamped my website to accommodate this new entry. Photographer Mari A. Schaefer helped me look my best. Tony Merlo offered moral support and listened when I needed to read passages aloud twenty times before I was satisfied.

I researched numerous online resources about ALS including those offered by the ALS Foundation, and read scientific papers on PubMed about the complex field of assistive speech technology. Tanya and Scott Sturgis generously lent their time and expertise to help me learn about assistive phone technologies. Any errors in the book are mine.

Finally, I must thank two of my former college roommates, Carol Corr Greis and Susan Simonian Meelhuysen, who were standing next to me the day an unexpected demonstration of religious expression passed below the balcony of our apartment. "Seems like something you could write a book about," Sue said. It took a while, but now I have.

Foreword

I've had the pleasure and privilege of working alongside Joanne McLaughlin for - well, never mind how many - years, both in the journalism trenches at the *Philadelphia Inquirer* and as fellow members of Philadelphia's acclaimed Rittenhouse Writers' Group fiction workshop. Our shared status as single moms trying to juggle demanding careers with fierce writing ambition further cemented our bond. The day job kept our kids fed; the writing workshop fed our souls.

She was even the model for a character in my first published novel, a dear friend whose killing spurred my protagonist to action. (Sorry about the murder thing, Joanne.)

And while I treasure so many aspects of our friendship, one that touches me especially deeply has been the privilege of an early look at her novels. Her trilogy, *Never Before Noon, Never Until Now,* and *Never More Human,* is like Joanne herself, whip-smart and funny, heartfelt and deeply informed. Who knew how seamlessly vampires blended into the prog-rock world? Testament to the strength of her trilogy: with each book, I wished for an accompanying Court of Cruelty soundtrack, so compellingly did she portray the undead rock stars.

Her fourth novel, *Chasing Ashes,* is both a departure from those earlier books and a leap forward.

In it, reporter Laura Cunningham takes her last shot at determining the fate of a friend who disappeared twenty-four years earlier, even as she deals with a marriage careening toward divorce and an attractive and very attentive ex-husband who just happens to be the cop who investigated the fire in which her friend went missing.

In the near-quarter-century since Kate McDonald's disappearance, Cunningham has gone from college journalism student to a Pulitzer Prize-winning investigative reporter, and now has the skills, along with the added benefit of current technology, to do her friend justice.

McLaughlin's own considerable journalism chops are on full display as she leads her protagonist through a harrowing investigation fraught with both physical and personal peril.

Laura Cunningham's wonderfully messy personal life—the cheating husband who wants to work things out, the fresh involvement of the ex now that the investigation is revived, a son from each marriage whose needs are always in conflict with the demands of the investigation—provides the flashes of humor that balance out the rising tension. Likewise, the observations of another of Laura's college friends who runs the local coffeehouse crackle with wit.

Chasing Ashes touches on social issues of the 1990s that remain relevant today, with its focus on the charismatic leader of The Challenge, the halfway house for troubled young people that went up in flames the night Kate disappeared.

Cults of personality often fail under scrutiny, and as Laura dives ever deeper into her investigation she realizes that almost nothing about The Challenge is as it originally seemed.

Which proves the maxim that every reporter learns early: If your mother says she loves you, check it out. Laura Cunningham checks things out, making for an ending that left me gasping.

-Gwen Florio is the award-winning author of eleven mystery novels and a literary stand-alone, *Silent Hearts*.
-gwenflorio.net

Chapter One

Laura
2016

No one can see where the fire singed me. My scars are well hidden. I breathe with effort, but not from smoke that seared my lungs. I ache, but not because scorched beams crushed any part of me.

My sleep-shattering, post-traumatic stress is real, and difficult to explain. I was not in the building that burned.

Google me. You'll find one Pulitzer Prize for Public Service Journalism and a dozen lesser-known awards. A Publishers Weekly *announcement that Saddington Nair Books had acquired Laura Cunningham's manuscript,* Bloodstrains. *A few follow-up press releases. Dig deeper and you'll find a divorce decree, a custody agreement, a property settlement. Though I have pretty solid stock in my professional world, my personal life needs some repair.*

What I want is to put that horrific event behind me. But I can't because they never found her. Twelve bodies, but not Kate McDonald's. And so, two young women vanished that awful day twenty-four years ago when The Challenge went up in flames. Ashes to ashes ...

My audience might stare, uncertain what to do once that oddly intimate little speech ended. Then finally, someone might applaud, and the rest might imitate. Clap for the crazy writer.

"True crime's always a hit with readers," or so everyone assured me. "True story, you're in this to right wrongs."

Publisher, publicist, national bookstore chain, a relentless choir singing, "Do it now, do it here! Today, tomorrow, every day new readers await!"

I waited, paralyzed, for too long. When the calendar flipped to that ugly milestone, the twentieth anniversary of Kate's disappearance, I knew I had to pull myself together. Pull together all the bits and pieces and interviews I'd been collecting and tell the Challenge Fire story no one else had told.

It took four more years to get here. *No more wasting time.*

Just do this, Laura, before it sucks the life out of you once and for all.

Chapter Two

Laura

Central Pennsylvania, October 2016

The familiar nausea swept over me, and the dizziness. A cup clattered next to my cheek, splashing coffee.

"Get your head off my table, Cunningham. You're a health-code citation waiting to happen."

I dared to open an eye. "I'm also your oldest friend, Baker. *Tu casa es mi casa.* My hair smells of French Roast now. Crap."

A plate crashed into my wrist, dusting my hand with cinnamon. "Eat your damn free breakfast, and get out and do what you came to do." Jane slid into the booth across from me and scowled. "You're not being waterboarded; you're reading from your new book."

"It's my publisher's own version of torture: 'This is your turf, Laura.' Hah! More like, 'We have to sell the bugger. We'll market it to the captive audience, the poor students for whom Steve Brightman will make it required reading.'"

"Return to the scene of the crime, of course. Or the alleged crime, like there's any doubt." Jane kicked me under the table. "Buck up, girl. Get it together. Do it for Kate."

Why the hell else?

The publicist was expecting me at the university's main library in an hour. Demand for tickets for the reading far exceeded expectations, so the event had been moved there from the campus bookstore. I sat up and scraped damp hair away from my mouth, gulped some tepid coffee, and licked cinnamon powder from my thumb.

Jane rattled the plate. "Is it even possible to drive the demons out after all this time? I love you and hate you for dredging up those memories, even the good ones, but I understand why you thought it was necessary. Did writing the book help?"

"Did not writing it help? Kate is still gone; Andrew Michaels might still be alive. It was my fault. …"

"Bullshit," Jane hissed. "We all knew what Kate was up to, more or less."

"More or less the part where she ran into a hell where people got killed." I drained my cup, pushed the cinnamon bun away, unable to eat. "How do I look?"

Jane polished a teaspoon with a paper napkin and held it up as a makeshift mirror. "Not like you drove more than one hundred miles from your house in Philly to get here. Not like a forty-six-year-old woman who doesn't sleep more than three hours a night, that's for sure. You always look great. It's why I despise you."

She stood and kissed the top of my head. "Go make them want to finally solve this thing, so we'll all get some peace. If anyone can do it, you can."

"Stage fright, remember? I hate speaking in public."

"You'll hate yourself more if you don't. This aisle isn't wide enough for more strenuous cheerleading, and I have other customers to take care of. So leave, Laura. Now!"

I set foot onto University Avenue for what seemed like the first time in forever, grateful for the flats I grabbed from my closet at the last minute. The downtown strip had transformed, with new apartment towers and new boutiques flanking Trilby's, the dive-bar-turned-coffeehouse Jane now owned. But on the other side of that asphalt divide …

Cold sweat dampened my underarms and my forehead. Taking baby steps, I made it to a bench off the campus mall, put my head between my legs and vomited, just missing my shoes.

Jane liked to say it had been therapeutic for her to move back to this town, that she believed Kate would turn up one day and need to see a friendly face. I had avoided this place as much as possible. Why immerse myself in Kate's absence when I couldn't get past it wherever I lived? Jane couldn't either, not really. Neither could Nick.

Oh, dear God, Nick. I prayed he would stay the hell away.

The bell tower's clock tolled 9:30. I dragged myself from the bench, hoping the publicist would have gum or mints. Something to take away the taste of my fear.

The dean of the College of Communications stepped up to a podium in the university library's packed lobby.

"If you're here today, you've heard of the fire at The Challenge. Last I looked, it was still ranking high in our search analytics, not too far below the football team, the alumni association, and a blog that reviews the local bars. So you know about the questions that surround the fire even now."

Steve Brightman paused for dramatic effect. Quite the master of ceremonies, my brother-in-law.

"*Bloodstrains* is a memoir as well as an exposé of what the authorities missed in their investigation of The Challenge fire. I was Laura Cunningham's editor for years in Philadelphia, so I can tell you this: She is a brilliant, tireless journalist with a unique perspective on what happened here in March 1992—a tragedy she reported on for this school's newspaper, the *Informed Student*—and felt personally as well. Kate McDonald,

Laura's childhood friend and college roommate, was never seen again after the fire. They were seniors when Kate died or simply vanished—neither has ever been determined. It gives me great pleasure to introduce the author of *Bloodstrains*, Pulitzer Prize winner Laura Cunningham."

I managed to stand, walk over to Steve, and let him hug me. "You got this, kiddo," he whispered. "This is your story to tell."

Tell it again, and again. I fixed my eyes on a girl wearing a blue hat with red woolen braids hanging down from the ear flaps. Then I launched into the talk I'd revised too often to count.

"Ten students were found dead on March 19, 1992, at The Challenge out on Allegheny Highway, on the grounds of this university. The Challenge was considered a haven for young people in pain because of addiction, abuse, family issues, you name it. Young adults looking for a safe space, a place where they could live and thrive. The internet was just becoming a part of our daily lives back then. Students enrolled here weren't required to have computers or email. And not everybody had cellphones. It was still possible to hide from the larger world, or to get lost in someone else's.

"Not found in the ruins of the fire—or rather, not definitively identified—were the remains of Andrew Michaels, the nondenominational preacher who founded The Challenge, or those of my friend Kate McDonald, one of the editors at the *Informed Student*, the campus newspaper. Forensics teams were divided on whether remains discovered outside the building the day after the fire belonged to Michaels, though a formal inquest later concluded they did. For Kate, no remains were a match.

"The investigation that followed, and some evidence cited in the early lawsuits that resulted from the fire, showed The Challenge to be a sham, almost a cult, and Andrew Michaels to be a charismatic figure who bent vulnerable individuals to his will. Kate McDonald walked into that world trying to find the truth behind the brutal death of a friend she believed had died at the hands of Michaels, either directly or indirectly, and hoping to bring Michaels down for the charlatan she believed him to be.

"*Bloodstrains* is Kate's story, drawn from her personal journals and articles she wrote for the *Informed Student*, as well as my own reporting based on public documents such as police reports, transcripts of the lawsuits filed by the parents of the fire victims, lab results from DNA and other tests performed by the county medical examiner's office and discussed by expert witnesses at the inquest, and other sources. What my book reveals is how so many institutions failed Kate and those ten students, their families and friends, and all of us, in the process."

I paused for just a few deep breaths to calm myself before reading from the opening chapter. Toward the back of the crowd, I spotted Steve with his brother, my husband, David Brightman, for whom fame had always been a turn-on. Depending on the success of this book, I could well be facing a second divorce, though to be honest, even the hottest bestseller might not prove to be enough to save our marriage.

In a corner behind them stood Nick Fabrizzio, my ex-husband, whose police work I was about to dissect.

Some might say *discredit*.

Chapter Three

Nick

Central Pennsylvania, 1992

Challenge Fire, suspected arson, suspected homicide, 19 March 1992

Evidence inventory #319/6a/vic13

Journal (verbatim 10 December 1991 entry) of Katharine McDonald, missing, presumed dead:

The morgue attendant pulled back the sheet. Jason's face was broken, swollen, and there was a purplish-blue indentation where his right eye should have been. His lower lip was mostly torn away, hanging by a string of skin. I gagged, grabbed on to the edge of the table in case I passed out. I stared at the body, feeling like I wanted to cry, like I should cry, but I didn't. I don't know why.

"Do you need a minute, Miss McDonald?"

"Jason Goldstein, who did this to him?" I asked the detective, someone named Fabrizzio, and a cop in uniform whose name flew past me on the half-mile drive in the squad car from my apartment. Fabrizzio nodded but said nothing. Must have been a signal that the uniformed officer should respond.

"We found ID on him, but nothing with a local address," the officer said. "We didn't want to call his family unless we were certain who he was. Your name and number were in a notebook we found at the scene, along with the words, 'Trilby's at 9.'"

"Jason didn't show up. I waited for an hour, left a note with the bartender, then went back to the *Informed Student's* office. Jason knew where to find me."

Fabrizzio dragged on a cigarette, blew a couple smoke rings. "He stood you up?"

"Wasn't a date. He was always late anyway, so, like I said, I went back to work."

"What was it, if it wasn't a date?"

"We were supposed to talk about an interview Jason had done with a girl living at The Challenge. We'd gotten tips about weird stuff happening out there, a dozen letters with Connecticut postmarks that talked about people worshiping Satan, having sexual congress with the devil, and performing ritual mutilations. I'm one of the editors at the *IS*. I assigned Jason to report the story and—"

"Calling the police didn't occur to you?"

"We thought it was a prank. Why not just go check it out? We do it all the time."

"One dead friend, beaten and carved up, is a good reason. You want to play junior reporters, fine, but whoever your pal crossed paths with last night was no amateur."

Fabrizzio, Detective Smug, just shook his head.

"The officer will drive you back to your apartment. Don't leave town, Miss McDonald. We'll be in touch. I assume someone can vouch for your whereabouts last night?"

"You think I could do something like that to Jason?"

"Just don't leave town, Miss McDonald. I mean it. Christmas break can wait a day or two, so we can catch your boyfriend's killer."

"He wasn't ..."

I stopped. There was no point arguing.

Guess I don't have much choice but to stay here for a while longer when everybody else goes home. It's not like I'm under arrest. Detective Jerk can't keep me here for too long, right?

Chapter Four

Laura

Central Pennsylvania, October 2016

Black, permanent marker ink stained the sleeve of my white blouse, and my right hand cramped from signing books. The publisher had sent five dozen, which sounded overly optimistic to me, but only three copies were still unsold. I flexed my fingers, shook my right wrist, then felt a hand clamp around it. A warm hand with a fierce grip.

"Sign one this way: 'To Damian, from his mom and dad, and Kate.' A nice keepsake, don't you think? I mean, he asks every once in a while why we broke up. He reads this, he might gain a few insights."

Nick let go and removed a book from the short stack. Someone took his twenty-five dollars and handed him a receipt.

"Damian's already read the book," I informed him. "He thought he should, in case you might want to talk about it someday."

"That changes things. How's this instead for an inscription: 'To Nick, with regret'?"

"I don't think so."

A throat cleared behind him. Nick stepped aside to let a young woman buy a copy and get my autograph. She said she'd heard of the fire but didn't realize there was still so much mystery surrounding it. Mystery, I agreed, and suffering, for all concerned. She shook my hand and promised to post a review on Goodreads.

I scanned the room for David and Steve, but they were gone, no doubt contemplating martinis and steaks at the local country club. That's where the Brightman brothers bonded.

What would they talk about, I wondered, besides my need to spill my guts about Kate and earn back the advance my publisher had given me on an initial print run of 15,000 copies?

"The Bright Lights split right after your reading. Heard it all before?" Nick paged through the last book on the sales table.

I noticed my publicist approaching him. "Do you want that one too? I'm Karla, by the way, with Saddington Nair Books. You must be Nick Fabrizzio, I recognize you from the newspaper photos we reproduced for this hardcover edition. Lovely to meet you after ... well, it feels like we've already met." Karla thrust her hand out for him to shake.

Nick fished out his wallet, took Karla's hand, and put two twenties into it. "Yes, I'll take this one too, for, um, my attorney."

I had sent him a galley copy of *Bloodstrains* – God, I hated that title – and had asked him repeatedly to tell me if he thought it unfairly represented him. Did he even read it? Everything in the book was true, every blessed detail about the investigation and his part in it.

One detail, I left out: that he had slept with Kate. Nick did everything by the book, but before the fire he had gotten closer than he should to a young reporter. *And then a second young reporter*, I imagined him reminding me as I watched him go.

"Are you okay?" Karla shook a bottle of ibuprofen at me.

"A headache. Thanks." I popped two without water. *A really big headache, he always was.*

"You just got a text." Karla pointed to my phone. It was David, saying he'd booked a room at the Inn of the Alleghenies, the swank place out by the country club. "Some alone time for us, since Drew and Damian will be with my mother. No need to drive home tonight, so we can do dinner with Steve. Invite Jane."

Witnesses were a good idea, in case one of us tried to strangle the other. And Steve's latest divorce was almost final, so why not invite Jane? Obviously, the Brightman boys hoped to get lucky tonight. Given today's crowd, I'd say David was aroused before his brother had finished introducing me. Why not enjoy a rare moment of his appreciation?

I texted Jane*:* "7:30 at the restaurant at the Inn. Wear something slinky." I needed something slinky of my own to wear. On my way to the library, I had passed a dress shop. I could stop there.

In the library office where I had left my bag and coat, I changed from the heels I wore for the reading back into my flats. I waved goodbye to Karla, whose job also included settling accounts with the bookstore folks.

Nick caught up to me before I made it off campus.

"Let me buy you dinner. You haven't eaten anything all day, have you?" He knew me too well.

"Sorry, I'm dining with the Brightman boys. I need to buy a dress fit for the midweek cocktail crowd at the Inn." I pushed past him.

"We need to talk, Laura."

"We've talked about our son and your attorney. I'm not seeing any other topics of mutual interest here."

"Dinner suggests you're not driving back tonight. Where's Damian? Where's Brightman's kid, for that matter?"

"Damian and Drew are staying with David's mother, who volunteered to pick them from up school and chauffeur them back there tomorrow. Beatrice knows that Drew fusses about going to her house without Damian, and that I wasn't about to let Damian stay in our house by himself. Fortunately, Nana Bea loves your son as if he were her own grandchild."

Nick steered me over to a bench, squeezing my elbow just enough to convey that we would be sitting as we continued this conversation. "Damian could have stayed with me, you know."

As if he had informed me what his schedule would be for the week. Police detectives worked unpredictable hours. So did reporters. Our visitation arrangement tended more toward fluid than formal.

"David was driving in from Manhattan. It was either bring the boys up here with me or send them both to Nana Bea's. Damian didn't give me an argument about that. You know how he can be about David."

"You and Bright Light Number Two didn't come together. Interesting. Trouble in paradise, Elsie?"

The old nickname, the one he always used when teasing me into bed. Nick leaned in, took my face in his hands, and kissed me hard. He ran his tongue across my lips until I opened for him. Until I realized what I was doing.

"What the hell was that?"

"You make me want to kiss you," he growled, then stalked away.

It started like that, all those years ago, when Nick was looking for Kate and her possible killer and I was the roommate frantic for the answers we both hoped to find. Something made him want to kiss me, and something made me want to kiss him back.

We called it grief, then we called it love, and then it tore us apart.

Chapter Five

Laura

Central Pennsylvania, October 2016

White-hot flames rose to singe Kate's eyebrows. Her sleeve ignited, the fabric falling away to ash. I squinted through the smoke and yelled again, louder this time, "Come with me! Follow me!"

Kate's shoes melted into the wood. Her legs burned as the blaze intensified. "I can't! Don't go! Don't leave me here!" She reached out. Her fingers crumbled …

I startled awake, my heart pounding. *Where was I? Where was Kate?*

A hand touched my back. I spun around, fists covering my face.

"Laura, it's okay, it's me."

I closed my eyes, focused on my breathing, and tried to slow my brain.

David pulled me to his chest and wrapped me in his arms. "Shh, it's not real. It's just the dream again."

Not real. Just the dream.

"She's on fire and can't escape. I can't reach her. The flames keep pushing me back."

He eased me down and tucked me into the curve of his body, pulled the blankets over us, smoothed damp hair away, and kissed along my throat until the tension ebbed and I could think again.

"You weren't there. You couldn't have saved her." His voice was gentle but frustrated. "What will it take for you to believe that?"

How many times had he asked and gotten only anguished silence in reply? How long before he fled and left me to my nightmare for good?

The pad of his thumb swiped at a tear. "Shh," David whispered, his voice caressing my ear. "I'm here."

As if cuddling could detour me away from the dream and my memories. "Distracter" had been David's role from the start. It wasn't his fault that it wasn't enough, though he was certainly to blame for other things, the things he did to distract himself. I savored, for now, the warmth of his hands on my breasts, the weight of his leg over my hip, the tickle of the graying curls on his chest as he moved against my skin.

"Come to Manhattan with me. Mom can keep the boys another night. I only have a few hours of editing to do. We can have dinner, get a little drunk."

A phone buzzed. Mine.

"It's Steve, probably reminding me I'm supposed to speak to his 1 o'clock class. Bet he made the students pre-order *Bloodstrains* to prepare a barrage of questions for me today. I can't blow this off."

It was already 9:30. Crap. "Plus, I'm due at the bookstore at 11 for a mini-signing, whatever that means."

David flipped me onto my back and settled himself between my thighs. "Means we're losing valuable time."

I let him distract me again.

"What do you want from this book? I mean, are you just on a juice cleanse here, or do you really think there's something new to discover?"

Steve posed his questions from the back of the classroom, ceding the front to me. A dozen heads swiveled first in his direction, then in mine.

I eased myself up onto the desk. "When the questioner is the head of the College of Communications, you forgive 'juice cleanse' cracks."

"When he's also your brother-in-law, you put up with it, right?" a cutie with a man bun offered from the second row.

I shrugged and smiled at Bright Light Number One, as Nick dubbed him years ago. Steve laughed. "I warned you we'd come gunning for you, Cunningham."

That he did. Time for me to step into the teacher role.

"What I hope to accomplish with *Bloodstrains* is this: To get Kate McDonald officially declared a victim of The Challenge fire, and to push for the investigation to be reopened from that perspective," I explained. "Kate's parents say even that much would bring them some closure, no matter what a new investigation revealed. Of course, if the McDonalds thought any new information warranted it, they would have to pursue legal action against the university independently. They couldn't retroactively join the settlement the university reached with the other victims' families. The administration clearly was motivated to settle after the fire marshal concluded that the Challenge building was an uninhabitable firetrap even without the evidence of tampering its electrical system showed. With the settlement, the civil court trial on that matter was resolved, and the university admitted no negligence in its oversight of The Challenge.

"But my goal with *Bloodstrains* is broader in another important way. While it's true that no body identifiable as Kate's was found at the Challenge site, the evidence suggesting that the charred corpse discovered outside the destroyed building belonged to Andrew Michaels wasn't definitive either. A forensic pathologist testified to that effect at the inquest that took place months before the university's settlement with the families. My contention is that the fire marshal's overall investigation was incomplete at best, riddled with inconsistencies at worst—and that, as a result, fire officials handed the municipal police force a mess from the start. I began to gather information supporting my argument almost immediately, though it wasn't until the twentieth anniversary of the fire that I recognized writing this book was my best chance to aim a spotlight at The Challenge that couldn't be ignored."

In what was probably less than two minutes, I had unpacked two and a half years of intensified research and a lot of legal twisting and turning. Steve's students seemed unfazed by the complexity. Hands shot up immediately. A young woman in the front row stood. I invited her to speak first.

"So you have someone missing and presumed dead but not categorized as a victim, and someone presumed dead by virtue of what you consider dubious evidence. Your book devotes a lot of pages to the fire scene—not the actual building but the area around it, like the spot where they found Kate McDonald's car. I get that the 'old building, questionable wiring, no smoke detectors' thing never cut it for you, but wouldn't another investigation just cover the same ground?" she argued. "You have interesting theories, but are they persuasive enough for the authorities to reopen a case they closed a long time ago?"

"Crowdsource it!" Man Bun said, getting to his feet. "I'm serious. We, this class, we walk the scene. We look at the stuff the police stashed away in an evidence locker back in the day. All that's public. Maybe we can find some tech-savvy volunteer to scan and scope and infrared-photograph everything within two miles of The Challenge location and see what's still there to see. Every one of us will have a different way of approaching this thing because we have none of the preconceptions the authorities had in 1992."

Steve moved up the center aisle to the front of the room. He leaned against the desk where I was sitting and chewed his lower lip. He used to be my editor; I recognized what that meant.

"Crowdsourcing. Not the worst idea I've ever heard, Brandon."

Maybe not the best idea either, if he asked me. Steve didn't.

"Angel, what do you think?" he asked the young woman in the front row.

"Yeah, I can see it," she said. "We do it like an Innocence Project investigation, like proving what really happened is a matter of life and death today, because who knows, maybe it is. Maybe there's a reason no one has ever figured out what happened to Kate McDonald."

A blond, frat-boy type in the last row stood. "There are only five weeks left to this academic session, and that's barely enough time to sort out where to start. But, Professor Brightman, you tell me that next session, instead of some dull municipal finance exercise in data-based reporting, we'll be reviewing all the physical evidence to establish who might have done whatever resulted in that fire, reading the journals and the filings and anything we can get our hands on, I'm signing up today. Keep the class to just us. We can divide up the work and decide what's important and what's not. We'll do a killer job."

I also knew this about Steve Brightman: Few things got him fired up more than a roomful of enthusiastic reporters.

"Laird makes a good point," he said. "We'd need the next few weeks to work out a strategy, plus get the police and the district attorney's office on board. Maybe some of the lawyers for the dead students' parents will help, too, off the record, on issues unrelated to the terms of the nondisclosure agreement included in the settlement."

Steve stepped away from me and closer to his students, as if to advocate on their behalf. "Laura, do you think you could be available to consult regularly, either in person or on a video feed?"

I fished my phone out of my purse to check the schedule Karla updated daily: six book appearances planned, mostly on the East Coast, a couple events in Ohio. I could wangle a few days off at the newspaper and figure out what to do about my kids as we went.

"Yes, but we can't just run at this like crusading zealots," I cautioned. "We have to be sure every step makes sense and take really careful notes. People's professional judgments will be called into question, people whose cooperation we need to do this right. We have to dig with a mission."

Steve extended a hand. "We're in if you are, Laura."

I shook on the deal. What the hell, maybe these new eyes would see what no one had before. Not me, not Nick.

Jesus, Nick. I had to tell him before he heard about this from someone else.

Chapter Six

Laura
Philadelphia, October 2016

Gone only two days and the boys were giving me the full "Mom, you abandoned us!" routine. The eight-year-old was kicking my seat, bouncing around the Volvo as much as his shoulder harness allowed. Beside me up front, the fifteen-year-old scowled, earbuds plugged in to signal the full depth of his sulk.

"Mom, Mom, is Dad coming home tonight too? He said he might."

Knowing better than to touch me while I was driving, Drew landed a kick into Damian's shoulder through the space over the console, earning the withering glare of his big brother.

"I don't think so, baby. He didn't seem totally sure this morning, but it sounded like he'd have to be in New York much of the day." In the rearview mirror, I watched Drew deflate. "It's only Wednesday, sweetie, and Daddy promised he'd be home this weekend for your soccer tournament."

"I hate his new job." Drew sunk back and let his seatbelt lash him to the upholstery.

I hated David's new job too, mostly because I wanted it for myself.

"Why don't we just move to Bucks County? Or don't you *want* David to take the train home every night?" Damian pinned me with a look that would do his detective father proud. What did he hear when I thought he wasn't listening?

"Don't start." I adjusted the mirror and calculated how much closer the truck behind us could get to my rear bumper. "We don't know whether the *New Yorker* job will be permanent. They're getting to know each other."

Drew's head popped up. "They'll like my dad. Everybody likes my dad."

"I don't." Damian poked his earbuds back in place.

We were still thirty minutes from home, traffic gods willing. I fantasized about a nice cup of tea in my cozy, updated Victorian, maybe with a splash of bourbon.

"Does he have to be so mean all the time?" Drew complained.

"Google 'male adolescent mood swings' and get back to me."

I heard Drew typing on his phone, then heard a ping on Damian's. He laughed and texted something back. Behind us, Drew giggled.

"What did you send him?"

Damian shot me a look of total innocence. "He didn't know what adolescence was. Couldn't spell it either."

"Mom, what's *test toaster* ...?"

"Testosterone?" I eased over into the exit lane for the last expressway stretch before home. "That's the stuff that turns sweet little boys into young men. It's what makes Damian taller and hairier and grouchier every day."

"Hungrier too, Nana Bea says."

"Yeah, like now," Damian said. "Can we stop for food?"

I was starving, but no way was I spending another minute more in this car than I had to. "You have an essay to finish, don't you? I'll call for pizza or whatever you guys want and have it delivered."

The pizza guy was turning out of our driveway as I approached it. Standing at the garage, holding two white boxes and a two-liter bottle of soda, was my ravenous teenager's father.

"Dad, can you stay for dinner?" Damian jumped out of the car and liberated Drew from the Volvo's backseat.

"Mom, he can stay, can't he?" Drew wrapped his arms around Nick's waist.

"I paid for dinner. You bet I'm staying." *Try to stop me,* Nick's wink said.

Drew took the soda from Nick, punched in the garage door code, and dragged him into the house.

"He likes my dad better than you do." Damian reached into the station wagon for the two backpacks and phones.

Liking has nothing to do with it, I reminded myself as I wrestled my gear into the house and tried to forget that on-campus kiss.

Nick didn't just show up at this house unannounced, not anymore. Someone must have clued him in to what transpired in Steve's class. I silently cursed the likely culprit, my brother-in-law.

An hour passed. We ate and cleared the table. Once the boys finally nailed themselves to their homework, I turned the sound up on the kitchen TV so Nick could deliver his message, loud and clear. I wasn't about to take this outside. If he wanted to throw a tantrum with the kids upstairs in their bedrooms, it was on him, and he knew it.

"Interesting chat I had with Bright Light Number One a little bit ago," he seethed at low volume. "What the fuck, Laura, first you write the fucking book, and now you've got Scooby-Doo and his junior detectives asking for the case files and whatever is in the evidence locker." He poked two one-dollar bills into the swear jar on the counter near the microwave.

"It's a graduate-level journalism class. No cartoon dogs that I could see."

"I know what *your* malfunction is, but what is Steve Brightman's deal? He's the head of the communications school, so what's he doing teaching a class, let alone joining this fucking quest of yours?"

I pointed to the jar. Nick pounded another dollar into it.

"Steve's school, Steve's rules, as long as he meets educational and industry standards for the course. He's bored and hates the administrative and fundraising part of the job. Plus, he's getting a divorce. Another divorce."

"And this is safer than sniffing around Jane like a German shepherd?" Nick turned on the faucet and ran water over the plates in the sink, opened the dishwasher, and started to load it like he owned the place, which he used to.

"Sniffing? Jane hasn't said anything."

"Jane Baker is sexy and smart, and Steve's been hot for her for years. He stops by Trilby's every day for coffee and something sweet."

"You know this how?"

"I used to be a cop in that town. People see things and pass the gossip along."

"Jane's a big girl. She can take care of herself."

"And Steve can be a jerk, which you know because you worked for him before you married his dickhead ambitious baby brother." Nick pulled a five from his pocket and tossed it at me. "Steve called and asked me to speak to his Junior Danger Rangers about the fire, lay the groundwork for what we did and why we did it, and provide whatever other help I could. Why the police department never pressed the case for declaring Kate a victim, et cetera. He said you were on board with his class getting involved. Jesus, Laura, are you *that* desperate to flog your book?"

I had poured what was left of my soul into *Bloodstrains.* That was one button Nick didn't get to push.

"Get out of my house, now!"

Nick slammed the dishwasher door. "Adios, boys!" he shouted up the steps, then grabbed his coat from the bench in the foyer and stormed out to his Jeep.

This was why we split. He knew every part of me, and still he didn't get it.

Didn't understand why a year's worth of Kate's journals littered our home office, a tower of memories I wouldn't put aside, couldn't put aside. Questioned why I continued to keep file folders stuffed with old printouts describing Jason Goldstein's funeral and the notes Kate took about those letters from Connecticut—the ones that stopped coming for a week after Jason died then resumed after the *Informed Student* published Kate's story suggesting a link between the letters and his murder. Asked exactly what I expected to find in the books I hoarded about arson and kidnapping and FBI profiles from notorious cases.

Boxes full of nothing that bore down on me like a boulder gathering snow in an avalanche. No matter what I did, I couldn't get out of its way. It crushed me.

Chapter Seven

Nick
March 1992

The Firebird idled on the left shoulder, almost obscured by the gray haze swallowing the road. Headlights on, driver's door open, a Supergirl keychain that Nick recognized as Kate's hanging from the ignition. He scrambled back to his car and gunned it, taking the final quarter-mile to The Challenge at a suspension-destroying clip.

Cinders lit the night, thick like fireflies, swirling evidence of an inferno ahead. Nick's radio crackled with chatter: "All units, all units." Then, behind him, sirens blared; he had to get out of the way of the ladder trucks. The wail grew louder. He drove up an embankment, abandoned his car, and ran.

Kate must have done the same thing. How far ahead of him could she be?

A great wall of heat threw Nick down onto his hands and knees, dirt and rocks scraping his exposed skin. He struggled to his feet, saw the beams of the fire trucks' spotlights. Heard the roar of angry orange flames licking at every inch of what was once a commercial dairy barn, now a residential counseling center. He picked his way through the hoses, deep in mud created by water cascading from the third story of the wood-and-stone structure. Too much wood, too little stone, the building was probably a goner. As for anyone inside The Challenge ...

"Back up! Get out of here!"

Nick flashed his badge. "I'm looking for someone, a young woman who was headed this way less than thirty minutes ago," he shouted.

A yellow helmet nodded toward the heart of the blaze. "Everybody I have is up at that structure, Detective, all men in full gear. Haven't seen anyone yet that didn't arrive on a fire truck, and we're still battling our way inside. Hope your girl wasn't anywhere around when that fire started."

Nick planted his feet; a chemical swamp formed around them. "A Pontiac parked on the side of the road back there is hers. The door is wide open, and the engine is running. She has to be here somewhere."

A sudden blare sent the firefighter running toward the building. A flash of light blinded Nick for a second, then he thought he saw someone on the roof. A second explosion rocketed flames higher.

No more than a heartbeat later, the roof collapsed.

Chapter Eight

Nick

Central Pennsylvania, October 2016

He didn't know where Laura's head was anymore. Kate's disappearance had nearly destroyed her, destroyed their marriage for sure, and now this book, this need to dredge it all up again. But they'd been in it together from the beginning—he couldn't let her go wherever *Bloodstrains* led with only Steve Brightman's Justice Kids beside her. As if this were only about justice.

Boxes filled the back of his Jeep, everything he'd asked his old buddies at the local police department to let him bring to Brightman's class, plus a few odds and ends Nick had saved on his own. His notebooks. Photos he took at The Challenge scene once the tight-ass fire marshal finally agreed to let him near it. Photos of Kate's car, and receipts from the towing company that dragged it to a state police garage to be picked clean of stray gloves and old textbooks, tubes of lip gloss and sticky soda cups, prints and fibers and hair and skin and whatever else she had left in it. The knit green scarf with the university logo Kate was wearing when she'd barged into his apartment building six weeks earlier and ended up in his bed, a line he should never have crossed.

Nick pulled into a visitors' parking lot and checked his phone. Brightman had texted the location, a room near the College of Communications offices commandeered for the remainder of the term. When Nick arrived with a fraction of the Challenge Fire archive, a projector and several laptops already lined a long table.

"Please, God," he muttered, "no PowerPoints."

Sitting with her back to a whiteboard and looking almost as pale was Laura. Nick handed her his bottled double-shot espresso. "You look like you need this more than I do."

She cracked it open, took a sip, and winced. "Too sweet."

"Yes, I am, but I'll behave today, I promise. Too many impressionable reporters in the room."

She rolled her eyes and handed him her book. "In case you didn't bring one of your copies with you. We'll be referring to *Bloodstrains* as we establish protocols, et cetera."

Nick took the closest possible seat. Annoying Laura always kept her sharp, though it didn't much help with his focus. Fortunately, the esteemed professor saved the day with introductions.

"You've already met Laura Cunningham, whose book inspired our project," Brightman said. "Meet Detective Sergeant Nicholas Fabrizzio of the Philadelphia Police Department, who was a member of the municipal police force here when the fire at The Challenge occurred. Nick, welcome to the graduate seminar in investigative reporting."

Nick stood, moved even closer to Laura, and waved.

"Most of you have already googled us, so let's get it all out there," Steve said. "Yes, Nick is Laura's ex-husband and the father of her older son. My brother, David Brightman, is her current husband and the father of her younger son."

Tension radiated from the very private woman to Nick's left. "We're one big, dysfunctional family, or should I say two?" she said, her voice hoarse after what Nick suspected was a bout of nervous coughing. "But you already know this isn't about us. It's about finding out what happened to Kate McDonald and what happened to Andrew Michaels, whose ministry attracted troubled young adults. It's about what the police discovered, and what they failed to notice."

Nick watched twenty-four skeptical eyes pivot to him.

"I agree with Laura. Those were different times, especially forensically. Police didn't readily see in the physical evidence things that they can today, and we didn't ask some questions we routinely ask now. The science has made all the difference, and technology has given our work a much broader, much deeper sweep. If fresh observation shows I screwed up in '92, so be it, if it helps us solve this thing. Did Andrew Michaels die in that fire? Did Kate McDonald? Let's find out."

"And let's begin as Nick and his colleagues did in 1992," Steve said. Nick flashed back to a tense roll call as Steve distributed copies of the fire marshal's report and the medical examiner's autopsies of the bodies found in or near the charred ruins of The Challenge, information released to the press at the time and reported by Laura and others. The students bent their heads to read.

Laura turned on the projector and a familiar image of the burned-out former barn appeared. Nick could still smell the smoke, feel the heat pushing him back again.

Over three hours, the class also began to drill into the summaries Nick and his fellow officers had written about the ten students whose bodies were pulled from the wreckage of The Challenge fire and the two non-students declared dead.

Brightman's crew picked up right away on the three victims whose names recurred in the reports and the investigators' subsequent interviews. Photos of those victims taken when they were alive, acquired by Laura from various sources, stared down from the projection screen, part of the slideshow she had prepared.

• Judith Wright, 20, for whom no parents had turned out to mourn, or to file suit over her loss. Blonde and pretty. Kate had mentioned in her journals a girl Jason Goldstein, murdered a few months before the fire, was supposed to meet in connection with those odd letters from Connecticut to the *Informed Student*. Kate believed Judy Wright was that girl. Kate told Laura about conversations she'd had with Jason in advance of the meeting.

• Stacey Endicott, 30, a registered nurse older than the typical Challenge resident. A striking redhead, word was she was involved romantically with Andrew Michaels. Though, as Nick recalled, no one he or any other investigator had interviewed could explain the exact nature of their relationship.

• Barry Poole, 21, who worked with Laura and Kate at the *Informed Student* and who was dating Kate at the time of the fire. His brother had been living at The Challenge and committed suicide there a few weeks earlier. Jim Poole, 23, had an arrest record and an accompanying diagnosis as a paranoid schizophrenic. *Andrew Michaels had acted like Jim's personal savior, some of The Challenge hangers-on recalled, though Nick couldn't see that there wasn't much saving to show for it.*

• And then there was Michaels himself, whose thin bio included only a six-month posting at an evangelical church just over the border from Erie, Pennsylvania, in Conneaut, Ohio, about a year prior to his arrival on campus. He was in his late forties or early fifties, about six feet tall, brown hair, brown eyes. *It was as if the man had parachuted in from outer space, Nick recalled thinking then, and now.*

Steve called for a lunch break, telling everyone to meet back in the classroom at 1 o'clock for a road trip to the fire location. Nick would have preferred to take his Jeep but agreed to travel with the group in a university minibus. That earned him one of Laura's rare smiles.

Time was, he would have done anything for that smile. Maybe he still would.

They trekked through the scene, shooting photos at the highway turnoff to the access road that led to the former dairy barn, and at the spot where Kate's car was found, and at the now-barren acreage where The Challenge once stood.

The grad students, their professor, and Laura trudged a little ahead of Nick, where sparse grasses had been done in by an early frost, to the place where the remains identified as Andrew Michaels had been found, 450 yards away from The Challenge building.

"In his official report, the fire marshal speculated that this person was thrown by the force of the second explosion, the one that caused the roof to cave in. He cited the fact that one of the firefighters, dressed in full gear, was thrown about 100 yards and suffered two broken legs," Laura said.

"That second blast sounded like cannon fire from an old war movie," Nick said. "When I learned that bullet casings had been found embedded in mud at the very edge of the fire location, I remembered a combat scene of a soldier confronting the enemy. But the casings seemed odd then. Still do."

The group stopped and looked back at him.

"Why would anyone have been up here with a gun? I thought The Challenge was a haven. A safe place."

"Excellent question, Angel." Steve Brightman turned toward Laura. "Any theories?"

"Only one ever made any sense to me: that Andrew Michaels staged his death, Kate saw him, and he made certain she would never tell anyone what she'd seen."

"Are you saying Michaels murdered Kate McDonald?" Brightman was talking to Laura but looking at Nick, who shrugged because, of course, he didn't know either.

"The physical evidence we had didn't point to it," Nick said. "And we didn't have much, period. The Challenge site was disturbed by heavy rains immediately after the fire—two inches in the nine hours that followed—and contaminated by the extinguisher foam that blanketed about an acre surrounding the building. We lost footprints, tire tracks. Who knows, maybe blood spatter. We couldn't assume that anything was as it appeared to be, so we had to focus on scenarios that seemed most likely. For that reason, we searched every square foot of the site twice."

Laura stared across the denuded Challenge property, looking as if she expected answers to rise like shimmering truth from the nothingness. Nick had done the same thing too often, on his own mostly, but occasionally with her at his side.

Meanwhile, everyone else was staring at *him*. They'd already read Laura's book.

"A week or so after the fire, we discovered something new at the spot where Andrew Michaels' remains had been found," Nick said. "Something that looked like a charred tooth turned out to have a serial number etched on it. We tracked it back to an Ohio dentist. The Challenge fire had been on the national news at that point, and I think our call asking for help in identifying one of the victims took her by surprise. She said, 'Who's Andrew Michaels? My patient's name was Michael Andress.' That led us on a hunt for information about Michael Andress that turned up only an expired Ohio driver's license with a photo that showed he had a beard, glasses and blond hair. We could find no current address for him, no phone number, nothing in tax records. Nothing from the federal or state criminal databases popped, certainly nothing with any connection to The Challenge. No cold cases or missing persons either. We ran the name for months after the fire, but it was a no-go each time. Bottom line: Though the tooth found at the fire scene was certainly the one implanted by the Ohio dentist, it wasn't relevant as evidence, and not worth pursuing further. Andrew Michaels might have used other names at some point, but we couldn't establish that, or that Michael Andress was one of them."

Expressions of reasonable doubt crossed several students' faces. Laura noticed them as well.

"Why did I include the Michael Andress photo in *Bloodstrains?* Because in the course of writing the book, I also tried to find the tooth's elusive owner—and I came up empty, even with the latest search tools available. That struck me as at least worth noting, given the controversial identification of Michaels' body."

A guy who reintroduced himself as Laird Morrison had paced the distance to the main road from where Kate's car was found. "What did Michaels drive? Where was that car?" he asked. "He didn't officially live at The Challenge, according to Ms. Cunningham's book."

"You're right, he was not listed as a Challenge resident," Laura confirmed. "His name wasn't on any Pennsylvania vehicle registration either. We don't know what Michaels drove, or whether he drove himself to The Challenge the day of the fire."

"Any other cars left behind here the way Kate's was?"

To Nick, Laird looked like a sports-car kind of guy. Laura didn't give him a chance to rattle off the inventory of vehicles the fire marshal impounded.

"None was left in a hurry the way Kate's was," she said. "There were two cars and a pickup truck. The fire marshal's office analyzed contents, drained fluids, swept for prints, fibers, dirt, everything you could test for in the early nineties, but they got nothing. The investigators were right back where they started."

"How do you mean?" Steve checked his watch, then stamped a booted foot on the cold, hard ground.

"Back to Stacey Endicott and Judy Wright and Barry Poole, except it was Barry's brother who owned the pickup and Jim Poole had been dead for a few weeks by then," Nick said. "All three vehicles were parked far enough away from The Challenge that the fire didn't reach them. Windows were open in Wright's car, so it was pretty much flooded by the rain. As was the bed of the pickup."

"Maybe that means something," Laird said. "Why would three drivers get out to walk that far to The Challenge? There was room to park out front, or at least that's what photos from before the fire show. I'd like to pursue the cars and see where they lead."

After twenty-four years, what was left to pursue Nick couldn't say. "The aim here is new eyeballs on old evidence. What are you thinking?" he asked.

"What happened to the vehicles themselves after they were searched and the title stuff got settled? Were they resold?" Laird asked. "Should be a VIN trail for all three if they were, and maybe insurance records we could use to track the new owners. If we find even one, that person might know something that will shed new light on the old crime-scene findings."

"And maybe," another student, Eric or maybe Derek, chimed in, "maybe there's some link between the cars and the people who bought them that wasn't apparent at the time. I mean, once you guys were done with the cars, you didn't give them a second thought, right?"

"We didn't, you're right. Those are all good points," Nick acknowledged.

Brightman was clearly pleased. "Anyone else thinking of a different line of inquiry based on what we've seen out here?"

Angel nudged the young woman next to her. "Tell them, Jess."

Jess walked into the center of the circle they had formed next to the bus. "I'd like to delve more into the car owners themselves, or at least into Barry Poole and Stacey Endicott. It feels like we're missing some connection beyond what Ms. Cunningham documented. It's a just a hunch, but—"

"Hunches are good," Nick said. "You'd be amazed how much police work starts with a hunch and ends with a significant arrest. What do you think, Laura?"

His beautiful ex-wife almost smiled, despite the burden of misplaced guilt she carried around. "Every hunch is worth playing," she agreed. "Every lead is worth chasing. We're not leaving anything up to chance."

Nick knew she might have added, "Not this time." That she didn't was heartening.

Steve slid the bus door open. "Jess, Angel, you have your assignment then. We need to get back to campus, but I want to hear more ideas on the way. Start thinking, people."

Laura let the students file past her. "Worth it?" she asked Nick.

"After the registrations were checked and the vehicles searched, we didn't much consider them relevant. As for Poole, Wright, and Endicott, if an unknown connection reveals itself, that would be great, I'd take that. And if one doesn't, well, it won't be the first time we've failed."

"No," Laura said, just above a whisper. "We excel at failure, don't we?"

Steve gunned the engine. She and Nick hurried aboard.

In advance of the daylong class and Challenge site tour, Bright Light Number One had offered to put Nick and Laura up at a local hotel, so they'd brought overnight bags. Excellent plan, Nick agreed, when the day turned out to be physically and emotionally grueling. Driving back to Philly right afterward would not have been a good idea.

Steve also had invited them to have dinner with him at a little Italian joint just off campus, a gravy and pasta place that reminded Nick of his grandmother's kitchen. Nonna Fabrizzio had made potato gnocchi to die for. The thought of them made his mouth water.

Since Jane evidently had the same effect on Steve, Nick casually suggested that Laura ask her to join them, to distract him from any potential spying for his brother. Good old Jane could also fill in any awkward silences. She would want to know all about that day's quest for clues and offer unsolicited insights.

Where Laura was willowy and auburn-haired, reserved and graceful, Jane was blonde and bosomy and opinionated. She suffered few fools, and let you know it. The four of them knocked back more Chianti than they should have and ripped through antipasto and pasta courses, but they passed on dessert in favor of espresso and limoncello.

Jane kept Laura laughing and talking until she couldn't hold back her yawns. "This little baker needs to be up at 2 a.m. Professor Brightman, you'll give me a lift, won't you? I'm on your way."

Somehow, Nick kept a straight face. Jane winked at Steve to seal the deal then stood, smoothed her skirt, and leaned over to plant a kiss on her best friend's ex-husband.

"For once, Laura's not wound tight as a drum," she whispered. "Reminds me of when you two were close."

As if Chianti was all it would take to bridge that distance.

Laura flashed a key card. "I'm in three-oh-eight. You?"

"I'm in two-ten. Feel like hitting the bar first? Have a nightcap, assess what, if anything, we accomplished today?" Laura hadn't taken one easy breath at the fire scene. Nick knew she was terrified they wouldn't resolve anything. Maybe more terrified that they would.

"I have a bottle of Jack Daniels in my room. Better than sleeping pills. Care to share?"

She didn't need to ask twice. Which she knew.

"Go ahead up," Nick said, pulling out his phone. "I have to alert the honchos I won't be back at my desk until about noon tomorrow."

That was a lie. Even with her brother-in-law otherwise occupied, this town had too many eyes—he and Laura should not be seen anywhere near an elevator together. Which Laura recognized, he figured, since she didn't question his need to check in with his division supervisor.

"Rocks or water?" she asked.

"Rocks. I'll be right up, I swear." How many times had Laura heard that in the dozen or so years they were together?

When he entered the room through the slightly open door, Nick found Laura sitting in an elegant wing chair, grasping a cut-glass tumbler of bourbon, and clad only in a pale pink bra and panties.

"I could have been anyone walking in here." Nick examined the lock.

"No, you couldn't be anyone but you, Fabrizzio."

When exhaustion set in, Laura sounded like Bette Davis after too many cigarettes, as if her voice were dragging the weight of her body along. Nick added water to the few fingers of Jack she'd poured into his ice-filled glass. A clear head might be important.

He sank to the floor, leaned against the bed, and studied her. "Comfortable? You look, well, like you want to be."

"Mmm." She sipped her drink. "What I want is to be home, and as far away from this town as possible. I didn't count on having to be here so much, or anywhere, for that matter. I thought I'd just write the book and video-chat my way through some author interviews."

Nick could see her nipples through the lace of her bra. "We don't have to do a postmortem, Elsie, we can just drink and ponder the unfathomable—as usual."

"Tired of futile pondering. Too many things still stuffing my mental file drawers. Screw that."

Amen. He'd felt the same impotence since Laura left him ten years ago for David, though not literally so as he sat looking at her now. It would be better not to still want her, not on top of everything else.

So he sat there, aroused, and watched her drink, which she did not do often. When she did, there was a reason. When the bourbon level dropped to the bottom third of the bottle, he plucked the glass from her hand.

"Talk to me. About today, about this book, about the kids."

"Or maybe about David," she said, "and how he's banging some publishing executive in Manhattan and barely seeing his son."

"Which of those bothers you more: the banging or the neglecting?"

She unfolded her pale body from the chair, slithered to the floor, and crawled across to him, putting her head on his shoulder.

"I'm driving him away, like I did with you. Kate is always in bed with us. Having a Pulitzer Prize-winning wife was a turn-on for David. Having a crazy one isn't as sexy."

"You want my opinion? David Brightman is an entitled, manipulative ass."

Nick could say a whole lot more on the subject, most of which Laura had already heard: that David had worked as relentlessly to campaign for her affections as those corrupt state legislators did in trying to discredit her reporting. And that she let him, while powerful men were gunning for her.

Then again, maybe she just needed to be loved by someone who wasn't carrying the same emotional baggage.

"You're not crazy, Elsie. Never have been. You're the sanest woman I know."

"Poor you." Laura took his half-full glass and drank it almost dry before Nick could snatch it away.

"You didn't answer my question. What bothers you more, David's infidelity or his neglecting Drew?"

"Does it matter?"

Nick kissed her forehead. Held her as she cried, until she fell asleep against his chest. Laura loved David; of course she was upset he was cheating on her.

Was she right about Kate having been in bed with them, too? Would they have gotten together in the first place if not for Kate's disappearance?

Oh, yeah, he believed in fate, or as much as a cop could. Laura was so quiet, so unlike her unstoppable whirlwind of a best friend. So unlike him. Nick felt like the frog who had found his princess, a piece of himself he didn't know was missing.

They hadn't solved Kate's disappearance, though. It broke their hearts, then it broke them up.

Chapter Nine

Nick

Central Pennsylvania, January 1992

The buzzer. Someone was downstairs, leaning on it. "What!" he snarled into the receiver.

"It's Kate McDonald."

He must still be asleep. "Who?"

"Katharine Theresa McDonald, of the Broomall, Pennsylvania, McDonalds, fine examples of white middle-class suburbia. Buzz me up, Fabrizzio. I don't think you want me yelling at you from the lobby at two in the morning."

Nick debated hanging up and heading back to bed. "Go down to the diner. I'll meet you there in fifteen minutes."

"No way."

"I spent half the day leaving you messages about the Jason Goldstein case, and you show up here? How the hell did you find me anyway?"

"Phone book, N.A. Fabrizzio. What's the 'A' stand for anyway?"

Nick buzzed her up and pulled jeans over his naked behind.

She looked like a refugee from a punk band. He went hard the minute he saw her. Not good.

"What do you want, McDonald?"

Kate threw down her backpack and keys and sank onto his manure-colored couch. "My day job is college student. At night, I'm investigating crimes you boys haven't managed to solve."

"What about that?"

"I know who Jason was meeting the night he was killed: Judy Wright, a junior who lives fulltime at The Challenge. She went to high school in Erie, but she's originally from Groton, Connecticut."

"The place with the nuclear submarines?"

Kate looked at him like he was insane. "I talked to some girls Judy lived with pre-Challenge, but nobody has heard from her since that night. She used to call all the time, they said, crying and talking about feeling like a prisoner at The Challenge, and wanting to go home."

"To Connecticut?"

"They didn't know."

Kate pulled a bundle of letters from her backpack. "All from this week. All postmarked 'Groton' again. Nonsense about the devil again."

A furnace banged, and heat blasted the room. Kate took off her jacket and peeled off the sweatshirt underneath it. "Feels like it's ninety degrees in here."

In a white T-shirt, her nipples lighting up as the air hit them, she was, no question, hot.

Nick stared at her breasts. "Anthony. The 'A' stands for Anthony."

She caught him looking and smiled. "Tell me you don't distract that easily. Judy Wright, new clue, remember, Detective?"

Letting her come up here was a huge mistake. He wondered whether it was only his first of the night.

Chapter Ten

Nick

Central Pennsylvania, October 2016

Steve Brightman strolled into class, waving his phone. Nick knew what was coming—Laura had texted him seconds earlier.

"Laura regrets she can't be back with us today," Steve announced. "A TV station in Binghamton has booked her for a spot about *Bloodstrains* on its 5 o'clock news show. Can't pass up that kind of publicity, and she's promised to give our endeavor here a shout-out, so let's get cracking on a plan for the next week."

He half-sat on the desk, one leg anchoring him to the floor, "Detective, impressions after yesterday's outing?"

One thought struck Nick immediately: that Steve, like his brother, enjoyed the spotlight, however dim and indirect it might be.

"You bet," he said instead. He grabbed a chair and turned it to face the class. "First off, the vehicles are a great place to start. State DMVs are pretty reliable sources of data that are regularly updated. So are car insurance rolls. You avoid the choppy recordkeeping and time lags you sometimes get when you're trying to track down a property's history. If the VINs for the two cars and the pickup found near The Challenge weren't tampered with, we could get a few new leads.

"Second, there's a lot of information in the civil court filings about everybody but Judy Wright, Stacey Endicott, and Barry Poole. None of their relatives sued the university. If Laura's TV interview reaches even one person who can tell us more, that's great. Regardless, we should comb through what we do know. Anything that seems promising, we chase. There are enough of us.

"Finally, we have time to do the work, which my colleagues and I didn't have enough of in '92. No newly grieving families to consider, no inquests or hearing deadlines to meet. Let's talk to as many people face-to-face as possible. Database research is fine to a point, but serious investigative work starts with seeing what can be seen in person."

Angel's head popped up from her tablet. "What are you thinking?"

"That we split up the people who need interviewing," Nick said.

Angel counted eager faces. "So maybe two of us each for Wright, Endicott, and Poole; Laird and Eric on the cars; and the rest of the class on the other victims, to see if there are connections we missed."

This girl will make one hell of a reporter someday. Or maybe one hell of a cop.

"Okay," Brightman said, "Laird and Eric, you're set. Let's decide who's doing the rest and get to it, people. Big jobs ahead for us."

Nick planned to spend the next week doing some extracurricular sleuthing of his own, scratching off scabs and opening sores. If Laura could take the pain, so could he.

Chapter Eleven

Nick

Central Pennsylvania, November 2016

"Nailed it!"

Heads turned Laird's way. "Nailed what?" Nick shouted from the front of the room.

"Judy Wright's former foster sister bought her car out of salvage. Eric and I ran Judy's name and the buyer's through every Pennsylvania database we could think of and got a pop on Erie County Children's Services. Annie Karpinsky was in the foster care system there the same years as Judy Wright. She lives in Conneaut, Ohio, now."

Eric waved a printout. "They lived with Richard and Debbie Boyle in Erie from 1985 to 1989, when Annie turned eighteen and left. Judy stayed with the Boyles one more year, until she aged out of the system, then came here for college. The VIN shows the car was previously registered to Richard Boyle, who transferred the title to Judy in 1990."

Steve Brightman beamed as if he'd done the digging himself. "Well done, guys. Shows this team merits all the good things Laura said about us on TV last week."

Laura applauded. "You absolutely deserve it; this is the first bit of new information in twenty-four years. New eyes see new things. New technology will be hugely helpful too, I think."

"I have to agree," Nick said. "Following the child-welfare paper trail might have taken months back in '92. Now, a couple of you work on it a few hours, and voilà! We have a connection and a shot at new information to fill in those gaps about Judy Wright."

Steve stood, marker in hand, at a whiteboard. "Where do we go from here, gentlemen?"

"Check out Annie Karpinsky, see what turns up," Laird said. "Maybe she just needed a car. Or maybe she has a criminal record and could somehow be implicated in the fire. We talk to her in person, find out more about Judy Wright and what Karpinsky knew about Judy at the time of her death."

Emma K., one of two Emmas in the class, spoke for the first time Nick could remember. "Shouldn't we look into the foster family too, the Boyles, just to be sure we know as much as we can about Judy's life before her involvement with The Challenge?"

"Yes," Nick, Laura, and Steve responded in unison.

"Now, you're getting it," Nick said. "Investigators work backward while also moving forward and sideways, making connections. If Andrew Michaels is still alive, and if Kate McDonald is truly dead, we'll find out by following the trail of connections."

"No such thing as coincidence?" Steve asked.

"Sure, there is. People are born and live and die at opposite ends of the same city every day. Then again, you have to ask: Is it a coincidence that before he founded The Challenge, Andrew Michaels worked just across the state line from Erie—where Judy Wright and Annie Karpinsky lived in a foster home—when he was assigned to a church in Conneaut, Ohio, where Annie Karpinsky lives now? We can't know unless we follow that thread as far as it leads."

Steve stopped next to Angel's and Jess's desks. "Do you two have anything to report yet? If not, I'd like to have Laird and Eric walk us through their process. It could be a help in your search as well as everyone else's."

"Nothing yet," Jess said, "but what *they* found, the former foster sister, that's exactly what I was talking about. How many more connections are there?"

"Then Laird and Eric have the floor. Tell us what you did, step by step."

"We started with Judy Wright," Laird said, "because she seemed to have no family, no one who would have acquired the car later. But what she did have was a long list of foster homes."

Family, in this case, being a relative term.

When Steve called for a lunch break in the day's four-hour class session, Laura walked toward Trilby's.

"Hey, wait up!" Nick called.

She turned and gave him the patented Cunningham left-eyebrow arch—Laura's expression of exasperation, dismay, name it. "I'm taking Damian tomorrow night," he said. "It's my mother's birthday."

"Yes, I remember," she said. "It will also give me some time alone with Drew, so he can process what's going on and ask questions."

"Process what, or shouldn't I ask?"

"My book. Why suddenly I'm traveling up here all the time. Why his dad never comes home during the week anymore. Just the normal stuff you chat about with eight-year-olds."

"Questions never really asked, and with no clear answers anyway?" Nick remembered being tongue-tied as he tried to explain their split to Damian, when even the right words seemed wrong.

Laura turned away and crossed the street. When they reached the opposite side, he grabbed her arm.

"What do you want, Nick? You think I don't know I'm the problem with my marriage? I'm done today. Send Steve and the class my regrets, but—"

"Nope, you'll be back. You may be many screwed-up things, Cunningham, but a coward is not one of them. Tell me how I can help. I'll take Drew with us tomorrow night, if you'd rather put off the conversation."

"Oh, that wouldn't be cowardly at all." Laura kept walking. Nick beat her to the door and opened it.

"How about this? Drive with me to Conneaut this weekend. We'll question Annie Karpinsky, maybe the Boyles over in Erie, too. We'll learn more about Judy Wright."

"Fabulous plan, I'll just drop the boys with David's mother again so I can jaunt off somewhere with you. That won't confuse Drew."

Fair point, but Nick knew there was no way Laura could resist the first opportunity in years to dig up something new on The Challenge fire victims.

"We can bring the boys with us, fake everyone into thinking we're this sweet little family."

"You've taken leave of your senses, Fabrizzio."

"Why not? A sweet little family staying in two rooms at a motel. We can leave the kids watching TV or a movie for a while. Hell, why not take them to Karpinsky's house with us, tell 'em to fire up their phones and keep busy."

Kids could be disarming, especially if someone was nervous. Laura was thinking the same thing.

"Maybe," she said. "Let me contact Annie Karpinsky first, to see whether it makes sense to head out there at all. Then we'll discuss who makes the trip."

Getting Laura to go along for the ride was critical. So was getting Annie Karpinsky to buy his presence there. If some random cop showed up at the door, anyone might have second thoughts. He had no jurisdiction in the environs of the university anymore, let alone in Ohio. There was no investigation beyond Laura's, so he had to hitch his badge to her book and imply that his role was related to *Bloodstrains*. Which it was. It wasn't like he had anything personal at stake—just his reputation and the need to put an end to the dread that he had missed something, before or after the fire, before or after Jason Goldstein was murdered, that might have saved all those people, Judy Wright included, and maybe Kate.

Something that might have saved his relationship with Laura if only he had been able to find it. Here she was, looking for it again, by herself.

No, not by herself anymore.

Laura opened the door to the coffeehouse and held it for him to follow her inside. He didn't.

"Let me know what you decide, Elsie. You know how to reach me."

One whistle, and he'd run to her. But she never was one for whistling.

Chapter Twelve

Nick

Central Pennsylvania, March 1992

He watched her stare at the door to the morgue and struggled not to cough and startle her, smoke from the fire still scraping his lungs. It was hard to manipulate a wheelchair when you could barely breathe, Nick had discovered. Especially hard to do so unnoticed.

He moved closer. Laura Cunningham looked beautiful, and so sad. They had met a few times—the student newspaper was the only press in town. Today, her auburn hair was pulled back into a severe ponytail, accentuating the redness of her eyes, and the puffiness of the skin under them. She clutched a white T-shirt streaked with the mascara her tears had left behind.

Nick couldn't hold back another cough and banged the wheelchair into a row of fiberglass chairs. She jumped at the noise.

"Anyone tells you different, don't believe them: Fighting fires is the worst job on the planet. Anyone who volunteers to do it is nuts, and career firefighters aren't paid nearly enough."

She managed a laugh. "Good thing you decided on another line of work, Detective Fabrizzio."

"This part of the hospital is off limits to the public, Ms. Cunningham. As you can see, I'm a paying guest, though not for much longer, I hope."

She shifted the T-shirt from hand to hand. "I called Dr. Louie. He said he'd get back to me when he knew something. I'm not sure I believe that. It's been almost three days."

Nick understood her impatience. The waiting was tough, even though he recognized the pressure Joe Louie was under.

"He has postmortems to do, plus grieving families, hysterical university administrators, and me to deal with. Joe's a good guy. He's not stonewalling you, Ms. Cunningham. He's just busier than any one county medical examiner should be right now."

If Nick hadn't been dodging the medical staff and staking out the morgue himself, he wouldn't have known she had been sitting here every day. She needed one of the bodies to be Kate, still unaccounted for since the fire. According to daily updates on the investigation, Joe Louie had identified all but one female pulled from the ruins of The Challenge. Nick wasn't sure if that put the odds for or against Kate's obviously distraught roommate.

"Go home, Laura. As soon as we know something, I'll call you. I have your phone number, and also the number at the newspaper."

She shook her head. "Not a good idea for you to be a source, Detective, given your relationship with Kate."

He stared at the shirt in her hands. Nick had dropped it off at the *Informed Student* office more than a month ago, after that night Kate showed up at his apartment.

"She told you?"

"No, you just did."

Laura leaned closer, as if sharing a secret. They were now, he supposed.

"Kate McDonald is my best friend, my sister. Find her, Detective. Don't make me regret trusting you like she does."

Chapter Thirteen

Nick

Conneaut, Ohio, November 2016

Annie Karpinsky flung the door open, waving the copy of *Bloodstrains* Laura had overnighted to her. She threw her arms around its author. "Thank God you found me!"

The sight of Laura arriving with a plainclothes Philadelphia police detective plus her two sons didn't rattle Karpinsky one bit. And as they discussed what she had read in the book, Nick decided he liked Annie, for her un-arched eyebrows and the unblinking certainty that if she had known Judy Wright was in trouble, she would have moved heaven and earth to get to her.

"I didn't know, though. I heard from Judy exactly twice in the three years between when I left the Boyles' house and when she died. I wasn't in a good place back then. I wasn't in any shape to help anybody. I was in Youngstown, waitressing, if you can call it that. Mostly, I was getting paid to give old men blowjobs ... oops, sorry." Annie nodded toward the boys staring at her kitchen TV mere feet away.

He saw Damian's head rise. Nick lifted his phone, then tapped his temple until his son popped earbuds in again. Unlike his big brother, Drew was absorbed in the superhero saga unfolding on the screen.

"You were saying?" Nick prompted Annie to continue.

"Right, so I thought Judy was safe at school. My foster family forwarded a letter she sent me at their house. Judy told me she was in love."

"In love?" Laura asked. "What else did she say?"

"Wait a minute, forwarded how?" Nick interrupted.

"Rich and Debbie's son, Teddy Boyle, lives in Youngstown. They mailed the letter to him, and he tracked me down to deliver it," Annie explained. "I moved around a lot then, but I used to call Rich and Debbie occasionally to tell them where I was living, so they wouldn't worry. Worry as much, I guess I should say."

"Teddy Boyle lived with you and Judy at his parents' house?" Nick wanted to clarify that relationship.

Annie shook her head. "He's about ten years older than I am, already out of college by the time Rich and Debbie took me and Judy in. When he brought me the letter, it was the first time I'd seen Teddy since my last Christmas at the Boyles' house. The next time I saw him was when he came to tell me Judy was dead. Didn't think it was right to tell me about our sister on the phone, he said. Took him more than a month to find me that time. Junkie hookers can hide pretty good when they want to."

She sank back into the sofa where she was sitting with Laura. "Judy was my little sister, and I didn't even sense she was dead," Annie said, sobbing. "I didn't know for half a year that she had burned up and died!"

At the sound of Annie's crying, Drew inched toward her and his mother, silently asking Nick what he could do to help.

"It's OK, buddy," Nick said. "Go back to the TV."

Laura put her arms around Annie.

"I got straight when I found out. Hitchhiked to Pennsylvania, down to the college, and found Judy's car at the impound lot where Teddy said the cops took it. Bought it for seventy-five bucks to cover the title and registration—no storage fee, they said, they just wanted the car out of there. Sold it for four fifty and checked into rehab for four days, because that's all my money could buy me. Worst four days of my life, but it was enough, it was worth it. I came back to Ohio, here to Conneaut.

Got cleaned up and, not looking like I was dead anymore, got a real waitressing job. Met my husband, had my kids, but I never forgot my baby sister. I swear I would have saved her, but I didn't know."

It was clear to Nick that Judy Wright was to Annie what Kate had been to Laura. She moved back a bit, to restore some professional distance, he supposed.

"As you read my book, or at least some of it, you saw the blind alleys the police chased down before deciding that all they knew for sure was that ten students and two other people died at The Challenge," Laura began. "The authorities ruled Andrew Michaels was dead because the evidence leaned that way. Kate McDonald was nowhere to be found. There was no body, and no evidence that there should have been except for her car at the fire scene and the story she was investigating. Did the Boyles tell you what they were hearing then?"

Annie wiped away tears, then blew her nose loudly with a tissue Nick grabbed from a box on the kitchen counter.

"Rich and Debbie couldn't legally claim Judy's body, Teddy said, but by the time he found me they had already paid for her to be buried. They couldn't sue the university because they had no legal standing with their foster kids once we turned eighteen. Eventually, the other victims' families weren't even allowed to talk to them because of the lawsuits, so they only knew what they read in the newspapers." She picked up *Bloodstrains* again and hugged it to her chest. "Your book was a terrible revelation."

Nick's gut told him Annie knew more than she realized. When she put the book down, he picked it up and flipped to the photographs in the middle. He tapped on the black-and-white driver's license shot of Andrew Michaels issued in Pennsylvania and the license from Ohio issued to Michael Andress.

"Did Judy know this man, Andrew Michaels, when you lived with the Boyles? Is it possible she followed him, maybe to a post here in Conneaut? Or maybe to the university when he founded The Challenge?"

Annie stared at each grainy picture, alternating between them, taking in the differences in the men's appearance. "I don't think so. Judy never mentioned anything."

But she leaned in again to study the image of Michael Andress, blond, bearded, and with wire-frame glasses. "This one, though—something about him reminds me of the guy Judy was in love with. She sent me a picture of the two of them. It was real blurry, like someone took it from far away."

Laura shivered, as if a ghost had rushed past her. "Do you still have that picture?" Nick asked.

Annie walked into the kitchen, opened a drawer, and returned with an envelope. Drew followed her back to the couch, then climbed up behind his mother as Annie handed the snapshot to Nick. "See what I mean? He's blond and tall, too. Skinnier, though, with longer hair."

Nick saw something else and handed the photo to Laura. She two-fingered a pair of reading glasses from the purse at her feet.

"It's Jim Poole."

"Who?" Annie and Drew asked at the same time.

"His brother, Barry, died in the fire with Judy," Laura said, tucking her son close. "Jim Poole committed suicide a few weeks before the fire."

"Barry Poole was dating Kate McDonald. We think he was the reason she was at The Challenge that day." Nick tried to keep his voice neutral, tried to push away that memory.

Drew peered at the picture. "He kind of looks like that man with the glasses in your book, Mom. Is that his dad? I look like my dad."

Little guy had a point: Jim Poole could have passed for Michael Andress's son.

They stopped for dinner. The kids devoured pizza and drank enough soda to power a rocket. Laura nibbled at a slice, picking off rounds of pepperoni and stacking them before Nick, like she used to. He ate them, like he used to.

Once they hit the highway again, he feared hours of sugar-fueled bouncing, but ten minutes past the on-ramp, the boys quieted down. A cartoon theme sang through the speakers of Drew's tablet. In the rearview mirror, Nick saw Damian's eyelids lower.

When he watched the road again, he found Laura checking on him.

"You good to drive? I can take over for a while."

"Only six hours more until home. I can do that in my sleep."

"Not funny, Nick. Maybe we should have gotten a couple rooms after all."

He squinted as they passed the bright lights of a motel billboard. "I don't see your publisher picking up the tab for this trip, do you?"

Plus, the drive back eliminated any need to argue with Drew about why he had to stay in his mom's room instead of with Damian. Eliminated the smirk Damian would no doubt have plastered on his face as Nick and Laura bluffed their way through an age-appropriate and unsatisfactory explanation why *they* could not share a room.

Laura slipped out of her boots and redirected the heat registers toward her feet. Nick forced himself to watch the taillights ahead. "So what do you think? Follow up with the Poole connection?" Interrogating her was a good distraction.

She stifled a yawn. "I think we have a ton of work to do first, and one hell of a lot of explaining why we went all the way to Annie Karpinsky's house without Laird and Eric, since they were the ones who located her. I knew once we contacted Annie, we'd have to move fast. I was right, I think."

"No question. She needed someone to assure her Judy's death was important. That someone was you, Elsie."

Laura reached into the console, grabbed his coffee cup and sipped the lukewarm brew. "Was Jason Goldstein killed because Judy Wright revealed something about Andrew Michaels and the Poole brothers?"

"Might have happened that way."

Before he could think about diving into the Goldstein case again, Nick was determined to retrace some very old steps. Back to northern Pennsylvania, to Bradford, to interview John Poole, Jim and Barry's father.

Poole had been less than talkative when he'd interviewed him in '92. Nick had put it down to grief. Maybe there was more to it.

Chapter Fourteen

Laura
Philadelphia, November 2016

"My dad's here!"

Sure enough, there was David, silhouetted by the garage light. I pulled into the driveway, stopping just short of his feet, challenging him to get out of my way.

Drew bounded out of the Volvo. "Dad, Dad, we went to Ohio to see somebody from Mom's book. She was nice and we ate pizza, and then we drove all the way back home." He wrapped his arms around David's waist and buried his face in his father's chest.

Damian speeded past them and headed for the basement. To Nick, he shouted, "Peace out, Dad. Text me about the game."

"You guys are going to a game?" Drew peeled away from David and looked hopefully at Nick.

"Sixers and Nets, kiddo. You're welcome to come if it's okay with your mom and dad." Nick grabbed his files from the Volvo's trunk and waved goodbye. "I'll give them some time to talk about it."

"Coward," I accused as he passed me.

Drew tugged his father inside. I collected empty water bottles and stray candy wrappers from the car.

What the hell, David? Of all nights to just show up, you had to pick this one, despite the messages I left saying I was taking the kids out of town and might not be back until Sunday. What's going on? Did you come home for more clothes and books so you could to move to New York permanently?

On top of the dryer sat his suitcase, assorted shirts and underwear and socks rolled into wrinkled balls inside it. "Screw it." I tossed a detergent pack into the washer and loaded in the clothes, setting the cycle to permanent press, cold rinse. The sound of the rising water was soothing.

When I opened the dryer, kids' laundry spilled out. Of course. As the boys needed clothes, they came down and found them. No one ever carried the clean things upstairs; nothing ever got put away. No one gave a damn, and most of the time, that included me. I vowed to set a better example. Sorted and folded: Drew's Spiderman briefs, Damian's boxers, and a thousand dingy tube socks of different sizes and different degrees of being worn-too-long. Whatever, not quite white was not quite white. They'd figure it out.

It was relaxing, meditating on the wash and the rinse and the spin. When the machine clicked off, I shook the wrinkles out of David's button-down shirts, rebuttoned them, and set them on to tumble for twenty minutes.

"It's the middle of the night, what are you doing down here?"

"Playing domestic goddess."

In a T-shirt and pajama bottoms, his feet bare, David sat on the stairs, dragged a hand through still-thick blond hair, and rubbed his eyes. "Hiding, you mean, and lying to me. That's not like you, babe. What the hell, I come home to surprise you and—surprise on me—there's your ex-husband's Jeep parked on the street in front of my house. Then my son tells me you and Nick drove him and Damian all the way to Ohio and back in one day because of your book? How is that appropriate?"

"How dare you imply that Nick and I would do anything inappropriate in my children's presence! Who's the one who's been unfaithful all these months? Certainly not me."

David padded over to the dryer, wedging me into the small space between it and an old kitchen table. He brushed his lips across my cheek, stroked my right wrist with his thumb. "We're so good together, sweetheart. You left him for me, remember?" He grazed his knuckles along my breast. "We have something great here. I don't want to lose it."

"Prove it, then. Drop her. Work the *New Yorker* job from home or come back to the newspaper—your six-month leave of absence is about over. Love this, David, love us. But if you don't, just go."

I backed up, pushing against the table and shielding myself with an overfilled basket of laundry. David reached for me, but I slipped away.

"I'm going to bed. Don't follow me."

He followed. Up the stairs to the first floor, up the next flight past the boys' rooms. I dropped the basket onto a bench in the hall and walked ahead of David toward our bedroom—*my* bedroom lately. "Don't try to come in unless you intend to stay for good. I mean it."

He laughed. "If ultimatums were the answer, I would have delivered one long ago. How's this: no more obsessing over Kate McDonald, no more falling over yourself looking for someone or something that will lead you to her. And how about as little non-kid-related contact with Nick Fabrizzio as possible, just because I'd like my wife to be *my wife*."

I shut the door in David's face and locked it. "That," I whispered from the other side, "is a most satisfying sound."

"Fine, I'll go. I'll take Drew to Mom's with me. Play Nancy Drew with Nick all you like, since it's what gets you off these days. Have a great time picking over the mystery of your dead-but-maybe-not-dead friend yet again."

He didn't say he was done with me. He never did. He didn't say when he'd be back. Maybe he wouldn't be.

Maybe it still mattered to me.

Chapter Fifteen

Laura

Central Pennsylvania, 1992

Incident Report, 12 February 1992, transcript

Charges: Suspected harassment, intimidation of witness

Location of interview: Squirrel Hill Court Apartments, 8:30 p.m. EST

Interviewer: Det. Glen Washington

Complainants: Laura Cunningham, Katharine McDonald, Jane Baker (who was not present for this interview)

Subjects of complaint: Rev. Andrew Michaels, James Poole, unidentified members (approx. 10) of assembled group.

Location of incident: Squirrel Hill Apartments #213

L. Cunningham: *Our apartment is on the second floor. Our balcony faces the parking lot, the ramp passes right under it, and you can see Squirrel Avenue and the Intersection with Fourth Street from the balcony. I didn't know what was going on at first, not until they came closer. Kate saw them heading our way and shouted for Jane to come to see, too.*

K. McDonald: *I was trying to sleep – I had a headache – but I couldn't. I had a creepy feeling, so I got up and walked into the living room to talk to Laura and looked out the balcony door. On the corner I saw this group of maybe a dozen people, some in front carrying signs, but others were carrying an open coffin. I couldn't see their faces because it was dark. It was about 7 o'clock, but they marched across Squirrel Avenue like it was a parade, then up the parking ramp. Car horns were honking like crazy because they were making a big show of it, taking their time, and the traffic was backed up in all directions. Everybody from our building was either out in the parking lot watching or up on their balconies, because it was pretty warm outside for this* *time of year. When the streetlights hit their faces, I could see that the people with the coffin were from The Challenge. I recognized Jim Poole in the coffin; I'm dating his brother.*

G. Washington: *The Challenge? You recognized these people? Both of you?*

L. Cunningham: *I didn't recognize all of them, but you could tell they were from The Challenge. Nobody else marches around with signs that say, "Repent! The prophecy is fulfilled!"*

K. McDonald: *I went out onto the balcony. I knew I was the reason they were there, because of the stories I had written for the* IS [*the* Informed Student, *the campus newspaper*] *about the murder.*

G. Washington: *The murder?*

K. McDonald: *Jason Goldstein's murder, which seems to be connected to The Challenge, or maybe someone just wants it to look that way. Anyway, when they got close enough for me to see them under the streetlights, Jim Poole sat up in the coffin. People started screaming. Our lobby door intercom buzzed, and Jane ran upstairs to get the building super; she was certain the crowd would try to get in.*

L. Cunningham: *The intercom phone rang, and I answered it. A man said he was Reverend Andrew Michaels and demanded to speak with Kate. I told him she wasn't available and that he was on private property and that I'd call the police if they didn't leave now. He said there was no need, that he wanted to talk to Kate about a personal matter. I told him he could tell me, that I wasn't putting her on the phone. He said he wanted to invite her to dinner so they could talk privately about the interests they had in common. I repeated what he said, so Kate would hear. She shook her head no, so I hung up.*

K. McDonald: *I leaned over our balcony rail so I could watch as he came out of the lobby. I saw an older man in a gray suit walk outside, and Jim Poole pointed up in my direction. The man turned – it was definitely Andrew Michaels, we had seen him before on campus – then he walked back inside. Our phone rang again. Jane came back with the building super, who had already called 911. Laura picked* *up the phone and handed it to me. I told Michaels I didn't see any interests we had in common, and asked why I should agree to meet him. "Because of the prophecy," he said. "Which maybe you just made up to serve your purposes," I answered, and handed Laura the phone to hang up.*

L. Cunningham: *Before I could hang up, I could hear him breathing heavily on the phone, as if he was too angry to get words out, but then he sputtered, "That's blasphemy, and you know it, Kate. If you know what's good for you, you'll meet me. I'll be at the diner at 10 o'clock." He hung up then, and Jane ran to the balcony. She said Jim Poole sank back in the coffin like he was dead, but then he heard the police sirens wail and hopped out. I could see everybody scatter and the guys who had been carrying the coffin scooped it up and ran. I closed the balcony door and pulled the curtain over it. Should have thought of that earlier, I guess, not that it would have helped. I've seen guys climb up to second-floor balconies. If they had wanted to get to Kate, they could have, in just a few minutes.*

Resolution: Complainants declined to press charges against Rev. Andrew Michaels, James Poole, and unidentified parties. Complaint closed without action, 13 February 1992.

*****Addendum to file, 26 February 1992:***

Subject of 12 February 1992 complaint, James Poole, discovered dead, 25 February 1992.

Medical Examiner determination: cause of death self-inflicted GSW, 24 February 1992.

Chapter Sixteen

Laura

Philadelphia, November 2016

A weight plopped onto the sofa beside me. "What did you do tonight, Mom, besides fall asleep?"

I squinted at the harsh overhead light. Took a minute to focus on an empty wineglass. On the floor next to it was a book I was reading—*would* have been reading if I had gotten past the second chapter. My big, handsome boy smiled down at me.

"Guess I dozed off. How was the game?"

"Sixers won ugly. Great seats, though. Dad traded up this time."

Nick bent and picked up the wineglass. "We deserve courtside."

Damian hauled himself to his feet and reached out a hand. "Come on, sleepyhead," he said, imitating me. "No reason to stay up, right? You don't have to wait for Drew to come home to bug me for a play-by-play."

"Don't think so." I ran my tongue across teeth that felt like a cat had walked over them. "Anybody want anything? Tea? Hot chocolate?"

"Pass. You grownups talk among yourselves. See ya, Dad."

I looked from my boy to Nick. So alike, yet not.

Nick dropped into a kitchen chair. He watched me as I filled the red tea kettle I'd had since college and set it on a burner. "What are we supposed to talk about, Laura? The absence of Drew and his father? I hear things are a little tense."

"Tense pretty much sums it up. Drew wanted everyone to be here at home for a change, at least until you came to get

Damian. He was still in his pajamas, playing video games this afternoon, when David announced that his mother was expecting them for a late lunch. Little guy went ballistic, started yelling that all he did anymore was go to Nana Bea's and asked why he couldn't stay in his own house with his own stuff, which of course made it my fault in David's eyes. Which, of course, it is, I've parked Drew with Beatrice so often recently."

I let that percolate until the kettle whistled. I pulled two mugs down from a cabinet and raised one in silent inquiry. Nick nodded.

"I don't think I can make the last two sessions with Steve's class before winter break. The timing is terrible. ... I don't want to put Drew through a divorce."

I sat next to Nick. He wrapped his hands around the mug I offered.

"David's not here much, and Drew already suspects the worst, if you ask me," Nick said. "Damian survived our split; he'll help with Drew."

"Adjusting to David's new job hasn't been smooth. Who knows what happens if we separate? David's not you, I don't know what to expect from him anymore."

"I'm so predictable?"

"No, but when you say you'll be here for Damian, you're here for him, and if you get hung up on a case, you let him know. Even when he was little, he never doubted you. I never doubted you."

I needed to shut up. Nick was my ex-husband, not my shrink, not my marriage counselor. Only David and I could fix this.

"Call him," Nick said.

My eyes went straight to the microwave. It was after 11 o'clock.

"Call him," Nick repeated and snapped his fingers to get my attention. "Tell David you want him and Drew home tonight. It's a forty-five-minute drive at this hour; Drew will sleep on the way. Trust me, Beatrice Brightman won't mind. She'll jump for joy at the peace and quiet."

No doubt about that. After listening to two unhappy males grouse all day, she'd be delighted to send them back home to me.

"I'll see what David says."

"Don't avoid the conversation when he gets here, Elsie, and don't let David avoid it."

Not like the last time, right? When the tear in that marriage got so big it couldn't be mended.

I threw my arms around Nick's neck, spilling his tea on his lap. "I can't do this again."

He pressed his lips to my temple, lightly, sweetly. "Neither can I," he whispered into my hair, then pulled back until I released him.

I didn't believe him, though: If Nick thought he could fix my marriage, he'd try.

Nick would fix *me* if he could. He had never figured out how, that's all.

I coaxed Drew's arms through jacket sleeves, untied his sneakers, lowered his jeans down skinny eight-year-old legs, eased the bedspread and blanket from under his body, then covered him. He smiled in his sleep, happy to be home.

I wasn't so sure about David, who hadn't said a word since carrying Drew in from the car. Who hadn't said much on the phone beyond agreeing to drive back to spend the night at our house instead of his mother's. He just stood and watched me with our son. I ducked under his arm and walked next door, to our bedroom.

"Permission to enter? If I'm sleeping on the couch, I'll need some pajamas and socks. This house is freezing."

I adjusted the thermostat up a couple of notches. In a minute, David would be too warm. A minute was probably all I would get.

"Do you want a divorce, David?"

"Do you?"

"I asked first."

He ran his hand over a two-day growth of beard. "Maybe. Sometimes, I think I do. I thought writing the book might help, but it never ends: There are always more questions, more doubts that tear you apart. You can't go back now, you have to see where the book takes you, I get it. But we *both* have to want to stay together. Are you sure you want to?"

I was sure of one thing: I didn't want this mess anymore.

"I want to try, yes. Two more sessions are left in Steve's class, but I'll call him and back out, or do them on a video hookup. Book appearances I have to do. I'm committed to three more, but they're all on the East Coast, a train ride away." I watched his face and saw the same fatigue I felt. "The holidays are coming, and I want us to be together. Work from home and be here with us, not in New York."

David sat on the bed, patted the space next to him. "What if it's not enough?"

"Beats me." I sat.

He wrapped his arms around me and kissed my forehead. "I'm in if you're in, Laura."

Was I?

Steve's rant ripped me from across a half-dozen county lines.

"Unbelievable! You go out to Ohio to interview the first lead in this case in more than twenty years without telling the people who made the connection for you. And now, you don't have the courage to explain yourself in person and give them the credit their work deserves? Get your ass here, and make sure your personal cop shows up too. Jesus, Laura, what the hell is wrong with you?"

My brother-in-law spewed over the phone's speaker as I poured cereal and made lunches. David heard every high-volume syllable from our home office one room over.

"Book leave's done, Steve, I'm back at work. I have children. Tomorrow isn't a good day for me to be away."

David ambled into the Monday morning wreckage that was our kitchen, shaking his head. *Don't piss him off more,* I understood the gesture to mean. David always bent over backward to please his big brother. No way was the fragile state of our marriage going to disrupt the Bright Lights' dynamic.

"Honey," David said sweetly and loud enough so his brother could hear. "I can be home tomorrow for the boys, I have edits I can do from here, and I'm sure you can switch up your days in the newsroom this week. Go, talk to Steve's class."

Chapter Seventeen

Laura
Central Pennsylvania, November 2016

My journalistic White Knight might have rescued me, but the dragon was not slain, merely quieted temporarily. That was clear the next day, as I rationalized for Steve's grad students why I chose to go face-to-face with Annie Karpinsky within hours of contacting her, turning her grief for Judy Wright raw again.

"Call it a gut feeling so strong I dragged my kids and Nick across the state of Pennsylvania with me. Annie needed to know that what she had to say was important. She needed to see how eager we were to hear her story and how important any insight into what happened to Judy might be right now. I regret I didn't include Laird and Eric, but I'm not sorry things turned out the way they did."

Eric looked disappointed but also less angry with me than either Laird or their professor. "It's hard to argue with the results you got." He squinted at Nick's cellphone reproduction of Annie's 1990 photo of Judy and her boyfriend. "You really think this could be Jim Poole?"

Nick projected the image onto the classroom's screen. So blurry, so grainy, it was almost laughable. Then he put up a 1987 campus look-book photo of Jim Poole as a freshman, his thin blond hair shorter and less ratty looking. Side by side, there was no doubt it was the same person.

"So," Eric mused, "Judy met Jim three years later, when she was a freshman, based on Annie Karpinsky's photo. We need to fact-check that."

Given what Annie had revealed about her drug use, not relying on her memory was a wise strategy. "We should dig into the *Informed Student*'s archives and the campus activities calendars and any old posters from the early 1990s. Jim Poole hadn't graduated by the time Judy Wright started classes here. Let's look for something, an event or a club, that might have brought them together."

All of them—Steve's students, Steve, and Nick—looked at me skeptically.

"Hey, this was pre-social media, remember? The printed word, it's how people navigated their way to concerts, university-sponsored mixers, that sort of thing."

"Mixers?" Emma Two asked. "You mean like networking?"

"More like speed-dating," Steve said. "Emma, if you and Jake could get started on that right away … there's a lot to cover, a lot of minutiae."

"We won't know if it's even going to yield anything, but we have to try." Emma Two was warming to her assignment. "We're on it."

"Nothing will be digitized. It's probably on microfilm, and going through it will take forever unless we narrow our search," Jake said. "How about we start with campus religious things, notices of church services? That way, we can blow past sports stuff and sorority crap."

Up on the projection screen, Nick flashed a photo of Andrew Michaels he had run through a facial-recognition program that also allowed for changes in hair length and beard, eye color and eyeglasses. Next to it, he put up a tweaked image that matched the dentist's description of the patient she knew as Michael Andress. Last, he put up Jim Poole's campus picture again.

Steve whistled from the back of the room. "Wow, there's a resemblance."

"Is there?" I asked. "Or it is just that their coloring and general facial types are similar? How do we establish a connection, if there is one?"

"Birth and Social Security records," Emma One offered. "Jim Poole would have needed an SSN to enroll here. But talk about a lot more digging, how many states do we check for birth certificates? Just Pennsylvania and Ohio? Those weird letters Kate McDonald had Jason Goldstein look into, those were from Connecticut. Do we check there too?"

"Adoption records," Jess said. "Since a lot of those aren't open files, there should be fewer to sort through and something might pop." She shrugged off her classmates' curious looks. "I'm adopted. I know these things."

"Really big haystack to search through." I tried to calculate how long it might take, even under the best circumstances.

"Yeah, but we might finally find that needle." Nick switched off the projector.

The really important needle I was sure was out there, if only we could figure out where to look.

Trilby's was packed, and I was beginning to think Jane had forgotten me. So I flipped through some work email, scribbled a few notes in the margin of a blank field-trip permission slip I found buried in my purse, and waited, nursing the latte she had made me twenty minutes earlier.

Nick stood in the aisle for maybe fifteen seconds before sliding into the booth across from me. I hated that I still sensed he was near before I saw him.

"That seat's reserved for the proprietor."

He slipped off the brown leather bomber jacket I gave him for our first anniversary and wrapped his fingers around my cup. "I used to be married to the proprietor's best friend. She'll indulge me."

"Ah, but will the best friend?"

Nick pulled the cup toward him, lifted it to his lips. "Think so, when she hears what I have to tell her."

I had left him with Steve's students not thirty minutes ago. We were due back there in another half hour. *What was so urgent?*

I slapped his hand, wiped the rim of the cup with my napkin. "A few minutes of peace in the middle of the day." I sighed. "That's all I wanted."

Nick's brown eyes warmed like dark chocolate. "I love it when you lie to me, Elsie, you're so bad at it. I should make you beg for this, since I've just frozen a few toes off outside, searching the trunk of my car for the right Challenge Fire case file. Something one of the girls said struck a chord."

"Which girl?"

"The one who brought up adoption records. In my interview with him about the fire, John Poole mentioned adopting his sons right after he'd married their mother."

"I thought you said he was belligerent and uncooperative."

"Oh, he was. The adoption comment surprised me at the time, because Poole didn't want to discuss his dead sons with me, period. Everything else I asked, I was lucky to get one-word answers from him. I don't know when or where the adoption took place, but wouldn't their bio-dad have to sign off on it? You know, consent and officially relinquish parental rights?"

Jane appeared with a mug of coffee and set it in front of Nick before nudging him farther into the booth. "Who relinquished his rights?" she asked, tossing a handful of half-and-half servings on the table.

"Barry and Jim Poole's birth father. Maybe," Nick said. Jane looked at me like I was supposed to know. "I worked with Barry for a year at the *Informed Student*. If he mentioned he was adopted, it didn't stick with me. I don't remember Kate talking about it either."

Nick caught the sugar dispenser Jane slid his way. "You're the adoption expert, Baker. Am I right about the consent thing?"

"Maybe, Detective."

Before she chucked a career in family law to run the coffeehouse, Jane often advised couples navigating the adoption minefield. Nick scooted up against the wall, so he could see her face fully. "Give me a few examples," he said.

Jane searched some mental file drawers. "Okay, let's say I'm sixteen and unmarried and my baby daddy's doing time in prison and I want to give up my child. Legally, the incarcerated dad can't control what I do, and in some states, even if I've acknowledged he's the father, the courts likely will uphold my right to choose—without his consent—who gets to adopt the baby. Or, and this is a rarer circumstance but it happens, let's say the father has mental health issues and is hospitalized long term for them., not just your seventy-two-hour suicide hold."

"Even if the parents are married?" Nick liked specifics, the more the better.

Jane eased out of the booth. "If a judge was involved, yeah, requiring the father's consent might be waived. Gotta run." She blew Nick an air kiss and smooched me directly on the cheek.

"Ready to go back and see teacher?" he asked.

No, I needed a few more minutes to map the new rabbit holes. Wish I had pushed Kate harder to do the same, to watch her back.

Chapter Eighteen

Laura

Central Pennsylvania, March 1992

I limped into the editors' office and dropped my book bag.

"What's going on? Barry almost knocked me down just now, said I'd have to find someone to cover his layout shift—that someone being me—and flew out the door."

Kate looked up from the computer keyboard. "I'm worried about him. Since they found Jim dead, he's been repeating all that 'Army of the Apocalypse' stuff his brother was always spouting, asking what if it's true, what if Jim had seen it."

I pulled off my left sneaker and the sock under it. "Blister." Kate dug around in her backpack, fished out a Band-Aid, and pushed it across the desk.

"Thanks, nurse." I covered the inflamed skin, replaced the sock, and tied the shoe twice.

Kate grabbed my hand. "If you're going to be laying out newspaper pages until two in the morning, you need to eat."

"You should talk." I pointed to an empty potato chip bag on the desk. "And it's only four o'clock."

"Now or never, Cunningham. And you're buying."

Of course I was.

Late afternoon daylight reflected off the journalism school's giant copper doors. It hung like a second sun rising for those of us student night owls who would produce the next day's newspaper. As Kate and I walked west to the edge of the campus, toward the diner, spring seemed possible after weeks of snow and sleet and, lately, death. We joined the parade streaming down the mall, not bothering to speak over the music screaming from boomboxes along the way. Nirvana and U2 and TLC, enough to make you deaf if you weren't already so distracted that you barely noticed.

We got the last open booth, the one in the back you couldn't see from the entrance so it was almost always available, according to Jane. She worked at the diner sometimes when someone called out sick, but she wasn't on today. I caught a waitress's attention as she headed past us to the kitchen. "Two cups of tomato soup, two grilled-cheese sandwiches, and coffee for me and my hardworking friend here."

The waitress rolled her eyes, took out her pad, and wrote down the order. Kate hummed "Twinkle, Twinkle, Little Star" until she vanished through the swinging door.

"I think there's more happening with Barry than grief over his brother. Not something I could discuss at the *IS*. Too many people."

"You're worried about Barry, naturally. We're all worried about Barry."

Kate tapped a finger to her lips. I got it: This was not to be repeated.

"Detective Fabrizzio says there was a note in Jim Poole's room at The Challenge. When the crime-scene guys went in, they found it wedged between the mattress and box spring on the bed. But it wasn't Jim's handwriting apparently, and when they showed it to Barry, he freaked out, Fabrizzio says, started crying and saying, 'Not again, not again.' Which makes no sense unless maybe Jim didn't commit suicide and someone killed him."

Our food arrived before I could decide how to respond. Kate swallowed a spoonful of soup, pushed it aside and bit into her sandwich. I decided against sampling the thick red goo and wondered why Fabrizzio would tell Kate any of that.

"The note said, 'The Lord Lucifer giveth, the Lord Lucifer taketh away. You remember Connecticut.' It sounds like something terrorists would do," she said. "You know, leave a note, take responsibility."

"Really? That's what Fabrizzio said, that it was someone taking responsibility for Jim Poole's death?"

Kate chewed a minute, then swallowed. "It's what my gut tells me. Fabrizzio didn't exactly show me the note. It was on his desk, in a plastic bag."

"And you read it upside down."

Kate winked. She scooped congealed cheese from between the bread slices and stared at it. "I'm going to The Challenge. I'll ask the good Reverend Michaels directly. He'll deny that he's behind it, and the Connecticut letters, but he knows who is, I'm sure of it, and I want to see his face when he does. I owe it to Barry, and to Jason."

My cup slipped from my grip and caught the edge of the saucer, spilling coffee onto the tabletop, drenching the stack of napkins the waitress had left. "You're not responsible for what Barry is going through. You weren't responsible for Jason either; you just asked him to report a story. You didn't know what he was walking into."

"If there's a connection between Jason Goldstein's death and Jim Poole's, don't I have to find out? What if this is the prophecy business Michaels was spouting that night he showed up at our apartment building?"

"And if it is, if Andrew Michaels is behind this, he's dangerous. Let Fabrizzio and the cops handle it."

She stood, pulling her coat after her. "Jason was my friend. I'm going."

I had to stop her. "Why would Michaels agree to see you now, with no notice, on his turf, when you didn't agree to meet with him under pretty much the same circumstances at our apartment?"

Kate looked back at me as if she'd just solved a riddle. "Maybe I don't have to demand to see Michaels. Maybe his girlfriend will let me in." She hurried toward the door.

I pushed my arms into my jacket and grabbed the check. "What are you talking about? Who is Michaels' girlfriend?"

Kate waited and let me catch up. "Stacey something. The person who discovered Jim Poole's body. I was there when she let Barry into Jim's room with a key so he could pick up his brother's things. She had a whole ring of keys. Maybe she's Michaels' spy, too. Maybe she'll trade a little of what she knows for a little of what she thinks I know."

Bluffing did not seem the way to go. "Don't play games, Kate."

"Don't call Fabrizzio to try to stop me, I'm going to The Challenge. Now."

Chapter Nineteen

Laura

Central Pennsylvania, November 2016

Steve's grad students huddled over printouts, crosschecking one against the next. Nick waved from across the room, where Laird was holding forth on procedures for requesting information under the state's Right to Know Act.

Emma One cornered me. "Something's going on. Brightman got called away, and he didn't look happy about it. He said we should start without him, that you were in charge."

Steve knew I hated being here; even the class knew it by now. The only thing that drew me back to this building and the memories that swarmed me the minute I stepped inside was the possibility we'd learn something new. Just one more week, and the university would shut down for the holidays. I wouldn't be back next term. But for now, it seemed, I was the boss.

I clapped my hands and whistled to settle them down, the way I did when I wanted my kids to pay attention.

"We were talking about public-records searches and scraping databases. You've been thorough but also pretty lucky. You've found unexpected connections among The Challenge fire victims in a deluge of details. A lot of the time, though, public records are a dark void hiding that one flicker of light you're desperate to find."

Nick pushed away from the window ledge he was leaning against. "These days, the slow business of investigation can sometimes seem even slower, there are so many sources to tap. But the upside of the data we can access from our phones is that the answers, once we finally locate them, can be excruciatingly precise. You might say beyond a shadow of a doubt."

"Good reminder," I said. "Before we broke for lunch, we were talking about adoption records specifically."

I turned and saw Steve standing at the classroom door, running a finger across his throat, a signal for me to shut up.

"It appears the university is upset by our efforts to develop new information about The Challenge fire," he said, anger imbuing each syllable. "I—we, I should say, have been ordered to cease and desist. Something about our being in violation of the nondisclosure agreement the university signed in settling the consolidated lawsuits filed by the victims' families."

"Bullshit," Laird muttered. "A lot of ass-covering, in case we discover something that shows even worse negligence on the school's part. This is a money move, that's all."

Steve pointed to his chest, then around the room. "State university employee, state university facilities, state university internet. Your tuition dollars are state university funds. Hell, even that printer belongs to this state university. I'll fight them on this, but in the meantime, we are done here."

Stalking to the corner where the printer perched semi-balanced on a chair, Laird liberated a box of its state university-owned reams of paper. "Dump everything in here now—spreadsheets, thumb drives, notebooks. They can knock us out, but not our work."

Steve needed us gone immediately, that was clear. I grabbed my coat and bag and headed for the hallway. Nick cursed behind me as we started down the fire stairs to the campus mall.

"Wait, take this with you," Laird shouted, rushing to catch us. He shoved the box at Nick. "None of us knows what's in here, not all of it. Plausible deniability."

Nick hoisted the box onto his shoulder. "No such thing, buddy."

"Well, then don't forget who dug up the information for you." Laird ducked back inside and let the fire door slam.

"Now all we need is a non-university-owned table and a couple non-university-owned chairs, so we can sort through this," Nick said. "Trilby's again?"

I searched around in my purse, jiggled the key I located there. "Jane's. For emergencies, she says. This qualifies, I think."

Jane would be jammed at the coffeehouse for at least three hours more, enough time for us to get a good start examining and organizing what our student deputies had uncovered. I texted her that I'd be at her place with Nick because the university had kicked us out.

We walked a mile to the townhouse Jane bought five years ago, after her cardiac-surgeon husband divorced her for a younger woman. Nice, fat property settlement, more than sufficient to cover this purchase and what Jane needed to transform Trilby's from the dive bar of our youth.

Nick set the box on the coffee table and walked into the kitchen, returning a few minutes later with a bottle of bourbon and two glasses. He poured two fingers and handed it to me. "Drink. This is gonna be a slog."

"I need to keep a clear head."

"If your head gets any clearer, it'll be transparent. Damn it, Elsie." He filled about a third of his own glass and knocked it back.

Why argue? I mimicked him, and the alcohol's warmth coursed through me. *So what if it was only the middle of the afternoon?*

An hour later, the dining room table was covered with the grad students' gleanings to date, printouts and photocopies we had sorted into piles: driver's license and vehicle data, birth certificates, deeds, death certificates, voter registrations, Selective Service records. And their quest for connections wasn't even comprehensive—the first round of searches was only for 1990 through 1995, to account for the period shortly before and shortly after the fire. The class also checked adoption records back through 1962, to account for the range of ages of the fire's victims including Stacey Endicott but not Andrew Michaels. Because we had believed, naively as it turned out, that we had moments to spare, we had left Michaels out of the search for the moment—we couldn't be sure we had even a reliable birthdate for him.

Thumb drives, a half-dozen of them, would offer something useful, I hoped. I plugged into my laptop a purple drive with Disney princesses on it. A folder labeled "1992 PA Marriage License Applications" caught my eye.

Nick leaned in for a better view of the screen. "Organized by county and month of application. Could be worse."

I opened the January 1992 file for the county in which we were sitting, scanning through it. Students at the university would have been gone part of the month for the holiday break, and members of the faculty typically headed for warmer weather as soon as they could. "Several dozen here, but no familiar names."

February's file was denser, probably because of Valentine's Day. I opened and closed each entry.

"Jesus, can this be right?" I turned the laptop toward Nick, tapped a fingernail against a February 20 application. "James A. Poole and Anastasia B. Endicott. *Stacey* Endicott? Jim died five days later."

"She was supposed to be Andrew Michaels' girlfriend. Michaels slept in her room when he stayed at The Challenge, and she had the keys to other people's rooms. Everybody who lived there and was lucky enough not to be home at the time of the fire told the same story. How the hell did I miss this, Elsie?"

"You weren't looking for it. Why would you?"

Nick spun my chair to face him. "Did they get married? If they did, why did Jim Poole shoot himself? *Did* Jim Poole shoot himself? He had mental health issues—antipsychotic drugs were found in his room and were in his body at the time of his death. But what if everyone was just supposed to think it was suicide? And Judy Wright, where did she fit in?

"How did I ask none of those questions at the outset, Laura? How else did I fail this investigation? All those years I told you to let it be…"

The despair in Nick's voice was more than I could bear. I pressed my lips to his, slipped my tongue between them, let him lift me onto his lap and wrap his arms around me. I melted into him, his heat, so familiar.

He tasted like the devil himself and everything I knew was bad for me. Like this investigation was bad for me, like the book had been bad for me. Nothing between us was ever settled and over.

He swiveled me until I was straddling him. His hands on my behind, my legs wrapped around his waist; my skirt riding high, his erection close to the wet ache between my thighs, nothing but his jeans and my tights keeping his skin from mine.

I sighed, or maybe he did, and he stood and carried me until my back was against the wall and he was peeling my panties down and I was tearing at his fly and guiding him into me.

My body remembered his touch, recognized him, and tightened around him. Between kisses, I heard a little voice telling me to stop, but that voice was drowned out by another one moaning with pleasure.

He ran his tongue along my neck, in and out of my ear, and I couldn't tell if anything existed outside that room. Nick didn't say a word, just swept me back to the place we once existed together, a place we might still be if not for Kate and David and more guilt than any two people should carry as long as we had. Lights exploded in front of my eyes, and I dissolved in a sea of liquefied bliss until I hung limply in his arms, and he lowered us both to the floor.

Pressed against his chest, I could hear Nick's heart pound as if he'd just run a mile. He whispered what his eyes had already told me: He loved me, that much was not in my power to change—not when I left him, not when I married David and had his child, not today.

"Nick, I wish—"

"Shh, don't say it, don't think. Just feel how good we are."

I clung to him, knowing it *was* good ... and also impossible.

Chapter Twenty

Nick

Northern Pennsylvania, November 2016

He might have turned southeast toward Philly, toward home and his son and his job. That would be too close to Laura, though, and what they'd just done, so Nick turned north on the interstate toward Bradford. Another few hours' drive, and he'd confront the man who must know more about The Challenge fire than anyone had imagined.

John Poole had been an angry man twenty-four years ago. No doubt he was an old, angry man now. Poole was still alive, still living in the same mobile-home park.

A police buddy had agreed long ago to keep an eye on Poole for Nick. Two sons' deaths within two months would have been enough cause to worry about the man's mental health, but when he interviewed Poole after the fire, Nick had sensed in him something darker than grief. Nick hoped his gut feeling about Poole was wrong, that the darkness wouldn't manifest in violence.

Over the last twenty-four years, it hadn't. Nick knew Poole had recently retired as foreman at a plant that manufactured specialty lighting for shopping malls and hotels. Nick's source, a friend from the police academy well acquainted with the Bradford locals, described how Poole had put in long hours and socialized infrequently. Every six months or so, his truck bearing canoe and camping gear, Poole headed over the nearby border into New York, where Pennsylvania State Police jurisdiction ended, and with it, Dixon Bott's informal surveillance. Dix never suggested it was time to stop altogether.

If Dix had, Nick wondered, would he have agreed? All these years, had he been as obsessed with Kate's disappearance as Laura? And when Laura wouldn't let it go, was it just easier for him to believe that he had?

At the rest area before the exit he wanted, Nick stopped for gas, rinsed the distraction of Laura's taste from his mouth and fingers, and plugged in his laptop for a refresher on the research he'd done in the weeks immediately after the fire at The Challenge.

In 1978, John Poole had married Elizabeth Aldridge, a divorced woman with two young sons. Two years later, John came home late one night to find his wife dead in their Connecticut home, the boys sitting wide-eyed, covered in blood and surrounded by an array of knives. Elizabeth's ex-husband, Mitchell Aldridge, was arrested and charged with her murder. Aldridge waived his right to a jury trial, was found guilty by reason of insanity by a judge, and was sentenced to fifteen years to life in a state prison's psychiatric block.

During an August 1981 riot, fourteen prisoners took a half-dozen guards hostage, beat them bloody, then escaped in the pandemonium. In the manhunt that followed, ten of the escapees were quickly apprehended. Two more fugitives were fatally wounded by police, and their bodies were found early the next day. A third wounded man had drowned in a backyard swimming pool near the prison. About four weeks later, the fourteenth escapee was discovered dead in a flood-control basin several miles away. The man wore Mitchell Aldridge's prison jumpsuit but was otherwise unrecognizable because of advanced decay, newspaper reports said.

Given the circumstances of his wife's murder and his sons' deaths, Nick doubted John Poole would be happy to see any detective, let alone one he thought he'd put in the rearview mirror almost a quarter-century ago. Nick didn't care. Those newly discovered links between the Challenge Fire victims told him Poole had done his best to divert the 1992 investigation away from his family.

No advance warning, this was a total cold call. Nick frankly couldn't wait to see the look on Poole's face when he recognized him.

He felt lucky when he saw a pickup in the driveway, less so when he realized the truck was up on blocks, missing its two rear tires. Nick banged on the screen door. Poole was well into his seventies by now, maybe a little less apt to hear right away.

Or maybe not. The door opened immediately. Poole looked surprised for a second, then his expression reassembled into disdain.

"Should have known I'd see you again. Your woman, the writer, she send you?"

Nick quickly hid his own surprise—Poole knew about *Bloodstrains*.

"Ex-wife and, no, she didn't." Nick stepped around Poole and inside before the door could slam in his face.

"Said everything I had to say back in '92, Detective … Fabrizzio, right?"

Poole knew damn well what Nick's name was, it had been in every news report about the fire and the lawsuits the victims' families filed against the university.

"Not sure what I could possibly do to help your Laura Cunningham—excuse me, your ex-Laura Cunningham—sell more books," Poole said.

Nick took a seat in the kitchenette, enveloped by the stale odor—hot dogs maybe—that hung in the air. "Not what this is about, John. I don't give a damn whether the book sells, though it's interesting that you know about it."

Poole kicked a chair across the trailer. "Then what the hell do you want from me? This is my life: this sad excuse of a home, an old dog, and a sidelined truck."

He shook with fury or frustration, maybe both, Nick couldn't even speculate, but he could tell Poole had kept it bottled up for too long. Nick stood and walked to the refrigerator. He found a couple cans of beer, popped the top on one, and handed it to his reluctant host.

"Twenty-four years after the fact, what I want is what I've always wanted, John: the truth. Your sons' relationship to The Challenge suddenly seems to be a pivotal part of the story, and you're the only one left to explain why that is."

"If you'd seen your mother murdered the way Jimmy and Barry did, you'd go looking for someone to help you, too."

"Then tell me about that."

He growled like a cornered animal. "What they saw? How about what the cops agreed to keep out of the official record, so they'd forget they saw it? Small, shallow knife wounds, dozens of them, on our sons' hands and on Elizabeth. Mitchell wrapped the fingers of an eight-year-old and a ten-year-old around the blades and cut those boys until they obeyed his order to stab their mother with him. There were so many knives and so much blood, the boys were drenched in it, their mother's, and their own. They were horrified at what Mitchell made them do, horrified at what their mother watched them do before she bled to death."

Poole gagged, bent over in his chair to keep down whatever he had last eaten. "Years of therapy couldn't erase that memory." His voice rasped, dragging pain along with every word. "Didn't matter where I moved them, my boys couldn't help but remember Connecticut."

The words chilled Nick as he remembered the letters sent before and after Jason Goldstein's murder, and the strange note found in Jim Poole's room after his suicide.

"Tell me about Jim."

Poole dragged his sleeve across his eyes to wipe away tears, and reached down to pet the black Labrador resting a paw against his boot. The dog licked his hand. "Jim didn't die in the damn fire you and that Cunningham woman are so obsessed about."

Nick watched John scratch behind the dog's ears, relax a little as the Lab rested his head against his leg, maybe the only comfort left to either one. "The fire killed Barry, but Jim had already died at The Challenge. He put a gun to his temple there five days after applying for a marriage license."

"Jimmy would never have married that tramp," Poole said. "A nice girl loved him, and he loved her."

Not a fan of Stacey Endicott's then, but maybe of Judy Wright. "Was there a wedding?" Nick asked. "Did Reverend Michaels perform the ceremony? Wasn't Stacey Endicott *his* girlfriend, too?"

Poole stood and flung open the door. "You can leave now, Detective. Yeah, my boys were messed up, losing their mother the way they did, but I raised them as Elizabeth would have wanted me to. The way I see it, Stacey Endicott was the reason Jimmy died, one way or the other. You figure out why, you let me know. Seems you got no trouble sticking your nose where it doesn't belong."

Nick didn't move from his chair. "How did you meet Elizabeth Aldridge? How did you come to marry her?"

Poole glared. "None of your goddamn business."

Message received. Nick slapped his business card down on the kitchen table. Poole slammed the door so hard behind him, Nick heard the trailer shake.

About six miles up the road, he pulled into a pancake joint to decide his next move—the day had thrown any number of wild pitches at him. Mindful of his 51-year-old body's cholesterol levels, he ordered an egg-white omelet with a side of turkey bacon and a cup of coffee. He connected to the restaurant's Wi-Fi and started poking around.

"God bless the great state of Connecticut for its many gifts," he whispered after a particularly fruitful search yielded the judge who had approved the adoption paperwork for John and Elizabeth Poole in the matter of James and Barry Aldridge: Leslie Anastasia Endicott of the Connecticut Probate Court. That was a familiar name.

Coincidence? Nick doubted it. He might have been a twenty-seven-year-old newbie detective when the ashes of The Challenge fire were first his to sift through, but he sure as hell wasn't one now.

Omelet consumed along with three more cups of black coffee, Nick headed south toward Philadelphia. For now.

Chapter Twenty-one

Nick

Philadelphia, November 2016

"Not without me, you're not! You're going to Connecticut, *I'm* going to Connecticut!"

He listened to Laura's quick, sharp shouts. He was the only one she ever screamed at, if Damian, their son, the volunteer spy, were to be believed.

"No sense in two people driving several hours on a mission of impossible-to-determine utility." He knew Laura would argue two heads were better than one, but the reality was that three dozen years had passed since the day of Elizabeth Aldridge Poole's horrific murder. "The house where the crime occurred is still standing, I've confirmed that, but will seeing it reveal anything? Long shot at best, I'd say."

Music rose in volume on Laura's end of the line, some '90s boy band.

"Bea's here to consult about Thanksgiving, like I care what's going to be on this year's menu," Laura whispered into the phone.

"If I find anything, we'll go back together, Elsie, I promise."

"You're already on the road, aren't you?"

Laura hung up on him. She would be banging stuff around now, her mother-in-law within earshot and no doubt weighing whether and what to report back to her son. Fortunately, Beatrice Brightman liked him.

He pushed Laura out of his head as he navigated the access lanes from the New Jersey Turnpike to the Garden State

Parkway, eventually cutting through New York state into Connecticut.

The drive was dull, and he had been tired when he started out. By the time he reached an increasingly rural stretch of highway, it was nearly dusk, and Nick was yearning for caffeine, blinking away little spots darting across his field of vision. Blinking, when a deer darted in front of him. He slammed on the brakes but clipped the animal in its right hindquarter with his left front bumper. The deer stared, shook it off, and ran into the woods at the side of the road.

Nick hit the emergency flashers. He was easing over to the right shoulder to check that his Jeep was as uninjured as the deer, when he struck something else. A flash of metal told him it wasn't another animal.

Swerving wildly on the gravel berm was someone in a wheelchair, its right-side wheel a perilous inch or so lower than the one on its left. The chair hit a rock, tilted more sharply to the right for several feet, then somehow corrected itself and charged ahead, powered by other-than-manual means.

Nick jumped out. "Hey! Are you hurt?" He sprinted down the road, but the wheelchair accelerated, and his heart raced. He regretted that he hadn't been to the gym in weeks.

He bent over to catch his breath, closed his eyes, and prayed he hadn't done serious harm. When he straightened, he saw looking back at him a gaunt face, long gray hair pulled back severely, hand tethered to the mechanized wheelchair's controls. Quickly, the chair spun around and began to race down the shoulder again, what looked like a laptop banging against one of its wheels.

Damn it, he'd struck an old woman, or maybe an old man, he couldn't tell from this distance. At least the person was alive, and the chair was moving.

Nick jogged back to his Jeep and examined the right front bumper. A thin silver-and-black line sliced through the red paint there. He had to file a police report. Not a hit-and-run exactly—what was it, since he wasn't the one fleeing the scene? Nick hoped there was 911 service here in Wherever the Hell He Was, Connecticut.

Nope, no cell signal, not in any direction. He got behind the steering wheel and headed toward whatever town lay ahead, driving a good ten miles below the speed limit, just in case.

The sky delivered a cloudless autumn evening in the twenty minutes it took Nick to register the first sign of civilization: a diner, dinnertime customers in the lot. A police cruiser too. *Good.*

About a dozen red leatherette booths with Formica tables lined the window wall. A scuffed-up counter with red stools suggested soda fountain rather than eatery, as did the old drugstore sign next to a 1960s vintage pay phone. Nick caught the eye of the tall twentysomething guy who seemed to work there and was chatting up a young woman in a uniform Nick recognized as Connecticut State Police. Nick got close enough to read her nametag, "S.P. Endicott."

"Interesting," he mumbled to no one. "Maybe my luck is changing."

"Can I help you?" the trooper pulled back, her personal space more than a little invaded.

He pulled out his badge. "Detective Sergeant Nicholas Fabrizzio, Philadelphia PD. Sorry to interrupt, but I've been trying to call local police about an accident up on the highway. I hit someone, also a deer."

Some signal Nick couldn't interpret transmitted from the trooper to the guy behind the counter. She scrutinized his shield.

"Got a business card, Detective?" He handed her one. "Which is it?" she asked. "Did you hit a human being or a deer before you fled the scene?"

Don't play games, sweetheart. This cop is too fucking tired for them.

Nick dropped onto a stool, retrieved his shield, and put a little attitude into his answer.

"I couldn't get a phone signal. You are the first officer of the law I have seen. Consider this my official report of the incident, which I presume is in your jurisdiction, given it happened on that road just outside. Take out your notebook, or call someone in to take my statement for you, I don't care. My Jeep will show evidence of two collisions—body damage to the left front bumper from striking a deer, then paint scraped when I tried to pull to the right and struck a motorized wheelchair traveling westbound along the shoulder. Both the deer and the person operating the chair left the scene seemingly uninjured, but we wouldn't want to take chances now, would we?"

The trooper gestured to one of the booths. "Justin, we'll be over there."

"Coffee, please, and a cheeseburger, well done, would be great." Nick followed the trooper, noticing a menu on the counter. "Christine's," the cover read.

"I'd like to speak to Christine."

"Getting answers out of Justin's mother might be tough tonight," Trooper Endicott said. "That was her wheelchair you hit."

Nick scrambled to his feet. "Is she hurt?"

The trooper's hand clutched his wrist like an iron manacle.

"Calm down, Christine's fine. Woman thinks she's indestructible; she dares folks to do their worst," Endicott said.

"Rides along that damn road at all hours, has been clipped at least a handful of times that I know of. Justin checked her out before you showed up. You're right, she doesn't seem injured."

His own heart had just about stopped on contact with the wheelchair. "You saw her?"

The trooper released his hand. "Followed her in just now. Chair was wobbling a bit more than usual, but she was motoring, kicking up a storm of busted-up macadam like she always does. Banged up her computer pretty bad, though. She can't talk without it, like what's his name, that famous scientist."

What was she talking about, besides maybe a lawsuit in the making?

His burger and fries arrived in a plastic basket lined with a thick gingham napkin. Nick threw ten bucks down on the table. "I'll take this to go, if you don't mind. You have my contact information. I'll be around for a while tomorrow, for whatever the authorities need."

Didn't take him too long to find a motel. But before he could even think about letting his head hit a rock-hard pillow, Nick lifted Trooper Endicott's fingerprints from his shield and Diner Guy's prints from the plastic basket and ran them through the system. He checked out the registration of every vehicle whose tag he'd photographed before he left the parking lot, then dug in to research whatever records existed online for the diner itself. Any bit of information that might help explain the Connecticut-Challenge Fire connection.

A 1998 incorporation filing showed a sole proprietorship registered to a Philip Anderson, doing business as Christine's. The latest property tax filing listed the diner's proprietor as Justin Anderson, DOB November 1992. Nick tracked back eight years, to before Justin would have been legally old enough to own the business. The 2008 property tax assessment listed the owner as the estate of Christine Lawrence Anderson, DOB February 1969, so not an old woman after all. Listed as trustee for the estate was Connecticut Probate Court Judge Leslie Anastasia Endicott.

Busy woman, the judge, handling adoptions, estates. …

Because there was an estate, there could be paperwork on other public databases as well. Nick found in the property history a 1999 deed transfer, a $1 paper transaction in which Philip Anderson had turned the premises over to his daughter-in-law Christine and his grandson Justin, with Christine Lawrence Anderson listed as trustee.

Nick was nodding off at his laptop when he decided on one last search, of news sites this time. For Philip Anderson, there was no obituary. Also nothing that suggested Christine Anderson used a wheelchair because of a traffic accident or anything else that required police involvement.

There was, however, a 2013 obit for Judge Endicott. Listed as her lone survivor was a granddaughter, Stacey Poole Endicott of the Connecticut State Police.

Endicotts and Pooles, Pooles and Endicotts, right here with him in small-town New England.

In a place called Aldridge, of all things, according to the mud-spattered sign he had noticed just before the motel turnoff.

Nick set the plastic basket on the counter, its red slats scrubbed a bit raw when he'd removed the fingerprint gunk.

"Really didn't expect to see that basket again after you nabbed it, but thanks. Don't suppose you're returning the napkin too?"

"That was a little harder to clean in my motel-room sink before checkout time." Nick slid over a five-dollar bill. "Will this cover it?"

Justin Anderson laughed. "Wow, I'm not sure how I'll recover that loss. What can I get you today, Detective? Some vintage restaurant china? A straw or two?" He poured Nick a cup of coffee and dropped a handful of creamers alongside it.

"I'd like to talk to your mother. I'd feel terrible if I hurt her last night."

The smile left the young man's face. "She'll be all right, just a scrape on her chin; the visiting nurse checked her out earlier today. Her computer needs to go out for repairs, though, after bouncing against the wheels of the chair. She won't be talking much to anyone until it's fixed, might take a couple weeks. Stacey probably told you last night that Mom has ALS."

Not in so many words, she hadn't.

"But she can hear, right? I'd like to apologize in person before I head back to Pennsylvania today."

A frown crossed Justin's face. "I don't know. Mom likes her privacy. She hates that everybody knows everybody else's business here. She'll hate that now a stranger knows hers."

Yet she owned a diner with her name on it, and it was probably Aldridge's gossip central.

"I'm just passing through," Nick said. "Your mom's privacy is safe with me."

"I'll ask her if she wants to hear you out." Justin pushed through the kitchen door.

The diner was quiet for nine in the morning. A pair of older gentlemen sat in a booth, playing chess. Regulars, no doubt. The one facing Nick sensed his interest and acknowledged him with a nod. Maybe one of them was Philip Anderson—Justin had seemed content to ignore them.

Did he chafe at this life the same way his mother seemed to? Run screaming out of here every night he could, and hit the local bar with his buddies or a girl? All work was a lonely existence, as Nick could attest.

Justin emerged from the kitchen. "She's asleep, her caregiver says. The nurse might have given her something. Mom was pretty agitated last night after the crash."

Nick slid his business card over. "I'd still like to apologize, whatever way I can."

He gulped a mouthful of coffee and left, regretting that he'd disrupted Christine Anderson's bid for freedom, such as it was. Also regretting that he was too exhausted from his overnight research binge to check out the place where Elizabeth Aldridge was murdered and drive back the same day to Philly, where his actual detective job awaited.

Aldridge, Connecticut, merited a second visit, for sure.

No way Bradford was on his route home, but the events of the last twenty-four hours pulled Nick back to that part of northern Pennsylvania and John Poole. Connecticut had yielded lots of new questions. He knew nothing about how Poole had met Elizabeth Aldridge and come to marry her, but now Nick had met a state trooper whose name suggested she was both a Poole and an Endicott. Something he had to pursue, given the marriage license application Steve Brightman's class had found.

As he turned off the interstate, Nick's phone rang. He swerved when the caller's location came up as Bradford.

"Poole?"

"Hope you're happy, Fabrizzio, he's here."

"Who's there?" Nick could hear something heavy banging, possibly the metal door of John Poole's trailer.

A shot fired, the sound so ear-shattering Nick might have been standing next to the gun. "Hang up and call the police!"

"My Elizabeth is dead, my sons are dead, and now he's come for me. Full circle."

Nick's ear rang as he heard a sharp ping, then a thud, then silence. He stepped on the gas, popping his police light onto the dashboard and dialing 911.

John Poole was lying in blood right now, dead, Nick was sure of it. He floored it the forty miles between him and the trailer.

He found the entrance to the mobile home park cordoned off by state police vehicles. He parked, flashed his badge to a fresh young trooper at the roadblock, and asked for his old school friend.

"Lieutenant Bott is commanding the scene until we've determined there's no active shooter, sir."

"I was on the phone with the victim as it was going down. Whoever did this came for John Poole and no one else. Call Lieutenant Bott and tell him Nick Fabrizzio is standing here, ready to tell him what he knows. Better yet, let me pass, and I'll tell him myself."

"Wait at your car, sir."

Nick cooled his heels for who knew how long. Perched on the hood of the Jeep, he chewed a half-dozen sticks of gum and tried to reach Bott at least that many times.

And then, there he was.

"Honey, you know better than to call me at work." Bott winked, his blue eyes bloodshot.

"What the hell, Dix? I called this mother in. You could have at least left word with Boy Wonder over there." Fabrizzio shook Dixon Bott's hand, knowing he'd have done the same thing.

"Does it help if I say you were right, there was no active shooter in the trailer park? Then let me tell you this, too: I don't know what you think you heard, but this was no intruder getting in and shooting, not as far as I see. Looks to me like John Poole killed himself."

A crime scene van pulled up to the roadblock and was admitted into the staging area, followed immediately by an ambulance labeled "McKean County Medical Examiner."

"Did you record the call, Nick?"

"Happened too fast, there was no time. I was on the interstate's off-ramp, on my way here, when Poole made contact. I didn't call ahead to tell him I'd be stopping by to visit again."

"Again?"

"I was here the other day. Surveillance camera up there must have captured me."

Bott looked up, but shook his head. "Nah, that's just one of those phony things you can buy online to fake out burglars. We'll see what blood spatter, et cetera, tells us, but it looks self-inflicted to me."

"John Poole knew who was banging at his door, and he knew what would happen. 'He's come for me. Full circle,' Poole said. Doesn't sound like someone who's suicidal."

Bott's phone rang. He held up a finger and took the call. "Okay, I'll be right there."

Nick eased himself to street level. "If you want, I'll give my statement and get out of your hair. Just do me a favor: Make sure your CSU gives this one the works—DNA, soil forensics, the whole nine. Because if what I heard is really the way it went down, you'll find something."

Bott led the way to John Poole's trailer.

Chapter Twenty-two

Nick
Philadelphia, November 2016

"Laura Cunningham, your book, *Bloodstrains,* calls for reopening the investigation into The Challenge fire more than two decades ago. What do you make of word that John Poole, father of two of the book's central figures, was found dead in upstate Pennsylvania with a gunshot wound to the head?"

Reporters and video crews had staked out her front door. "All I know is what I've heard: that it looks like the wound was self-inflicted, but the police are also pursuing a tip about a shooter. Until that's been sorted out, I won't know what to make of John Poole's death."

Really, Elsie, that's the best you got? They ambushed you, the least you can do is push your damn book.

Nick sat in his Jeep around the corner, trying to watch a 6 o'clock newscast feed that kept buffering on his phone, trying to keep out of sight until the press ended its blockade of Laura's street.

"But what was your gut reaction when you heard, Laura?"

The live feed straightened out long enough for Nick to see her square her shoulders. "What else? That the fire had claimed another victim, its last, I hope. John Poole lost two sons in a matter of weeks at The Challenge back in 1992—the older one to suicide, the younger to the fire itself—and I still haven't heard a good explanation why either death occurred."

"Laura, Laura—"

"That's all, thank you."

Standing behind her, David leaned into the bouquet of microphones. "My wife's work deserves to be recognized, no matter how John Poole died. Laura has argued all along, and now through *Bloodstrains*, that too many questions about The Challenge fire remain and must be answered."

So, maybe not an ambush after all. When the cameras shifted to catch Laura and David walking inside, Nick got a better view of the driveway: four cars, including Steve Brightman's Mercedes convertible and his mother's BMW. Even one Brightman brother could summon a whole lot of local press on short notice. With both on the case, the Associated Press and the national networks probably were alerted too.

Nick stayed put until the news flotilla dispersed. He checked email to see if Dixon Bott had learned anything more; finding nothing, he texted Dix asking for an update. When he finally rang Laura's doorbell, there was no question the news crews had gotten a warmer reception.

"How nice of you to keep me posted about your trip to Connecticut. How good of you to just drop in now, when we're about to start dinner." She barely opened the door.

"Laura, let the man inside, then rip his head off. It's chilly out there."

Nick stepped into the foyer. Beatrice Brightman greeted him with a proffered hand, which he immediately kissed.

"You look like you could use a drink, Nicholas. Get him a bourbon, dear. I'll escort your handsome ex into the family room." Laura shot her a withering glare. Beatrice leaned closer.

"You push buttons she doesn't know she has. She's annoyed, but you're much smarter about her than my son. This John Poole business has put David on Laura's side and against you. Drew doesn't really count, of course, but Damian and I will defend you. Do your best to woo Steve, because he'll be the swing vote."

It took a minute for Nick to remember he'd arrived in the middle of Bea's annual pre-Thanksgiving descent on Laura and David, which Damian always enjoyed because it made his stepfather squirm. Beatrice lived in Chadds Ford, about an hour's drive away, but she insisted on a weeklong sleepover visit each November.

For full effect, they stopped, Bea's arm looped through his, at the entrance to the family room. "David, make sure there's a steak on the grill with Nick's name on it. You'll be staying for dinner, won't you, dear?"

David's glare matched his wife's. Nick smiled insincerely. Damian's eyes lifted from his phone. "Hey, Dad. Mom didn't tell me you were coming."

"Last-minute decision. I'm just back from a trip."

Steve Brightman's eyebrows rose. "I, for one, would love to hear all about it. Drew, you and Damian can handle setting an extra place at the table while the old folks talk, right?"

"You just want to get rid of us," Drew complained.

Damian shooed him into the kitchen. "Nah, they just want to get rid of *you*. Somebody has to keep an eye on the steaks. That would be *me*."

Beatrice waved goodbye to the boys and saluted her older son after relinquishing Nick's arm. "Nicely done, Stephen. Nick's obviously here to deliver information. Spill, Detective."

Nick perched on the arm of a leather loveseat. "I was a witness to John Poole's death—if you can call hearing someone being mortally wounded over the phone witnessing it. I was driving back from Connecticut, headed to Bradford to see Poole, when he called me. I heard someone force his way into Poole's trailer and shoot. John said someone had come for him. 'Hope you're happy,' he said, before the second shot killed him."

"And what the fuck did that mean?"

Beatrice slapped David's wrist, as if he were Drew's age. "Go on, Nick."

"An old friend is with the state police at the barracks near Bradford. I've given Lieutenant Dixon Bott a statement, and he's got his people scouring around Poole's trailer for evidence that corroborates my story. John Poole was not a happy man when I saw him recently, but also not what I'd describe as suicidal."

Laura stopped pacing and took a long drink from the glass she held, the bourbon Bea had ordered for Nick. "John Poole called you? A week after you visited him? As you were on your way back from Connecticut, where you went after talking to him about the day Mitchell Aldridge killed the mother of his sons? Who else could have known about that conversation, or your trip to the town where Elizabeth Aldridge Poole was murdered?"

"I know what I heard," Nick said. "If there's something to be found, Dix and his guys will find it. Poole didn't have a landline, only a cellphone, so there should be metadata on the call to me confirming the time and location."

David walked the room's perimeter. "Bott's a good guy, I worked with him on that juvenile-profiling series two years ago, but he doesn't exactly have the A-Team on his side there."

Steve, tracking his brother's movement around the room, nodded. "The county will send its detectives in; between them, they'll get it done. I'm not sure what more we can do until there's an official ruling on Poole's death."

"We can remember Connecticut, that's what. Find the dots in Pennsylvania and connect them to New England." Laura sounded so certain, and Nick hadn't told her about the rest of his trip yet.

"Remember Connecticut," she repeated. "The letters all said that, every one of them sent to the *Informed Student* before and after Jason Goldstein was killed. So did the note found in Jim Poole's room after he died, and the letters Kate got after her stories. We always knew they were linked to the fire, we just never figured out how."

David stepped behind Laura and pulled her into his chest, a possessive arm encircling her.

"Here's one link," Nick said. "West of Hartford, in the town where Elizabeth Poole was murdered and where Jim and Barry were adopted by John Poole by order of Probate Court Judge Leslie Anastasia Endicott, there's a state police trooper named Stacey Poole Endicott. I met her two nights ago. She's 26, maybe 27. The judge was her grandmother. The Stacey Endicott who died in the fire could be her mother, or her aunt or a cousin, or maybe Poole and Endicott are just common last names there."

"Threads that need tugging. Where are my students when we need them?" Steve refilled Nick's glass and handed one to Laura; his younger brother took several steps away from his wife.

"What else, Nick?" Laura knew him well.

He set the bourbon on the coffee table, watching the deep amber liquid swirl. "When I visited John Poole last week, he was different than he was twenty-four years ago. Still angry, no question, but also frustrated that after all these years you had left him no choice but to break his silence. He described what he saw when he found his wife's body, the knives he found in his sons' hands. Mitchell Aldridge didn't murder Elizabeth alone. He forced the boys to help him kill their mother."

Laura flung her arms around Nick, splashing him with her drink.

"*That's* what 'Remember Connecticut' means! Did John Poole send the letters?"

Nick shook his head. "John's last words tell me no."

"Then you and I have to go there to find out who did."

"Laura!" David barked. "I'm not sure you should stay for dinner, Nick. Make whatever plan you need to and text her the details. Get out of my house and stay away from my wife."

Ah, yes, your wife. Nick disengaged himself from Laura, and stooped to pick up the glass her lips had touched.

A plate sailed into the room, crashing to the floor near him and David.

"Don't talk to my dad that way!" Damian yelled at his stepfather. "This isn't about you and my mom, it's about her friend who's been missing for longer than I've been alive. Didn't you ever have a friend who meant so much to you, you didn't know what you'd do without them?"

Damian stepped between him and David. "A piece of Mom got lost when Kate disappeared, and she's been searching for it ever since. Am I the only one smart enough to figure that out?"

Nick knelt and began to pick up shards of china from the hardwood.

Beatrice linked arms with Damian. "Thank goodness you're so much wiser than the adults. Let's get Drew and eat, and maybe the rest of them can manage not to embarrass themselves further."

At the table, Beatrice seated Steve with the boys and Nick next to her, as far away from David and Laura as possible.

"I didn't raise two children without learning something about strategic separation," she whispered, never taking her eyes off her plate.

Chapter Twenty-three

Nick

Connecticut, November 2016

Floodlights drenched the driveway and front yard, enveloping them in a beam worthy of a hovering flying saucer and blinding Nick as he leaned on the doorbell of the house where Elizabeth Aldridge Poole had been murdered.

He heard just fine, however, the familiar click of a weapon's safety mechanism.

"It's Nick Fabrizzio, the detective from Philadelphia. Be pissed if you want, just don't shoot."

The lights dimmed slightly, to stadium intensity. Trooper Stacey Poole Endicott, in uniform, opened the door. "Expected you to come back. Didn't expect you at my front door before the sun showed its face."

His traveling companion offered her hand. "Laura Cunningham. We were hoping to catch you before work."

"You wrote *Bloodstrains*. I read it in one day."

They entered the house and stepped into the living room. Nick reached for the book on the coffee table. A packing receipt fell out. "Same-day delivery. Eager, were you?"

She pushed the door shut. "Wouldn't you be eager to learn what a new book had to say about the fire that killed your mother back in 1992? My grandmother, the judge, parsed every sentence about her death, and her life for that matter. But you're more interested right now in my house and its lurid history, especially in light of my uncle's death. Have at it, look around, there are no secrets here."

Nick doubted that. He trusted nothing about the smudge on the map called Aldridge, Connecticut. He walked into and out of the small kitchen, and poked his head into a powder room, recently installed by the looks of things—it didn't jibe with his understanding of the layout when Elizabeth Aldridge Poole was killed.

"John Poole was your uncle? And the Stacey Endicott who died at The Challenge was your mother?" Laura asked, testing the gnarled branches of that family tree. "All dead now, and John's sons, too, all those years ago."

Trooper Endicott lowered her long frame onto her sofa. She was slender as well, not built like her mother, based on the few photos Nick had seen. "I learned more from *Bloodstrains* than Gran ever thought to share. I knew John all my life, and he never said a word—not about this house, not about what happened here. He was my great-uncle by marriage supposedly. John's half-brother was Gran's third husband, but she never took his last name."

"Yet *you* have the Poole name." Laura sat on the arm of the sofa, the better to see under the broad brim of the trooper's hat.

Stacey tossed the hat next to the book, pulled a band from her ponytail, and shook her hair free. That was when Nick noted a resemblance to the other Stacey Endicott; she had been a redhead too.

"I added the name myself. Seemed like a good idea to show the family ties," this Stacey said. "Aldridge is a tiny place, inbred, you might say. I discovered that in a rather embarrassing fashion."

That got Nick's attention. "Feel like elaborating?"

"I hung out with Justin Anderson in high school, even though he was younger. I was a senior when he was a sophomore."

"Justin is the son of the woman whose wheelchair I hit on the shoulder of the highway," Nick reminded Laura. "He runs the diner."

"Right. So we were teenagers, and Justin was all adorable and horny, and things got a little wild one night, and we started taking off each other's clothes. Turned out he had this sickle-shaped birthmark on his left hip. I did too, which was enough to stop us in our tracks—he knew about as much about his father as I did about mine, and I knew absolutely nothing. I asked Gran, who raised me after my mother dropped me off with her when I was a baby and didn't come back. All she had to say was, 'Almost everybody in this town has an Aldridge or a Poole somewhere in the bloodline. Be sure to look before you leap, sweetheart.'"

Stacey walked into her kitchen, grabbed the pot from the coffeemaker, and ran the water to fill it. She pulled a gourmet-shop bag of French roast out of the fridge and her cellphone from her pocket, probably to text someone she'd be late for work. Or maybe to warn Justin Anderson what she'd just told them, whatever its significance.

Laura joined her at the counter. "Make it extra strong please. I'd really like to understand what's going on here."

Stacey added two more scoops and set the coffee on to brew.

Nick cleared his throat, hoping to pull the conversation back to Stacey's revelation. "Don't suppose you have a picture of this birthmark?"

She pointed to a desk at the far end of the living room. "I've been collecting vintage cameras since I was in Girl Scouts. Top drawer, you'll find a stack of yellowed Polaroid shots."

Nick sorted through the photos and set two side by side on the counter.

"This one," Stacey leaned in, "is Justin's hip, obviously."

Plus half his buttocks and a slight glimpse of his penis, Nick noticed, but, as she said, they were horny teenagers.

"And this one is me, naturally."

More of a side view, Justin was clearly the more discreet photographer.

Laura peered at the photos. "The Challenge fire burned a lot of the victims' skin. John Poole might have mentioned Barry had a birthmark, if he had cooperated with the investigation. Kate never mentioned one. Was there anything about a birthmark in Jim Poole's autopsy report, Nick?"

Not that he remembered. "Why are you telling us this, Trooper? You're right, we came to get a look at your house because a terrible event occurred here, and it now appears that event may have some bearing on another crime."

Stacey pounded her fist on the counter. "Do you really not get it? I want in. You show up out of the blue a few days ago—the detective who investigated the fire my mother died in—and on the same day, John Poole dies. I may spend my shifts writing speeding tickets, but I'm enough of a cop to know all that can't be random."

Definitely not random.

"Right now, John Poole's fatal gunshot wound is being viewed as suicide. But I was on the phone with him when the shots were fired, and somebody else was in that trailer. The last thing John said to me was, 'Hope you're happy, Fabrizzio, he's here.' Who the hell is *he*, Stacey? That's what we need to find out."

Stacey slumped back onto a stool. "You think the answer is in this house? Because if it is, I've lived with it for three years, and I haven't found it."

"Fresh eyes couldn't hurt." Laura filled three mugs with coffee. "I've been looking in the same places for so long, I just want to scream. I do scream, when no one else is around to hear."

Nick heard, without being there. He didn't have to be.

"Fuck, damn it all to hell, son of a bitch! AIIIYYAAHH!!" Bloodcurdling it wasn't, but Laura's shriek did sound cathartic.

"WHOOAAAAA!" he bellowed.

Stacey looked at them as if they were nuts. They had to be, to still be at this after all these years. "I'm not screaming, I'm hunting. Are we doing this together or what?"

"Damn right we are," Laura replied. "We hire a forensics team, and you book yourself a hotel room so we can tear this place apart." She waited for Stacey's shocked expression to fade. "Or," she strung the word out, "you pull every file related to Elizabeth Aldridge Poole's murder you can lay your hands on. Evidence bags, postmortem notes, blood-spatter reports, everything, and we go through it all meticulously."

When Laura was fired up, the way she was now, she was an unstoppable thing of beauty. Nick saw a very long weekend ahead.

Aldridge, Connecticut, Nick learned, wasn't an actual town. Didn't have a mayor, or any kind of government apparently. It was more like a settlement, where two centuries ago someone had acquired considerable acreage to build a compound for his family. Four hours in the public library had yielded a lot of local lore, and confirmed what Judge Endicott had told her granddaughter: Aldridges and Pooles dominated the local gene supply. An Aldridge man had married a Poole woman and settled here, where they were fruitful and multiplied. Most of their offspring did the same, mostly elsewhere though they eventually returned, and the cycle seemed to repeat itself for multiple generations. The librarian pointed Nick to a circa-1989 genealogy tome that estimated there were more Pooles by far than Aldridges in these parts. The settlement founder's many brothers-in-law had moved here with their wives and had many sons who had many sons, while the Aldridges mostly had daughters, now scattered around Greater Aldridge, such as it was. When Nick asked, the librarian said the community was named after Robert Lester Aldridge, the man who originally bought the land in 1814.

Nick had left Laura at Stacey's house to go over the deed, title history, and any other paperwork that accompanied the bequest of the house by Judge Endicott to her granddaughter. Before he headed back there, he pulled into the crowded lot at Christine's diner to pick up lunch for them both. He snagged the last seat at the counter.

"What brings you back to our roadside speck?" The proprietor set a coffee cup in front of Nick. Justin Anderson was a handsome guy; Nick could understand the younger Stacey Endicott's initial attraction. Nick also noted, for the record, that Justin didn't much resemble any of the Pooles he knew.

"Apologizing to your mother is still high on my list. Is she around today?"

Fatigue, and maybe some anger, flashed across Justin's face. Couldn't be easy running this diner and dealing with an ill parent.

"You pretty much destroyed her computer. It won't be fixed for a while, and that's if they can get some part they've had to send away for. So I've grounded her. It's bad enough she races around in that wheelchair when she *can* communicate. I'm not letting her go out with the old piece of crap we have to make do with, so of course, she's angry at *me* for that."

"Some company might put her in a more kindly mood."

He shoved a menu at Nick. "Or she might just be pissed at you too. No visits, sorry. Signal when you're ready to order."

"I'm ready now, let's do this." Nick wasn't about to let him out of his sight. "Two cheeseburgers, well done, ketchup and mustard on the side. Double order of fries, two pickles. Two sodas, one diet, one not, I don't care what kind. All to go." He slid another one of his business cards and one of Laura's *Bloodstrains* promotional bookmarks across the counter. "And I don't need your mother's computer to express my regret at having hit her wheelchair. The author of that book and I will be here for a few days, talking to Trooper Endicott, among others."

Justin turned away from Nick and the contact information he'd provided. "Your order will be up shortly. Since you're not eating here, I'd appreciate having the stool for a customer who is."

Fair enough, Justin wasn't going to make this easy. Nick relinquished his stool and stationed himself by the cash register, opposite the kitchen door. A waitress sailed out with a huge tray on her shoulder. Visible for a few seconds behind her was a gray ponytail, a woman in a wheelchair facing a guy hunched over a prep station. In the middle of everything, yet the kitchen seemed to run smoothly around her, as if the staff was used to her being there. Nick moved closer to the door, hoping Christine Anderson would turn her chair around so he could get her attention.

"Don't even think it, Detective. Your guilty conscience isn't our concern." Justin held out a bag. "Here's your food. Pay up and leave, before I call the police."

Nick did as ordered. He put the food in his Jeep, then wandered around to the back of the diner, to the delivery area. A ramp led to a solid steel door that was partially open. Nick was willing to bet it was the means Christine Anderson employed to escape when her son wasn't looking. Nick watched the door for a few minutes, then started back to the Jeep. The clanging of metal made him turn.

Christine Anderson sat poised at the top of the ramp. Her wheelchair hurtled down. Momentum threatened to crash her headlong into a dumpster.

Nick put his shoulder to the side of it and his weight into a shove. The dumpster rolled out of her path.

The wheelchair skittered about a quarter-mile to the edge of the diner property, then capsized, spilling its occupant onto the ground.

Nick dialed 911. "Get to Christine's diner now," he shouted.

He outraced the kitchen staff to the chair.

Christine's Mets cap lay in a puddle next to her. Her laptop was trapped under one of the wheelchair's armrests.

"Everything's going to be okay. The EMTs will be here any minute," Nick said, hoping to reassure her. And himself.

"What the hell! Get away!" Justin jumped over the side of the ramp and ran to them. "Damn it, Mom, you figured out how to open the automatic door even with that old, busted-up computer?"

He bent to examine his mother and freed the laptop. Nick knelt beside her. "Mrs. Anderson, I hope you're not hurt—not now, and not from our collision the other day. I'm Nick Fabrizzio. I hit your chair last week. I'm so sorry."

He moved a few inches nearer. In her green eyes, he saw tears.

"NO YOU," flashed on the screen of her computer.

"I thought you said she couldn't communicate without the machine that's being repaired?"

"Why the hell do you care?" Justin, exasperated, looked daggers his way. "You're trespassing back here. I should call the police."

"Your mother might be dead if I wasn't back here. Her chair was heading for the dumpster until I pushed it out of the way." Nick got off his aching knees but stayed low, where Christine could see him.

"NO YOU," flashed on the computer's screen again.

An ambulance came roaring around the diner, lights spinning, siren roaring, startling Christine. The EMTs lifted her back into the chair and wrapped her in a blanket, to prevent shock.

"NO YOU," the computer flashed a third time.

Nick swore he saw panic in her eyes. He worked his way past the emergency medical crew and diner staff, back to the parking lot. His Jeep smelled like old grease. He grabbed the bag of food, and tossed it into a trash bin. Nick sipped one of the sodas and hoped it would keep the few contents of his nervous stomach down.

Chapter Twenty-four

Laura

Connecticut, November 2016

Road salt and icy dirt soaked through my boots. Sleet stung my eyes, and a frozen spray hit me with every truck that passed as I trudged toward the diner Nick mentioned—at least I thought I was going the right way. Ninety minutes since he last texted. Where was he? Was I supposed to sit for hours in Stacey's kitchen studying scans of old paper deeds and marriage-license records for Pooles and Endicotts and Aldridges? If I had police credentials too, I could be examining the actual physical evidence Stacey requested, things removed from her house after Elizabeth Aldridge Poole was murdered there.

A truck horn blasted behind me. I turned, but headlight beams blinded me.

"You look like you could use a ride, young lady."

A face appeared through the front passenger-side window. It was Santa Claus.

"Don't you have work to get to, Santa, this close to Christmas? I'm not going far, just to meet someone at the diner down the road." Better he thought someone would notice if I went missing.

"Two more miles, give or take. Those boots of yours already look drenched," the man said. "Hop in, I'll drop you off."

The passenger door unlocked, but I kept walking, hearing all my mother's warnings about getting into cars with strangers, or in this case pickup trucks, and knowing too well another cautionary tale about a girl who disappeared. "Thanks, but I don't think so, not today."

The pickup inched alongside me. "You'll be a popsicle by the time you get there. I can call ahead to tell my grandson to greet us with a couple cups of hot coffee. I'll even let you drink them both."

Maybe I was being ridiculous. "Your grandson?"

"Justin Anderson, he runs Christine's. You can call him instead, if you like."

This was Philip Anderson? "Hand me your phone."

He pulled the truck onto the shoulder a little ahead of me and got out, swaying when he put weight on his right leg, and gave me the phone after entering his passcode. I searched his contacts, found the diner's number, punched it into my own phone, and hoped for a signal. When the call somehow went through, I put it on speaker, so Santa could hear too.

"Christine's, please hold," a woman said.

"Wait—" A James Bond movie theme song blared. Santa's truck idled, its exhaust warming me a little.

"Christine's, how can I help you?"

"Does the owner's grandfather live around here?"

"Uh, not anymore, he lives in Maine. But he does visit from time to time."

A beat-up Maine license plate hung from the rear bumper of the truck, its paint-on-metal pinecone looking like it had been crunched and pounded flat a few times. "Is he visiting now?"

"Don't think so."

"Hannah, it's Phil," Santa yelled into the phone. "I'm down the road a piece with this young woman. Vouch for me, please, before we both freeze to death out here."

On the other end of the line, Hannah let out a long breath. "Oh, thank goodness, all hell is breaking loose around here. Christine almost crashed her chair into the dumpster out back, and that nice policeman from Philadelphia saved her."

Santa looked puzzled. I knew how he felt. "The cop who hit Christine last week? Jesus, I'll be there in a minute. Let Justin know." He walked back toward the truck. "I'm needed, miss. If you're coming, it's now or never."

"Now, please." I climbed inside, and he floored it, barely giving me time to wrap the seatbelt around me. Heat poured from the dashboard vents, as if powered by whatever adrenaline pushed Philip Anderson's right foot down on the accelerator. Sweat pooled under my arms and soaked through my turtleneck.

Santa peeled into the diner's parking lot, kicking up broken asphalt and gray water. He bolted from the truck, surprisingly fast for a limping man in his seventies at least. I ran to keep up. Once inside, he disappeared through swinging doors leading to the kitchen. I followed.

"What in blazes happened here?" he shouted. "I thought her computer was broken. How did your mother get out?"

The look on a taller, much younger man's face suggested he was used to being dressed down in front of the diner's staff.

"She's not dead, you know, she needs to communicate. I hooked Mom up to an old computer I've been keeping for emergencies, and she did what she always does—sorted out how to get where she wanted to go. I didn't figure on her being able to open the automatic door with it, but she did."

Philip Anderson slapped his grandson's face. "You didn't figure? No one told you to think, so don't. Run this diner, keep that empty, handsome head of yours bringing some money in, and keep her in line, that's all I ever asked you to do, Justin, and you can't even manage that much."

A sugar dispenser clipped Santa's jaw. "Then you stay here and take care of her twenty-four-seven," Justin roared. "See how you like it, old man, instead of hiding out in the Maine woods with whatever odd bunch of souls you claim to be saving right now. I've spent the last eight years trapped in this diner with her. At least she's free to think what she wants—hell, she even goes where she wants, while I'm a goddamn prisoner. I'm done."

Justin tore off his apron and pushed through the swinging doors. Hannah hollered his name. I watched her chase him into the parking lot before the kitchen doors swung closed again.

"NO!" a robotic-sounding voice screamed. "BACK!"

Trying to maneuver past me was a wheelchair, the woman in it rocking it back and forth and powering it into a worktable, knocking pans to the floor as she plowed a path toward the door to the dining room. Philip cursed as the chair shoved him aside. He grabbed for one of its arms but missed. I ran past him and kept running, ducking shards of glass, as the wheelchair broke through the diner's front entrance.

"Someone call 911!" I shouted.

Ice on the ramp to the parking lot added to the wheelchair's momentum. Justin's van slid as he escaped. The chair skidded behind it, past a wooden fence at the end of the diner property.

I pumped my arms and legs to catch up, Philip Anderson wheezing behind me. I looked back, saw him bent over at the waist, gulping air, and Hannah, the cashier, arguing with him to come back inside before he had a heart attack. I turned toward the fence again and saw Nick's Jeep through the heavier sleet that had begun to fall. Squinting against the cold, I could see him sprinting down the shoulder after the wheelchair.

As the road curved to the left maybe a quarter-mile ahead, I lost them. A siren wailed and a car surged past me,

Connecticut State Police. I shook wet hair out of my eyes, scrubbed the water off my face with my sleeve, and walked until my heart rate was normal and my lungs filled with the oxygen they needed for running again.

By the time I reached the police vehicle that had passed me and another that must have approached from the other side, they had blocked the traffic lanes. A car horn blasted, earning the squawk of a siren from an unhappy trooper. More police pulled up, and an ambulance navigated past them.

I picked my way along the cars for a better look. The wheelchair lay on its side. Strapped into it, glass glistening in her hair, was a woman who had to be Christine Anderson. Nick helped an emergency tech right the chair, and a digitized cry cut through the chaos.

"BABY! JUST!"

Pure sorrow.

Sobs escaped from me, and Nick moved closer. "No, help *her.*"

I watched as an EMT removed Christine Anderson's computer from its tether so she could be examined. Watched as Christine stared at Nick, probably wondering why he was there and her son wasn't.

Chapter Twenty-five

Laura

Central Pennsylvania, December 1991

We took seats toward the front of the narrow campus chapel, just fifteen rows deep, sixty folding chairs all together. Quickly, the space behind us filled. I counted dust motes streaming along sunrays that shone pink through a stained-glass window. Next to me, Jane squirmed.

"I don't understand why Kate has to be here. Why we have to be here," she said. "It's not like she ordered Jason to his death. She's upset, I get that, but this—"

"We're here for Kate. She's here for Jason's parents. They just lost their son, for God's sake."

A short young man, brown hair tucked under a yarmulke, stepped up to a microphone and announced Reverend Andrew Michaels would be starting the memorial service momentarily.

Michaels? I caught Kate's eye as she turned to look back from the front row, only a little less surprised than Beth and Saul Goldstein.

A clash of cymbals, like some percussive heavenly host, vibrated across the space. A flute played a thin version of "Amazing Grace," and, clad in white, Michaels strode from the rear of the chapel to the front.

"My brothers and sisters, I welcome you in the name of the Lord Almighty, the lord of Abraham, Isaac, and Jacob, who followed the will of Jehovah before the promise of true salvation was prophesied and the form of the Messiah was known."

Hardly the nondenominational service Kate said the Goldsteins had been promised. Saul Goldstein's head swiveled, as if he were looking for someone to right this latest wrong. Next to him, his wife sobbed. "Baby, my baby!" echoed through the small space.

"Our son Jason has been cruelly taken from us," Michaels declared. "Join hands and pray that God, who is our heavenly father, eases Jason's pain and that of his dear parents, left here to grieve his loss." Michaels bowed his head and recited the Lord's Prayer.

A distraught Beth Goldstein slumped to the floor. Barry Poole rushed from a side aisle in time to catch her. Kate elbowed him away and drew Jason's mother into her arms, whispering something that seemed to comfort her.

What did she say, I wondered: "Just ignore the charlatan who's usurped your time to mourn?"

Standing at the chapel's altar, Michaels punched a button on a boombox, and accordion music replaced the flute—an up-tempo Klezmer beat with what I guessed were Yiddish lyrics replacing "I once was lost but now am found ..." I went to Catholic school, so didn't know much about Jewish services. Michaels and Company seemed equally clueless. Again, Beth Goldstein went down. This time, her husband caught her by the shoulders.

"I'm calling an ambulance for Jason's mother. This is ridiculous." Jane ran to the chapel's office.

"Turn the music off!" Kate rushed toward the altar and slapped the boombox until there was silence. "Don't you see what you're doing to the Goldsteins? If you can't get it right, or won't get it right, just get out and leave them to their tears."

Michaels nodded, gesturing to Barry to claim the boombox. He started away, then paused before the Goldsteins. "May Jesus give you His peace as He has given it to me."

His wife's cries rising again, Saul Goldstein beat Barry to the boombox and threw it into the center aisle. "We were expecting a university chaplain. Who the hell is that?"

He glared at those of us assembled: some journalism professors, Jason's roommates, some kids from the *Informed Student*. Kate whispered into his ear.

"Andrew Michaels can go to hell!" Saul Goldstein threw a folding chair down the aisle, too.

Kate, stroking Beth Goldstein's hair as she cried, locked eyes with me.

Could this have gone worse?

Chapter Twenty-six

Laura

Connecticut, November 2016

A blanket slipped from Christine Anderson's lap into water puddled half-frozen at the side of the road. Sleet changed to snow as we waited for the EMT to finish checking her for injuries.

"Can't you get her out of this weather? She has to be cold."

A state trooper noticed me, a civilian standing where she shouldn't be, and waved me off to the other side of a barricade. "Can't move her until we're sure we won't do her harm, miss. An ambulance equipped to handle the wheelchair will be arriving any minute."

"At least get something dry to cover her with. You're dressed for this weather, she's not," I peered at his nametag, "Scott Wozniak."

Nick shot me an "atta girl" look. The trooper shrugged out of his parka and draped it across Christine's shoulders.

"You," the digitized voice, now reattached to its owner, crackled.

"You're welcome, Miss Chris. Sorry if you're cold." Wozniak bent, kissed her cheek, then straightened to his full height. "My mother is the cashier at the diner," he explained for my benefit.

Hannah, yes, the woman who also witnessed Philip and Justin Anderson's argument.

My teeth were chattering by the time the second ambulance arrived. Two EMTs lowered a ramp and rolled the wheelchair aboard. Within minutes, it was heading down the highway, lights flashing red.

"Another uneventful afternoon in Aldridge, Connecticut. I need to get out of town just to keep that woman safe." Nick put his arms around my shivering form.

"Don't." I pulled away. "What did the troopers want with you?"

Nick ran a hand through his still mostly black hair; a dusting of snow came away with it. "Officially, I was describing for them how she got from the diner to here with me chasing after her. Unofficially, I think they just want me gone. They're all old friends of Justin Anderson, and anything that upsets his mother seems to upset them. When Trooper Wozniak heard Justin bolted, he looked worried."

"Wozniak likes Christine. I thought Justin told you his mom wasn't much of a people person."

Nick leaned against the now-unnecessary barricade. "What he told me was she hated this town. That she felt trapped because of her ALS."

I stamped slush from my boots, longing for dry socks and warm slippers. "Guess we have to hoof it back to the Jeep. No rideshare service here, is there?"

He checked his phone. "Nope, and we only have about a half-hour of daylight left."

So we set out along the berm. I shoved my hands into my totally insufficient pockets, wishing my foul-weather soccer-mom gear was layered on me instead of at home in Philadelphia. We hadn't gotten far when a police car, its siren whoop-whooping, passed, did a mid-highway U-turn, and stopped beside us.

"Miss, please come with me," Trooper Wozniak said. "Miss Chris—Mrs. Anderson, that is—wants you to accompany her to the hospital. She won't go without you."

"She doesn't even know me."

Wozniak leaned over and opened the passenger-side door from the inside. "The driver says she's been kicking up a fuss with that machine since the ambulance left, typing, 'Her! Her!' He figured that had to be you, miss—sorry, what's your name?"

"Laura Cunningham."

"Then please, Miss Cunningham. Mrs. Anderson shouldn't become more agitated. Bad enough Justin isn't there with her, and it's her caregiver's day off. We're trying to find Chelsea now."

I looked at Nick to see what he thought.

"Go. I'll get the Jeep and meet you at the hospital. Maybe I'll bring Philip Anderson with me, if he wants a lift."

"That's not a good idea, sir," Wozniak said. "Philip and Miss Chris don't get along very well. It'll just upset her more."

That settled it. I got in, fastened my seatbelt, and turned to see Nick resume his trek back to the diner's parking lot.

"You won't be long, Miss Cunningham. They'll check out Miss Chris and send her home with her caregiver, once they track Chelsea down. It's not like Justin to take off that way. Seems no one was expecting Philip today."

Which explained a lot, I supposed. A complicated family, the Andersons.

"I wasn't sure what to make of the argument Justin and his grandfather had. Did your mother tell you? She saw them go after each other, too."

Wozniak started to say something but thought better of it. So we drove in silence until he stopped behind the ambulance's open back doors. He offered me a hand up, then vanished into the storm.

An EMT sat next to Christine, taking her blood pressure, her wheelchair harnessed into position for the ride. When he finished, he motioned me to take his place. "If you need us, talk into this." He pointed to an intercom.

"Belt!" the computer screeched. I buckled myself in.

"I'm Laura Cunningham, Mrs. Anderson, but maybe you already know that? I'm a friend of the police officer from Philadelphia, Nick Fabrizzio."

"No," the computer hissed.

"He's sorry for your accident the other day. Sorry he ruined your good computer. Your son said it could be repaired by tomorrow. But, of course, you know that. I don't mean to treat you like a child—I have two of my own at home, maybe I talk to everyone like that these days."

"Baby."

"Not quite babies, fifteen and eight, though sometimes they do act like babies, my boys."

"Just."

"Justin? Trooper Wozniak says his friends are looking for him. Meanwhile, maybe they've gotten in touch with your caregiver so she can meet us at the emergency room."

"Bin," the computer squawked.

The small, cracked screen read B-I-N, rather than B-E-E-N, which might have made more sense.

"I'm not sure I understand," I said.

Christine sighed, or maybe it was just a random sound, what did I know about ALS?

"Cab," the computer buzzed. "Bin."

Cabin, no mistaking that. Was Justin at some family vacation house? Someplace our state trooper pal Stacey might know about?

A nurse greeted us at the emergency room entrance, briefly staring at me. "Mrs. Anderson, your caregiver is inside waiting for you. A little paperwork, a little more poking at you, and that should do it. Chelsea will take over, and your friend here can go on with her business."

A blonde in her early twenties, insurance cards in one hand, toddler's fingers clutched in the other, rushed toward us. "Miss Chris, you're gonna give me a heart attack. I had to bring Cassidy with me, no time to find a sitter."

"Baby!" the computer squawked.

I touched Christine Anderson's hand. "That's my cue to go, I guess. It was lovely to meet you—"

"NO ME. NO YOU," the machine blared.

"Nice to know you too." I waved and walked off in search of a ladies' room, hoping to find a hand dryer I could aim down at my boots. My feet were more frozen than the puddles next to the highway.

Near the ER's sign-in station when I returned at last stood Nick, holding a pair of hospital-issue slipper socks and a cup of coffee. "Check my left pocket," he said.

In it was a chocolate chip cookie. I tore open the plastic wrap and bit off a huge chunk.

"You're asking yourself, 'How did I ever let this perfect man go?' Am I right?"

"Is the coffee hot?"

He lifted the cup to his cheek. "Not anymore, I've been standing here awhile, waiting."

"No way you're perfect then." I took the coffee and sipped. Barely lukewarm. The socks, however, were a gift from heaven.

His hands freed, Nick fished a wad of paper towels from his right pocket. "Kick off your boots and I'll pat them down. And let Nurse Nasty over there see you put on the socks. It took every ounce of charm I have, and a reminder that you came in with Christine Anderson, to convince her you deserved them."

More evidence that the people of Aldridge, Connecticut, loved their Miss Chris, even if she wasn't necessarily fond of them.

"I don't suppose going back to the diner for some actual food is an option?"

Nick shook his head. "I'm *persona non grata* with pretty much all the Andersons, and you know how the local cops feel about me. Best case, we hit a pizza joint and head back to Stacey's. We're on the road to Philly first thing tomorrow, and there's still stuff we need to do."

More database searches for me, more evidence bags for Nick.

"Wish we could stay until Christine has her fully functioning voice computer back. Bet she knows a lot of the local secrets." After the quarrel I witnessed between Justin and his grandfather, I was pretty sure there were more of them than one-syllable words could convey. More than Nick and I could find out in what was left of the day. Unless ...

"Christine said something about a cabin. What's another road trip, Detective?"

Chapter Twenty-seven

Laura

Connecticut, November 2016

We found Justin's van in the driveway, parked at the cabin's door. Stacey called him but got no answer.

"I'm sure I heard a phone ringing," I said. "Call him again."

On the second try, we all heard the ringtone. Stacey tested the door. It was unlocked, and so we walked in. There was Justin's phone, sitting on a stack of yellowed newspapers.

"He can't have gone far." Stacey pointed to the fireplace screen, which had been pulled away from the wood box.

Nick peered up the chimney. "The damper's open."

The décor was thrift-store shabby. A chunky sofa and a couple of rumpled easy chairs surrounded a produce crate-turned-coffee table; baskets and vintage suitcases offered quirky storage. Vinyl chairs and a Formica-and-metal table separated the central space from the kitchen. A long, faded rug led down a hall, presumably to bedrooms.

I poked around, nosy reporter that I was—you could learn a lot about a person from the things they owned. Mom that I was, I recognized the signs of a house where a boy grew up. Sports trophies marched along one wall shelf: soccer and Little League awards, a couple of karate medals like the ones Damian and Drew had earned. I saw an older stereo, with a turntable and a cassette tape player, on another shelf. Below them, a beat-up footlocker held LPs and tapes, some folk, some jazz. I flipped through—there was a classical album I remembered, *Scheherazade*, which Jane brought from home to our apartment after her mom's funeral. The music started to play in my head.

"Somebody's a big reader," Nick said, interrupting my internal symphony. I looked up to high shelves on the opposite wall, filled with mysteries, spy novels, and books probably from a college lit course—Orwell and Castaneda and Hesse. On the very top shelf, some large volumes lay flat, their spines difficult to read in spaces the light didn't reach. One looked like a yearbook.

Next to the couch, a trunk was crammed with toys, picture books, a stuffed pink pig, an aqua dog. An oversized bear wore a ratty college T-shirt exactly like the one I had put on a teddy in Damian's nursery. We had talked about that, Jane and Kate and I, how we'd dress up plush pals for the babies we'd have someday. I was the only one who had any.

"You can find those shirts from Harrisburg to Hawaii. Probably got it at a yard sale," Nick said, reading my mind.

"Stacey," I shouted toward the open door. "Did Christine Anderson go to college? Did Justin?"

She stepped inside, her boots dripping onto a frayed woven mat. "Justin's been doing online courses; he can't get to actual classes because of Christine and the diner. Can't devote a lot of time to those either. It's taking him forever, but he wants to get his degree as soon as he can. You never know what else could happen, he says. Like his mom, she was a few credits shy of graduation when he was born."

"So she left college? Which school?" Nick was interested now.

"She eventually got her degree. I don't know which school; you'll have to ask Justin."

That would have been the more direct approach, but would Justin tell us anything, given that we were strangers snooping around his cabin?

I wandered back to a bedroom and turned on the overhead light. Dresser, chest of drawers, nightstand, bed. Double-wedding-ring quilt on the bed, comb-and-brush set on the dresser. I slid open a folding door: toilet, sink, tub with shower, faded green towels, faded green rug. On the bedroom's remaining wall hung framed school photos of Justin, up until middle school maybe.

I reentered the cabin's main space just as its owner returned. Justin dumped an armload of wood at Nick's feet. "What the hell are you people doing here? Jesus, Stacey!"

"I've being trying to call you. Your mom's at the hospital again. They had to track Chelsea down to check her in."

"Doesn't explain why you'd bring *these* two along. This is the guy who ran my mom down, and I have no idea who this woman is."

"We've been over what happened on the highway that afternoon," Nick began, "your mom's wheelchair appeared out of nowhere."

"Coming here was my idea," I interrupted. "Your mother said you'd be here."

"Yeah, right, like you had a conversation." Justin grabbed his phone and pointed to the door. "Out now, all three of you."

"Wait, my name is Laura Cunningham. I was in the diner earlier. Your grandfather gave me a lift there, then I met your mother in the ambulance on the way to the hospital. She was worried because of your argument with him. When you took off, she took off after you. Not a good idea, it turned out."

He sank to the floor and stared out the still-open door, flurries flying in. "Mom's okay, right? You would have told me already if she wasn't."

"She wanted you. That's why we came here, to get you." Stacey sat next to him and wrapped him into a hug.

"But I can't be there every minute of every day to stop her getting out. She *wants* someone to run her over."

"That's not true."

"Isn't it, Stace? I better go call her, let her know I'm all right."

I followed him to the door and watched him walk toward his van to make the call in private. "There are no baby pictures here, not a single photo of Justin and his mother together that I can see. No pictures anywhere of his father. It's odd."

"So? You've been known to be a little camera-shy yourself," Nick reminded me, playing devil's advocate as usual.

Stacey pulled out one of the dining room chairs. Dust floated up as she sat.

"This place has always looked this way. I remember coming here when I was little, when my grandmother was looking into some legal thing for John Poole. This used to be his cabin. He said he came here to remember his boys, because this was their spot, Gran told me. But then he gave her the word to rent it, sell it, donate it, whatever. He just wanted it gone. Christine moved in then."

"Except she didn't buy it, my grandfather did." Justin pulled the door shut against the cold and shook snow from his wool cap. "She could never afford this place, but she convinced him that it would be good for me to get outside and play somewhere besides the diner parking lot. We'd come up here whenever she could get away."

"So the things here belong to you and your mom, or to John Poole?" I asked. The question did not make Justin happy.

"I was six years old when we moved to Aldridge with Gramps and he bought the diner. I was maybe eight when we first started coming to the cabin. Mom didn't throw John's stuff away, in case he wanted it someday, if that's what you mean. What difference does it make?"

I pointed to the books on the top shelf. "That yearbook up there, it looks an awful lot like one from my school."

Justin walked over and pulled it down from the shelf. Nick and I locked eyes the second we saw the cover—it was, indeed, like mine. How many times had we looked at the pictures of Kate in my yearbook, at her official senior portrait and the shots taken in the *IS* newsroom?

"That's when I graduated, 1992. And that's the university I attended. Whose yearbook is this, Justin?" I snatched at the book, excited and apprehensive at the same time.

"We found this here, I think, but I don't really remember. Mom said my dad went to college for a while but didn't graduate. I don't know where, he was already dead when I was born. Got thrown off his motorcycle and slammed into some rocks head first."

"So you don't know whether your father's picture is in this yearbook?"

He shook his head. "Never looked at it."

"What about your mom?" I pressed. "Did she go to college in Pennsylvania?"

"My mom told me she went to night school to finish her degree in computer science. She had a job writing code before we moved here. She's always reprogramming her wheelchair and her laptop, the good one, not that piece of crap she's using now."

Nick reached for the yearbook. "May I?" He pushed aside some junk mail on the dining table and opened it. "What was your father's name?"

"Aidan Anderson."

I flipped the book over. "Start here at the back because there's an index of all seniors who were expected to graduate that year. Some people on the list may not have—the yearbook went to press months before commencement."

We settled into the four chairs around the table and scrutinized photo after photo. Justin stopped at the *Informed Student* pages about midway through the book.

"That's you," he said, tapping one photo. Pointing to another, he added, "This is John Poole's son, the one who died in that big fire along with Stacey's mom. I heard about Barry Poole from Judge Endicott, Stacey's grandmother. She showed us an old newspaper article with his picture."

"Laura wrote a book about The Challenge fire. That's why she and Nick are here," Stacey explained. "Also because John Poole is dead. Nick heard him being shot—he was on the phone with John when it happened."

"Jesus, that's awful. I'm so sorry about your great-uncle, Stace." Justin jumped up, walked around the table to Stacey and stood behind her, kneading her upper arms. Over her shoulder, he stared again at the open yearbook, then moved closer and slapped his hand down on the largest of the *Informed Student* photos.

In it, about two dozen journalists-in-training sat amid boxy desktop computers. Some of us mugged for the camera; others played it more serious. Justin studied the faces. "Who's this sitting next to you?" he asked. "Why is she the only one not looking at the camera? She's on the phone with her head down."

I didn't have to see the picture to know who he meant. "That's Kate McDonald, my best friend. We think she went to The Challenge the day of the fire to look for Barry Poole. They found his body but never found Kate's, and no one has seen her since."

"Maybe you should have written a script instead. Sounds like a bad TV movie." Justin's phone rang, sparing him a nasty comeback from me.

"Mom? It's okay, I'm fine. Is Chelsea on the call too, in case she has to answer for you?" He put his phone on speaker and set it on the table. "Gramps didn't hurt me, don't worry about that. I'm pretty sure I didn't hurt him either. I'm at the cabin, you were right to tell Miss Cunningham to check here. We were just looking at that old yearbook John Poole left behind."

"No. NO!" I recognized the shrieking of Christine Anderson's computer.

"What's going on? Chelsea, are you there?"

A toddler whimpered in the background.

"They want to sedate your mom. She's still freaked out about what happened with you and your grandfather. The doctor is keeping her here at the hospital overnight, so they can do a brain scan tomorrow just to be sure nothing else is wrong."

"Hang on, give me a minute." Justin took the phone off speaker, then motioned as if shooing us away. "I need some privacy here. Time for you three to head back to town anyway. The diner can use the business."

Stacey kissed him on the cheek. Nick nodded. When Justin turned back to his call, I slipped the yearbook under my coat then followed them out to Nick's Jeep.

I'd been living with guilt about Kate's disappearance for years. This small larceny could batter my conscience only so much.

My laptop cast its pale light on the yearbook photo. The *Informed Student* staffers mostly smiled in the glow. A plastic cup appeared next to my right hand. I smelled bourbon, already a little diluted as the ice cubes stacked to the cup's rim had begun to melt.

"Except for Kate, you know what became of every person in that picture. You've worked with them, or exchanged Christmas cards with them, or gone to their weddings and their kids' christenings for the last twenty-four years." Nick sipped from an identical cup, standard U.S. motor-lodge issue. Alcohol mellowed his voice to warm, and he spoke much too close to my right ear.

I hoped the liquor would silence the voice in my head. "Why did Justin ask about Kate?"

"He didn't, he asked about the girl who was on the phone. Who was she talking to anyway?"

I dipped my nose into the cup, breathed in some of the bourbon's fire. "She was looking at an F, hoping for an incomplete, in a computer programming class and was running out of time to make up the work. Negotiations with the teacher were not going well."

"She didn't do the assignments?"

"Too much was going on, and that class was just one more thing. Jason Goldstein was dead; the threatening letters kept coming; Jim Poole committed suicide and she was trying to keep Barry from falling apart. I don't know how she managed to get him into the newspaper office that day, let alone into that picture."

Nick's breath brushed my neck as he leaned closer to the photo. "Twirl too many plates for too long and a few are bound to fall. Sometimes, you just can't will things to work out," he said, then straightened.

So true, as we both were aware.

"What time are we leaving tomorrow? How late can we push it?"

Nick put his empty cup next to mine, put his hands on my shoulders and massaged them. "Gotta be on the road early you said, so you can get ready for some book signing."

Crap, he was right, but I needed to do this more. "I have to see Christine Anderson. But I won't be able to get into the hospital before eight probably."

Thumbs dug into me. "You want to tell me why you want to see Miss Chris?"

"I want to show her this picture and see how she reacts, *if* she reacts. Maybe she was at the university when I was. Maybe she met Aidan Anderson there and Justin was conceived there."

Nick applied several knuckles' worth of pressure to the knot at the top of my left shoulder blade, hard meeting hard. Pain made the room spin. I closed my eyes and saw Christine in her chair, one-syllable riddles buzzing from her computer.

"University registration records for 1988 to 1992 showed no Christine Lawrence and no Aidan Anderson," he said. "Zilch."

I leaned into his hands. "Maybe they weren't fulltime students. Maybe they were working to scrape up enough tuition money. Does it matter? They met, and Christine got pregnant and Aidan was killed on some road. She had their baby and ended up living here in Aldridge, a place connected in too many ways to John Poole and his dead wife and sons. What do we have to lose by showing Christine the yearbook picture?"

He pressed kisses along my throat, and a spark sizzled down my body. I wanted what he wanted, more than was good for me. "Enough, Nick."

"Fine," he said and sat on the bed, a safe three feet or so away. "We'll go to the hospital tomorrow morning on our way out of town. But they might not let you see her, you know. It's not like you're family."

Chelsea, Christine's caregiver, would vouch for me, I hoped. Maybe they wouldn't let me see her, but I had to try. "John Poole may have been killed because we started asking questions. But which questions? Isn't that what we came here to find out?"

Nick stood and yawned. "Shut the investigation down for the night, Elsie. Get some sleep."

I locked the door behind him and powered down the laptop. I felt around in my purse for my phone and called David. "Hi. I miss everybody," I told his voicemail. "This town creeps me out, so I'm glad we're leaving tomorrow. Kiss the boys for me." I got into bed and surrendered to the exhaustion.

Not sure how long I'd been sleeping before the phone vibrated against my ear. I pushed hair out of my eyes. It wasn't a number I recognized. I stumbled to the window and peeked around the vertical blinds. It was still dark, but the sky was beginning to lighten. Very early morning.

"Laura Cunningham," I said, hoping I sounded more awake than I felt.

"My mother wants to see you. Assuming that you are, as her caregiver thinks, the person Mom means when she types, 'Her. Ride. Hospital.'"

"Assuming that I'm talking to Justin Anderson, and not some other mother's son."

He laughed, then thought better of it. "You're all Mom talked about last night, aside from some random repeats and goofy words we get when she's forced to use the crappy old computer. She likes you, I guess."

"I like her, too." How could I not admire Christine for wringing what she wanted out of life, whatever way she could?

"Can you come now, Miss Cunningham? To the hospital? She won't rest, and she's driving the nurses crazy. I have to get to the diner by 5 o'clock to relieve Hannah."

"I don't have a car of my own."

"I'll pick you up. Fabrizzio can get you later."

In fifteen minutes, Justin texted he was outside. I slipped on my coat, grabbed my suitcase and laptop bag, and shoved my phone into a pocket. As I started to open the door, I remembered the yearbook and stuffed it in next to the laptop.

Chapter Twenty-eight

Laura

Connecticut, November 2016

The night nursing supervisor let me into the room, never questioning who I was, or who I was to Christine Anderson. If Miss Chris wanted me and it was all right with her son, it was all right with the hospital. Good thing I wasn't a paid assassin.

I plugged my laptop into a power strip and logged into the hospital's guest Wi-Fi. I called up my website, enlarged the *Bloodstrains* book cover, and turned the screen around on the bedside table so Christine could see it from her wheelchair.

"I'm a newspaper reporter. This is my book."

"No," her computer buzzed. "NO. YOU. YOU. BOOK."

"It's about a fire almost twenty-five years ago in Pennsylvania. Lots of people died. My best friend, Kate McDonald, might have died there too, we think."

"BOOK. SEE," she replied.

I sat on the bed and turned the laptop back toward me. I clicked on a link that opened to the first chapter, and read aloud:

"The smell of smoke has not dissipated. It still hangs over this central Pennsylvania acreage, or maybe it just seems that way to those of us who can't forget what happened here in 1992. Those of us who lost loved ones, or think they might have but can't say for sure. Ed and Marianne McDonald walk this land every year, looking for something that cannot be seen: something that will show them where their daughter Kate is; reveal her fate that March night after fire overwhelmed The Challenge, killing ten students, an employee, and the group's leader. Maybe killing Kate too. There is no sign of her today, just as there was no sign of her after that night. She simply vanished."

As I finished, I was crying, just as I cried when I started to write the book, just as I cried almost every time I read those first sentences. I looked up from my screen to Christine's computer.

"NO. STOP," it said. "BOOK."

I looked at Christine's eyes. She was crying, too.

I searched my document files for an electronic galley and picked up reading where I had left off: my journalistic account of the fire, its likely cause, the laborious sifting through tons of charred building material for bodies, the widening search of the grounds beyond the building itself for evidence.

"NO. NO," Christine's computer tapped out. "SO. BAD."

"Almost too terrible to comprehend."

"NO. NO," it repeated.

Was she sympathetic? Agitated? I wasn't sure how to proceed, so I kept reading.

"BAD," the computer buzzed every page or so.

By the time I got to the end of the second chapter, the room had gone quiet. The patient was asleep, tears still bright on her cheeks. I took a few tissues from a box on the bed and gently wiped the moisture away. She didn't stir. I noticed a thin scar on her left eyebrow, a tiny white stripe amid brown strands. Some childhood mishap probably, like the softball I accidentally pitched at Kate's head during a practice game in middle school. I walked in the winning run and left Kate with a mark just like Christine's. She didn't talk to me for a week.

My memories and I eased onto the hospital bed, my back settled against the headboard. I wanted to sleep—it already felt like a long day, with a long ride back to Philly ahead. But an insistent vibrating in my pocket woke me. It was Nick. I slipped out of the room and into the hallway, ducking into an empty lounge area near the elevator to call him.

"Where the hell are you?"

"I'm at the hospital. I couldn't leave a note."

"Kidnappers break your fingers?"

I took a deep breath, much too weary to fight. "Justin called early to say his mother wanted to see me. We've been talking, Christine and I."

"How's that going?"

"I've been reading *Bloodstrains* to her. She's following the story."

Nick's end of the line went quiet for a minute. "Okay, that's good, I guess."

"Or maybe she's just frightened and grateful to have someone staying with her. Her caregiver has a little one, and Justin had to get to the diner for the breakfast crowd."

"Have you noticed, there's a strange vibe in this town, Elsie, more than just the ugly murder in its history. Justin seems to want out of Aldridge as much as his mom wants to escape in that wheelchair. Makes you wonder why he doesn't. I doubt she'd try to stop him."

Nick's instincts were good about these things, but we didn't have time to test them now. "Let me get back to Christine's room. How long before we leave?"

"Fifteen minutes, tops. I'll text when I get there."

I hurried down the corridor. Green eyes peered at me as I walked in.

"Sorry, I got a phone call. I won't be able to stay much longer."

"YOU."

"That was Nick on the phone. The one who hit you with his Jeep, then rescued you yesterday. He's my ex-husband."

"X."

"We were married for a while, but we split up a long time ago. Long story."

"NO."

That's all I needed, another Nick ally, as if Jane and Damian, maybe even Bea, weren't enough. Changing the subject was in order, so I retrieved from my bag the yearbook I'd taken from the Andersons' cabin.

"I went to this school. Did you?"

"GO," the computer crackled.

"You went there? Or you want me to leave?"

"NO."

Not the unambiguous answer I was hoping for.

"I graduated in 1992." I showed Christine the spine with the year on it. "My picture is in this book. I'll show you."

"YOU. NO YOU."

Better than *go,* I supposed. I turned to the graduates' headshots, flipped through the alphabetical listings to the C's. "That's me." I tapped on the black-and-white image of my twenty-two-year-old self. "Laura Eileen Cunningham, journalism major with a print concentration and a minor in political science. So predictable. Economics would have been the smarter way to go."

The green eyes blinked. They stared at the yearbook, then at me. "Same," the computer judged.

I flipped to the two-page spread about the *IS*. "Here I am again, at the center of the picture. I was editor in chief of the *Informed Student*, the school newspaper."

"THERE."

"I don't understand."

"THERE," the computer sputtered again. Whatever that meant to her.

Nick texted he was waiting downstairs. "My ride is here, Miss Chris. I have to go." I quickly packed my gear, stashing laptop, yearbook, phone and coat wherever they fit. Not registering any of what I was doing because I was aware that Christine watched every move, though she said nothing. As if she wasn't sure what to say.

I started for the hallway, then turned back to press a kiss onto her forehead.

"BYE." Her eyes filled again with tears.

I waved and rushed out before she could see mine.

I cried until we merged onto I-95 south, then cried some more until Nick pulled off the interstate for coffee and a pit stop.

"Even if Christine had her better computer, she might not have given us anything we could use, Laura. We can't know what's inside her head. We'll just have to follow the few crazy leads we do have."

He parked in an almost empty section of the lot and got out. "Are you coming? You need caffeine and food. We both do."

"Don't tell me what I need. I don't want coffee. I want to forget the look in Christine's eyes when I left. She didn't implore me to stop, or to stay, but those eyes. ... Another week in Aldridge, that's what I need. I know she'd tell me something."

Like why had she asked to see me, not just once, but twice?

"What if those one-syllable responses meant something else? The ones she gave me, and the ones she gave you. Everything she said, Nick, from the day you hit her with this Jeep until I left her an hour ago. What if we just didn't understand?"

He opened the passenger door. "'NO,' in capital letters. That's mostly what she said, or, 'NO. YOU.'"

"What if it meant, 'Know you,' as in recognize?"

What if we just didn't know where to look before. ...

"Her eyes. She talks with them, but it's more than that. Where's the yearbook?"

I scrambled over the console into the backseat, searching among the things I'd thrown into the car when Nick picked me up.

"Poking out of your laptop bag, under your coat." Nick and I reached for it simultaneously. I handed the yearbook to him and twisted my way into the front seat.

"Find the M's, Kate's senior picture. Her left eye."

"What about it?"

I leapt out of the Jeep, surprising him, and toppling the two of us and the book onto the concrete surface.

"Her left eye, Nick. Look at the scar in her eyebrow. Christine Anderson has one exactly like it!"

He hauled us upright and set me on the hood of the Jeep.

"It's her, Nick! Christine Anderson is Kate! We have to go back! Turn back now."

"Laura, lots of people have scars."

"I was there when Kate got it when we were kids. I watched her forehead heal. I know exactly how the scar slices over her left eye, zigzagging in there about a third of the way to her nose. Christine has an identical scar."

He looked at the picture again. "You're serious."

"Yes!" I jumped off the car and spun away from him. "I was reading to Christine, describing the fire, and I started to cry, and when I looked up she was crying too. She was seeing it all again. I know it."

"Wait a minute, hold up. You're exhausted, and you've been pounding away at this for so long. What if she's not Kate? What if you just want her to be?"

Deep breaths. Be rational, Cunningham, I told myself.

No one wanted to believe me more than Nick. If I couldn't convince him, I couldn't convince anyone.

"Since *Bloodstrains* came out, every lead has pointed us here to Connecticut—that was clear to you before it was to me. If I'm wrong, I'm wrong. It's just more wasted effort and dashed hope. But what if I'm right? Imagine what that means. We have to go back, Nick!"

"Get in," he said. He slammed my door, got behind the wheel, and peeled out toward the highway. But instead of looping around to the northbound ramp, he got back on the interstate heading south toward Philadelphia.

"I'm not saying you're right—plenty of reasons why you might not be. But if you are, Elsie, going back there is the last thing we should do. We need to get away from Christine until we know more. John Poole is dead for reasons we can only guess at. We need to sort out his killing before we put her in danger."

"What if we already have?"

Christine Anderson's secret has been safe for twenty-four years, I consoled myself. *Keep your cool, and keep your mouth shut. Nick's right.*

Still damp in my pocket were the tissues I'd used to blot away Christine's tears—there might be enough to test for DNA. Until then, like the good reporter I was, I opened my laptop and recreated from memory every computerized thing she had said to me, one monosyllable at a time.

Chapter Twenty-nine

Nick

Philadelphia, December 2016

The thing about crime, the ugly truth about it, is that all truth is relative. Junior Detective Lesson Number One, something he learned long ago: There are many ways to look at a crime, multiple perspectives to consider, even after the basic facts are established. It's only by examining every possibility that you get a sense of how what happened, happened. If you're lucky enough to have everything line up, of course, and in precisely the places where you're looking.

A little bad luck could blind the best investigators to the truth, or blindside them. Ruin prosecutions, destroy victims' families. Careers, too.

Not something Nick enjoyed contemplating as he watched the TV mounted over his favorite polished-wood Mount Airy bar. Up on the screen, Dixon Bott was acknowledging to a crowd of working press that, all prior signs to the contrary, John Poole's death in his home two weeks earlier had not been a suicide, but a homicide.

"How did the Pennsylvania State Police get this wrong?" a reporter asked.

"As I noted at the time, our findings were preliminary, pending forensic analysis of the crime scene and John Poole's body," Dix said. "Blood spatter, ballistics, and pathology results now corroborate the initial 911 report that Poole's fatal head wound was not self-inflicted."

"The father of one of the ten students killed in 1992's infamous Challenge Fire—a fire that's the subject of a book getting national attention right now—is shot to death weeks after the book's release. Are you saying that didn't raise red flags immediately, Lieutenant Bott?" The reporter shoved her microphone at Dix, daring him to dodge her question.

"Of course, it did. That's why we're standing here today. This case has been our top investigative priority."

It might be cold up in Bradford, but Dix was sweating bullets outside his barracks. This story had gone viral, thanks to *Bloodstrains,* and there was no putting the genie back in the bottle.

Make that *genies,* plural. Nick had called in a favor and asked a forensics tech to run the scant DNA sample Laura got from Christine Anderson against the sequences for possible Challenge Fire victims entered into the state's crime-lab archive in 1992. They were a perfect match for Kate McDonald. Also, a perfect motive for murder: John Poole's, assuming he knew the truth about Christine.

Potentially, a reason to want Christine dead, too—and the people who found her.

A blast of icy air struck Nick's back. In the mirror behind the bar, he saw Steve Brightman enter and walk toward him.

"Surprised to see you here, Detective Fabrizzio."

Nick didn't turn. "Likewise, Professor."

Steve had been warned to stay out of the *Bloodstrains* spotlight or risk losing his job. But Nick needed to trust someone with their discovery in case he and Laura did, indeed, end up dead. He also needed legwork done that couldn't readily be traced back to him. The old Irish taproom was both conveniently within walking distance of Laura and David's house, and a favorite of the Philadelphia Police Department's Northwest Detectives Division, where Nick worked.

A chance meeting, what else could this be? A little white lie compared with Kate's decades-sweeping fiction.

Steve ordered a craft beer Nick couldn't abide. He was on duty anyway and signaled the bartender for another cup of coffee. After some commercials, the noon news cut to an interview with Laura at a bookstore near Princeton, the latest stop on her hastily expanded *Bloodstrains* promotion tour.

"My sister-in-law is everywhere these days. Just heard NPR tease to an interview with her this afternoon."

Nick stirred milk into his coffee. "Things are popping in the John Poole case. I'll be testifying at an inquest soon, I suppose, since I heard the gunshots."

Steve tasted the foam on his IPA. "They have a suspect?"

"Not that I've heard. But Dixon Bott and the local district attorney have to lay out the case for murder now. Make noise about how the killer will be found and justice will be swift. The DA has to look good for the voters who just reelected him."

Steve watched Nick's face in the mirror. "Bang the drum about the old fire evidence and the lawsuits, the sealed depositions. The university won't be happy, but it also can't be portrayed as impeding a suddenly high-profile McKean County murder case."

Nick nodded. That pot needed stirring.

"A former grad student of mine, she's with the Associated Press in Harrisburg—" Steve searched the contacts on his phone. "If she raised a new fuss about the sealed Challenge Fire documents, the state Attorney General's office might bite. The DA and your buddy Dix could demand the meat of the 1992 investigation, and the university couldn't be seen as pushing back."

"My possibly botched 1992 investigation," Nick reminded him. "Your AP friend would have to detail what's publicly known about the contents of those documents: DNA samples from the fire scene. Also the DNA samples the families provided to verify victims' identities. What if John Poole was killed by a disgruntled family member seeking retribution a quarter-century after the fact?"

Steve stared at the TV. "What aren't you telling me?"

Nick brought the coffee mug up to his mouth, so his lips could not be seen in the mirror. Before speaking, he scanned the reflection of the room behind him.

"We know where she is," he said finally, "and so might John Poole's killer. I'm telling you, well, just in case."

The bartender dropped off a bowl of peanuts between his only customers. Steve scooped up a handful, crushed them, and examined the wrecked shells until the man moved out of earshot.

"Where?"

"Middle of Nowhere, Connecticut. You don't tell your brother, you don't tell Jane Baker, you don't even tell the university president when he fires you."

Steve dusted the shells from his hands. "All this time?"

"Unclear."

"Damn it, if I'm going out on this half-busted limb again, I need more to go on."

Nick emptied his coffee cup, stood, and left a few dollars on the bar. "Can't tell you more, but trust me. I'm not putting anyone else in danger."

In the mirror, Steve's reflection registered worry. "Laura?"

"Not that I know of, not yet."

"She's my brother's wife, the mother of his son."

"She's the mother of *my* son, too. She was *my* wife."

Nick pulled his coat from the back of the barstool and stalked to the men's room. He checked his messages, his news feed, the weather. He read and replied to some email. When he emerged, he saw Steve had moved to a table and was typing on his phone.

"Recreating our conversation?"

"You never said the document stuff was off the record. Don't try now."

Fair enough. "'Sources familiar with the matter,' that's as far as you go. Meanwhile, I need your students to check something else."

The kitchen door swung open, and the bartender set a burger, a side of fries, and the check in front of Steve. He snagged a few fries and signaled Nick to continue.

"Check Planned Parenthood clinics in the central part of the state. Who requested pregnancy testing or counseling from December 1991 through March 1992."

"HIPAA rules, Nick. They'll never hand the records over, if they even still have them."

Nick was well aware of the obstacles, and opportunities, old analog files posed. "Tell your students they need to push, and not to take no for an answer. To say they need names, that's all—no contact details, no job or insurance information, no personal data—they're just trying to confirm a tip police are pursuing. They should offer to haul old, dusty boxes or search microfilm, so clinic staffers don't have to."

"And if we get names, then what?"

He stole a fry. "Snail-mail a thumb drive with the list to this post office box. I'll keep an eye out for it." Nick wrote a New Jersey box number on a napkin and passed it across the table.

Steve chewed on a bite of his burger as well as the request. Nick put on his coat; he was already late getting back to the division.

"What if this person took a home pregnancy test instead?"

"That would suck," Nick admitted, "but I'm following my gut here."

He left Steve to digest a mountain of ground beef and carbs.

One thing he and Laura had not discussed about their epiphany in Connecticut was this: If Christine Anderson was Kate McDonald, who was the father of her son?

Damian bounded off the court, perspiring like it was July instead of two weeks before Christmas. The old boiler made the high school gym hot as hell.

"Dad, did you see that three-pointer? Didn't know I had it in me. None of those guys even stopped to defend against it."

Sometimes, surprise was the best strategy, Nick mused as his boy jogged to the locker room. *Sometimes, it was the only strategy, so long as you weren't the one being surprised.*

He'd hit Christine Anderson with his Jeep, had pushed her away from that dumpster, but hadn't recognized her as Kate. Whatever twenty-four years alone might have done to change her appearance was complicated by her illness. Her hair was long and gray now, her eyes no longer the bright, inquisitive green he remembered. When he compared his cellphone shots of Justin at the diner with the pictures of Barry Poole Laura had included in Bloodstrains, *he didn't see a resemblance – not that it would have proved anything.*

"Ready to go? I'm starving, Dad. Can we pick up burritos for dinner? There's that place downtown near the newspaper."

He'd have to order ahead, find a place to stop the car, and run in. "Let's just eat there. Parking will be cheaper at this hour. We might even find a spot on the street."

Damian loaded his gear into the Jeep, then settled in up front with Nick, pushing the passenger seat back as far as it would go. The boy had crested six feet a couple of inches ago. He was taller than his dad now.

"I'm really glad this is one of my nights with you," Damian said. "Nana Bea is staying at our house again because Mom is on her book tour, so Steve is there for dinner tonight."

"Thought you liked Drew's Uncle Steve."

"I do." Damian thought a minute. "What I don't like, I guess, is being the only non-Brightman there. When Mom's around, she helps balance things out. Not as much Ivy League perfection in the house."

"You feel like an outsider without your mom there?"

Large sneakers assaulted the Jeep's dashboard. "I'll survive. It's not the worst thing that could happen to a guy."

What would be?

"What if all your life people told you one story about your father, saying he had died before you were born, and then you found out it wasn't true? What would that feel like, do you think?"

Damian gave him the Cunningham look: eyebrow arched, nose scrunched as if he smelled something bad. "Who are we talking about?"

"A guy I met up in Connecticut when I was there recently."

"In the town you and Mom drove to around Thanksgiving?"

"That's the place."

Damian tapped those big-and-getting-bigger feet against the black vinyl of the dash. "What's the lie? His dad isn't dead after all, or he isn't his dad and someone else is and he might find out?"

Smart boy. "The second one."

A sample of Justin's blood or saliva could rule Barry Poole out. Managing to get either one without showing his hand wouldn't be easy.

"If this guy never knew his pretend dad, it wouldn't be that hard for him," Damian said. "If he can get to know his real dad now, that could help—if the real dad is alive, that is."

"We're not sure yet." Nick pulled into the parking deck closest to Laura's newsroom and found a space on the first level. Time to focus on the young man the two of them had created, their one great accomplishment together.

Although they had found Kate, that was no small feat.

About 9:30, Damian finally settled down at Nick's coffee table with his homework. Neither the schedule nor the setting Laura would have chosen, but at least the kid studied. Nick would have tried to bluff his way through tomorrow morning's history midterm on the Second Continental Congress.

He was working around Damian, tidying up their three-nights-a-week, two-weekends-a-month bachelor pad, when his new investigative partner at the Connecticut State Police texted for a fourth time. Nick stepped into the kitchen and called her.

"I've been trying to reach you for the last hour, Fabrizzio."

"I have my son tonight. We just got back from dinner. Figured you'd leave me a message if there was an emergency."

Stacey laughed. "Emergency, right. Nothing's happened in this town in years."

"Not since Elizabeth Aldridge Poole was murdered in the house you live in."

"Which is why I'm calling. Because John Poole once owned my house, a search warrant is being executed there as we speak. At the Anderson cabin, too, for the same reason, and at a handful of other properties, including the diner. Those Pennsylvania troopers want evidence John knew his killer."

Nick knew they'd scour every inch of John Poole's former real estate holdings for prints, fibers, DNA, and so forth. They would look for commonalities, but even that wouldn't be conclusive. Nick's fingerprints, for instance, would be at Stacey's house and the cabin and the diner, as well as Poole's trailer in upstate Pennsylvania, but he sure as hell didn't kill the man.

"Keep me posted. I'll do the same on this end."

Damian's head shot up from his textbook. "Soda?"

"Fridge. I'm on the phone for work," Nick said.

"Right." Damian stayed put on the couch.

Stacey chuckled into Nick's left ear. "How old is he?"

"Fifteen. You heard, huh?"

"I heard. So funny, those deep voices that barely speak a syllable at a time."

Sort of like Christine, or rather Kate, reduced for now to communicating like a teenage boy. "Was Justin like that?"

"Still is; no great conversationalist there."

"Does he talk to his grandfather?"

"Not if he can help it. Justin's happy Philip is in Maine most of the time. Philip Anderson has a nasty temper, and you don't want to cross him. Justin mouthed off a couple times and got slaps that knocked him on his backside, talk around the diner says. Before she got sick, Miss Chris took a few slaps from the old man, too, Justin says."

Now there was an interesting insight into Kate's life: the father-in-law from hell.

"On paper, Philip Anderson comes off well, providing financially for his daughter-in-law and grandson for years. Maybe he never lets them forget that?"

"My grandmother once asked Phil why he'd bothered to bring Christine and Justin to Aldridge when she clearly did not want to be here. I remember his answer. It was so loud Miss Chris must have heard it back in the kitchen: 'Because *she* doesn't get to decide.' Justin always said that was why his mom loved the cabin, because it was the only place where she could escape."

At the cabin, Justin had said he and his mother moved to Aldridge when he was six years old. *Why there of all places?*

"Did your grandmother and Philip Anderson grow up together?"

"Don't think so, but maybe. Gran said the three of them just pulled up one day in an Airstream trailer after Phil bought the diner. He came to get the keys from her. They lived in that trailer until he built them the house in the back."

Static crackled over the line, Stacey must have been in her cruiser, driving between cell towers. "Say that again—"

"I said they all lived in the Airstream until Phil built the house behind the diner."

"So he and your grandmother weren't friends, she just did his legal work? That's odd, isn't it, for a judge to have private law clients?"

"Gotta go!" Stacey shouted over the blare of her siren.

Who the hell was this guy, and how did Kate and her son end up under his thumb? Nick fired up his Philly PD laptop and tapped into Maine's Bureau of Motor Vehicles. Seventy-three Philip Andersons, thirty-six Phil Andersons, twenty Phillips with two l's, and a couple dozen with first initials preceding the name Philip, not to mention still more who spelled the last name

Andersen. Narrowing his search to a range of birthdates would shorten the list, but he'd still have to open each file to see whether the man in the accompanying photo looked like Santa Claus. That's how Laura had described Phil; Nick had never seen him face-to-face.

Rusty old red pickup had been Laura's only recollection of the truck Phil was driving when he gave her a lift. That far north, it probably described half the trucks on the road. A plate number would have helped Nick cross-reference the truck's registration with Anderson's name. Much quicker.

"How much longer you plan to stay up?" he asked Damian.

"Hour, maybe? It's not that late, Dad."

It wasn't. "Okay, back to work then. I have some to do, too."

Another day, another haystack in yet another state.

Within forty-eight hours of his chat with Steve Brightman, Nick got an alert that the state attorney general had filed paperwork in Pennsylvania's Commonwealth Court, arguing that any and all documents relating to the 1992 Challenge Fire should be unsealed and made publicly available. In response, the university filed for an order restraining release of the documents.

Within seventy-two hours, an emergency hearing was scheduled in Commonwealth Court, and lawyers on both sides were urged to present their best cases immediately rather than drag the matter out indefinitely. The university tried again for a restraining order but was denied, since John Poole's murder had been deemed by the court to be sufficient cause for prompt action.

In Columbus and Indianapolis, Laura gave interviews noting that unsealing the documents would be only the first step. Finding something in them that might help solve John Poole's murder and answer lingering questions about The Challenge fire was far more important.

On December 19, the Monday before Christmas, the documents were unsealed. State troopers, led by Dixon Bott, made a show of transferring to the McKean County Courthouse some files pertaining to DNA and other evidence, in hopes of proving whether Poole's killer was linked to the fire in which Poole's own son had died. Laura traveled back to Philadelphia that day, and thus was incommunicado at the most inconvenient times. The McKean County District Attorney's office filled in for the media whatever information gaps it could. The university declined to comment, citing the advice of counsel.

So for now, the big story—the one immediately available, and seized on by the press—was how much the university had spent in the 1990s to settle with the victims' families and make their consolidated lawsuits go away. The payments were largely equivalent from family to family, but the attorneys' fees amounted to several million dollars over that total payout. The newly released information was as Nick mostly expected it to be. A few forensic revelations from the documents might come in handy, but he knew it could be weeks before any emerged.

The Wednesday before Christmas, he and Laura were on I-95 heading north to Maine, driving through morning haze on the way to book events. David wasn't happy about Nick's presence on the trip, but had spared him the snide comments as they were leaving.

Nick had brought a long list of Maine Philip Andersons to check during their forty-eight hours together—Laura had promised to be home for the long holiday weekend. One other list awaited, one Nick hadn't expected so soon.

He was grateful for the smokescreens, natural and legal.

Chapter Thirty

Nick

New England, December 2016

Laura scanned the pages.

"How did you get Planned Parenthood records?"

"Don't ask, don't tell."

She pushed her sunglasses up into her hair. "Lot of names here."

Nick eased into the left lane, passing a bread truck with a smiling bear painted on its side. "Yep, but no Kate McDonald, and no Christine Lawrence or Christine Lawrence Anderson. You two were like sisters, you knew how Kate's brain worked. Anything look like a fake identity she'd assume for a pregnancy test?"

Laura flipped her glasses down again. "Her mother's maiden name was Italian, Cellini, I believe. Nothing like that here."

Cars slowed in the passing lane in front of the Jeep. Nick tapped the brakes and signaled a move into the center lane of traffic. "Grandmothers' names? Other high school classmates? Favorite movie stars?"

She started to rub a finger over her left eye but stopped herself. "A torn contact lens is the last thing I need right now. I only have one extra pair with me. Don't want the book-buying public to see me in my bifocals."

"I hear the readers in Portland like their true-crime writers to look studious. Hold the glasses in your hand as a prop, to calm your nerves."

"Why not? Nothing else works. Saddington Nair arranges author events for *no one*. Karla was shocked when the company agreed to set up that on-campus launch, so I'm pretty sure she can't imagine whom she offended to get stuck with me and my stage fright on a weeks-long book tour."

Lately, Laura's publisher couldn't do enough for her, given the buzz *Bloodstrains* was getting because of John Poole's recent murder. All her fine work, her Pulitzer Prize, yeah, they were nice, but they were beside the point. Those skyrocketing sales were all the credentials Saddington Nair required.

"How much longer to Portland?" she asked, for what had to be the tenth time. To Nick, it felt like driving Damian to camp every summer. Leaving just after 3 o'clock in the morning had put them ahead of the New York City rush hour, and they'd managed to clear Connecticut and Massachusetts fairly easily.

"We're about two hours out," he said. "I'm pulling off for lunch and gas next chance we get."

"I can't eat, Nick, not before a meet-and-greet."

"Your meet-and-greet isn't until seven o'clock tonight, and I don't want you passing out on me. Karla can be your nurse when we get there, but in the meantime, I'm the chauffeur, and I'm starving."

Chauffeur-bodyguard, but he didn't want her worrying about that. Not that he wanted to, either.

"My butt is sore, so I may as well get out and walk around. Try to find a place that sells more than burgers and tacos, okay?" She fluttered her eyelashes at him and mouthed, "Pretty please."

Nick pushed away thoughts of that butt and batted at the pages, which she'd tucked into a cup holder. "Do that thing you do, read these out loud to yourself. I promise you a wilted salad if you can come up with a name."

She retrieved the printouts, then squinted at something. "This list ends in March 1992. Where's the rest?"

Nick pointed to a sign advertising food and fuel. "I didn't think later dates were relevant, so I didn't ask for them."

"Why wouldn't they be relevant?"

"Because the fire was on the nineteenth of March and Kate immediately disappeared."

"Tell me you remembered it can take a while for a woman to know she's pregnant. What if Kate didn't suspect until April, even May or early June?"

Nick logged into his phone with one hand and gave it to Laura. "I admit it, I screwed up. But check my email for something labeled *half year*. There's a file attached that covers tests through the end of June at one women's center, a fairly busy one based on the length of the list. I didn't print April, May and June out, but maybe the names will expand enough to be legible."

"I'll forward it to my tablet, and we'll see." A few keystrokes on his phone, a few on the tablet, and Laura had that list in her hands. "Reading through this could take a while."

Nick eased off the accelerator and cruised the mile to the off-ramp. When he pulled into the rest area parking lot, Laura was smiling.

"Catherine Earnshaw, April 28. That could be her."

"Who's Catherine Earnshaw?"

"Just Emily Bronte's heroine in *Wuthering Heights*, Kate's favorite book. If I'm right, she left a clue she knew someone might recognize."

Nick got out of the Jeep, walked around to the passenger side and opened the door. "Then why isn't Catherine Earnshaw sitting in that wheelchair now? And whose maternity records should we search for, Cinderella's?"

Laura stepped out, and he slammed the door behind her. "How the hell am I supposed to protect her—and you, for that matter—if every answer brings another twenty questions? Where *was* Kate, or Christine, or whatever she was calling herself in the weeks between the fire and that clinic visit? Where was Justin born, and where did they live until he was six, when Philip Anderson apparently dragged them off to Aldridge, Connecticut?"

Nick took a deep breath, trying to slow down his brain, though what he really wanted was to smash his fist through the windshield. He rushed into the rest area building, straight into the men's room to throw some cold water on his face. In the mirror, he saw the same man who was always there, but he felt ancient, tired of wandering this endless, dangerous maze.

When he re-entered the hall of fast food and junk souvenirs, Laura gave him a cup. "This is decaf. Say thank you."

She put her hand over his hammering heart. "Nothing ever changes, does it? I want to be home baking Christmas cookies and wrapping presents, I really do, but instead here I am, still obsessed, chasing answers to still more questions. And I dragged you back into this. I'm sorry."

He didn't want her sorry, he wanted her with him, safe.

"We found Kate. We have to keep at this until we know the whole story." He lifted her hand and pulled her toward a table. "Hot shots like us, what's it gonna take, another twenty years?"

Karla twitched beside him.

"Are publicists always this nervous?"

"Oh, yeah," she said. "Especially when we're almost out of books—again. No matter how we try to predict demand, we can't get enough. There's always some TV report that brings more people in."

"Selling out of books is a bad thing?"

She scowled at Nick and snared the bookstore manager for a quick huddle.

More than an hour ago, Laura had moved from the podium to a table to sign copies of *Bloodstrains*. She shook her fine-tipped marker. Karla materialized at her side with a fresh one, and added a few books to the stack awaiting the buying public.

Nick eyeballed the line for sales. *There might be enough copies after all.*

The author stood and stretched. "Occupational hazards: stiff neck and writer's cramp. Give me a second to work the kinks out." As her fans applauded, Laura scanned the crowd and smiled at Nick.

Why did she get so rattled before these things? She had done well, as usual.

Laura's focus shifted across the room, and something changed—Nick saw it in her face. She sat quickly and hard, rocking the table. Karla rushed in with a bottle of ginger ale, but something told Nick more than low blood sugar was the cause. He walked up the side aisle toward Laura, hoping to see what she had seen. Nothing but people holding books, chatting among themselves. Nothing out of the ordinary.

Casually, he retraced his steps, moving past the rows of chairs set up for Laura's appearance and onto the main sales floor. Past the tables of classic English literature, bestselling novels, and picture books. Past the café and the obligatory mugs, tins of tea, and bags of gourmet coffee. Past the board games and the art books and the other impulse-buy options lined up near the registers, where more people with copies of *Bloodstrains* waited to pay. Typical bookstore sights and sounds.

"Thank you, everyone, for coming this evening," the voice of a store employee said over the public address system as Nick ended his second circuit through. "And thanks especially to Laura Cunningham for those fascinating insights into her new book."

A wrap, at last, on one very long day.

Karla, looking no less stressed, waved Nick over. "I have to settle up with the store and then call ahead about books for tomorrow's stop in Bangor. Go on without me. Laura needs to eat, and soon."

Her job, Nick guessed, was the kind you did in your twenties and hoped you survived with enough energy left for the rest of your life.

One final autograph signed, Laura yawned and searched for her coat. "What time is it?"

"Eight fifty-five. Closing time is 10 o'clock, according to the sign at the front door, so we don't have to go if you don't want to, but I'm more than ready. I saw a little Italian joint down the block. A few slices of pizza and a glass of wine, and you'll sleep like a baby tonight."

She nodded and let Nick steer her outside. In the few minutes it took to walk to the restaurant, Laura looked over her shoulder twice. Inside, she asked the hostess for a booth then slid into it so she could see the entrance. Nick moved in across from her, rearranged the flatware and napkins, and handed her a menu. Laura raised it, shielding her face.

"You want to tell me who you're hiding from?"

"You can't hide from someone who's already seen you and knows you've seen him. I want to see if he followed us."

"Who are we talking about?"

"I'm not certain."

A waitress stationed herself on Nick's side. He ordered two glasses of Merlot and a large white pie with green peppers, and waited for Laura to challenge him about not consulting her. She didn't, which worried him. When the wine arrived, Laura gulped some, coughing when it became trapped in her throat. He moved over to her side of the booth, patting her back until the liquid went down.

"Enough, Elsie. Tell me who you saw."

"Probably just power of suggestion. Because we're in Maine, I thought I saw Philip Anderson. It looked like him, but also didn't."

"Let's pretend I'm a cop. Describe Phil Anderson to me."

More slowly this time, Laura sipped at her wine and closed her eyes. "Early to mid-seventies, maybe five-ten, five-eleven, though he walks with a limp and is a little hunched to one side, so he might be taller."

"Which side?" She opened her eyes and saw Nick taking notes on his phone. "Right, he was favoring that leg after getting out of the truck."

Nick wished he had ordered a whole bottle of Merlot instead of just two glasses. "Coloring? What was he wearing?"

"White hair was poking out from under a red wool cap, so I couldn't say how much he might still have on top. His ears were completely covered by the hair. Bushy gray eyebrows, brown eyes, I think, wire-rim bifocals, the kind with the line that goes straight across the lens. His skin was flushed, but it was cold and wet that day. He was wearing one of those red plaid flannel jackets that looks like a shirt but has a quilted lining, and blue jeans and duck boots."

"Demeanor? Facial expression? Was he a pleasant guy, civil?"

"I wouldn't have gotten into his truck if he had been creepy. He was polite, which is why I was surprised when he started yelling at Justin, then slapped him."

Their pizza arrived, bubbling and smelling how heaven would if its primary components were mozzarella and garlic. The waitress served each of them a wide wedge and moved on to the next table. Nick folded his and bit off half. Laura picked off the pepper slices one at a time and ate them first, like she always did.

"What about the man in the bookstore?"

"He didn't look like that," she said, finally lifting the slice to taste it. "No hat, a full head of red hair. From where I was sitting, I couldn't tell whether there was any gray in it. He had a metal cane, propped up against his right leg."

"The kind with feet, for stability?"

"No feet."

Nick pushed his phone away. "The guy in the bookstore didn't look like Philip Anderson, so what startled you? Did he say anything? Did he buy a book and ask you to autograph it?"

She shook her head.

"Are you sure it wasn't just someone who stopped to hear your talk but didn't buy a book?"

"He did have the book, I saw it, and he stared at me like the nuns used to in grade school. Like he knew all my sins."

Of which there were very few, as far as Nick knew, though that wouldn't stop her from fretting over some perceived wrong that might require absolution.

He pushed his wineglass her way and tapped it until she drank.

Two hours, the entire pizza, and much more wine later, he dropped off Laura at her hotel room; she was slurring her words but still able to walk a straight line in heels. In his room, he opened his laptop and located the running tab he kept on everyone connected, even tangentially, to The Challenge fire. Nick pulled off his boots and read into the early morning, refreshing his memory on the Anderson family tree as they now understood it.

The distinctive birthmark made Barry Poole the most probable supplier of half the chromosomes that produced Justin Anderson. Barry died in the fire in 1992. Pregnant, Kate chose—for reasons still unknown—to let the world wonder whether she was dead, and may have called herself Catherine Earnshaw, at least for a while.

Twenty-four years later, John Poole, Barry's adoptive father, was murdered within hours of Nick's introduction last month to Justin and his mother, known to her neighbors as Philip Anderson's daughter-in-law.

John's wife, Barry's mother, Elizabeth Aldridge Poole, was neither an Aldridge nor a Poole except by marriage, nor was her family originally from Connecticut, according to police and newspaper reports when she was killed in 1980. So she wasn't the source of the birthmark. That left Mitchell Aldridge, her murderous ex-husband, who died after a prison break in 1981.

Which led Nick no closer to why Kate chose to become Christine Anderson, widow of the possibly non-existent Aidan Anderson, whom Justin believed to be his father.

Knowing he wouldn't sleep, Nick opted to delve into the pile of Philip Andersons he had culled from the Maine Department of Motor Vehicles. There had to be a face Laura would recognize.

"Hope you rush-ordered at least a hundred books. Crowd looks even bigger today."

Karla sighed. "We're in Bangor-effing-Maine, for God's sake. Nobody lives here, Nick. How is a week-old NPR spot still pulling them in?"

"It's not. A little while ago—on NPR and every other major news outlet—the Pennsylvania State Police announced they had a person of interest in John Poole's murder."

An hour earlier, mere seconds after receiving the alert, Nick had phoned Dixon Bott.

"Not me, is it?"

"You're a lucky guy, Fabrizzio, calling in that report of shots fired while you were still forty miles north of Bradford." Dix sounded stressed and very tired.

"Who then?"

"You won't believe it," he whispered. Nick heard a door creak, then shut.

"Try me."

"Nobody can appreciate more than you how nuts this case just got. We're looking at Mitchell Aldridge."

"No fucking way."

"Talk about a big payoff from the crime-scene units that swarmed John Poole's trailer and those places he used to own in Connecticut," Dix said. "Two days in Stacey Endicott's house alone, and they even had that diner closed for half a day. Aldridge's fingerprints were all over Poole's trailer—they were identical to those taken when Aldridge was arrested for killing Poole's wife. We're still processing what we pulled from the cabin."

"The day Poole died, that trailer looked like John knew someone was coming for him and he had given up," Nick said.

"The dust, the water running over greasy plates piled in the sink. Stuff strewn everywhere. In your shoes, Dix, suicide might have been my first call too. When I visited him days earlier, it didn't look that bad."

Somehow, John Poole fit the past to the present. Did he know Mitchell Aldridge was still alive? Where had the man been all this time?

Before heading back to the bookstore for Laura's appearance, Nick had reviewed the notes from his conversation with Poole. Read an old newspaper clip detailing the manhunt for Mitchell Aldridge and the others who got away amid the chaos of the prison riot. Scanned earlier press accounts of Elizabeth Aldridge Poole's murder and an original police report he was able to access. Saved a grainy head shot of Mitchell to his phone. *Might come in handy.*

He was itching to talk to Laura now. If Karla hadn't heard news of the arrest, Laura probably hadn't either. Nick knew they had gotten tied up on a conference call with Laura's agent and reps from Saddington Nair. Much haggling over book availability and contract bonuses and boosting the second print run for *Bloodstrains* was all Laura managed to tell him when she and Karla emerged from the bookstore manager's office minutes ago—moments before she ran into the ladies' room to comb her hair and calm her nerves.

Promptly at 3 o'clock, the store manager introduced Laura. She stood at a podium, in a space similar to what they'd seen the night before in Portland. Copies of *Bloodstrains* sat stacked on a table nearby as Laura launched into the horror story that still kept her awake at night.

While she read from her book, Nick monitored the store, on alert for the red-haired man seen the previous evening. He had already eliminated each Philip Anderson under sixty in the

DMV files. With a couple dozen left, it might be easier to print the drivers' pictures and spread out the remaining Phils for Laura to consider and round out her description.

She had just started to take questions when a cable-network reporter standing at the rear of the group asked whether Laura would comment about the day's developments in the John Poole case. A videographer and sound tech stood poised to move closer.

Nick stepped into Laura's line of vision and nodded. Apologizing for the interruption, Laura invited the TV crew to come forward.

"Laura Cunningham, new details surface almost daily that substantiate your book *Bloodstrains* and its call for re-examination of evidence from the fatal Challenge fire in Pennsylvania in 1992. Today, law-enforcement officials in Bradford, Pennsylvania, announced they had a person of interest in the murder of John Poole, whose son Barry died in that fire.

"Sources close to the investigation say that person is Mitchell Aldridge, who was the first husband of John Poole's wife, Elizabeth Aldridge Poole. Interestingly, Aldridge was convicted of *her* murder more than thirty years ago, and he himself was declared dead after a prison break," the reporter said. "Tell us, Laura, what do you make of this new development?"

Heads turned as the bookstore crowd looked from the TV reporter to the author. Karla nudged a copy of *Bloodstrains* closer to Laura, catching the videographer's attention long enough for him to swing in for a shot.

"I'm stunned," Laura said, and paused to sip some water. Nick noticed her hand trembling. "John Poole found his wife dead and her two young sons sitting in her blood. He helped put

Mitchell Aldridge in prison. If Aldridge has been alive all this time, I can't imagine how he eluded police, or why he would go after John Poole now."

Nick knew she could very well imagine but didn't dare out loud. Not if they wanted to protect certain people in the town named for Mitchell Aldridge's ancestors.

"The thirst for revenge is never quenched, is that it?" asked the reporter.

"It's a good theory. Now, if you don't mind, I'd prefer to take questions from these nice people who came specially to hear me talk about my book."

The audience applauded. The news crew took the hint.

Every available print copy of *Bloodstrains* had an owner by the time Laura capped her pen, stood, and stretched her arms over her head.

"One hundred hardbacks, plus twenty-five eBooks at the counter," Karla said. "Point-of-sale nonfiction numbers like this, I personally have never heard of or seen." She gave Laura a quick hug, grabbed her briefcase-size purse, and vanished into the crowd.

Nick opened a fresh bottle of water and handed it to Laura. "No strange, red-haired men today, or none that I saw."

"I didn't have time to look around, but I'm glad you did, Nick. What a crazy day."

To be followed by a long drive tonight. He was due back on duty tomorrow, and Damian had extracted from Laura that promise that she'd be home for his holiday basketball tournament. Nick saw Karla schmoozing with the bookstore manager, so he put on his best charming-detective smile and asked if he might print out a few photos related to the Poole case.

When he was finished in the manager's office, Nick rolled up the pages and flashed her a salute.

With New England's weather obligingly clear and conducive to a smooth eleven or so hours of driving, plus a couple of breaks, Nick estimated they'd arrive in Philly about 6 o'clock Friday morning. Early enough for Laura to see the kids start the day; early enough for Nick to go home, shower, and consume sufficient coffee to keep him vertical at work. She had been smart to take the day off. He would be more interested in gaining access to the police department's databases than sleeping once Laura identified Kate's/Christine's putative father-in-law.

He tossed the printouts into her lap well before they hit the interstate. Laura trained her phone's flashlight on each driver's license picture. The face she finally recognized was Philip Number Eight.

"Could this picture be any worse? Even by low DMV standards, it's terrible. His chin is down; his eyes are half shut."

"You're sure it's him? I thought you said Philip Anderson looked like Santa Claus."

"Add a hat and a full white beard, and it's him. According to this license, he lives in Augusta, or at least he did when this photo was taken almost three years ago."

It was a place to start, a first step toward unraveling the tapestry of Kate McDonald's post-fire existence.

"Philip doesn't come down to Aldridge much anymore, Stacey said. Doesn't that seem strange?" Nick asked. "Your daughter-in-law is gravely ill, your grandson has to juggle a business and provide for her care, and you don't visit?"

Laura folded the printouts in half and folded them again. "Hannah, the cashier at the diner, acted as if his being in town was nothing out of the ordinary, and also like he was the cavalry come to rescue them after another of Christine's mishaps. Maybe Phil lived there full time after Christine got sick? It's possible, depending on how old Justin was then."

"We need to build a timeline, starting from when the three Andersons showed up in Aldridge, Connecticut, to when Christine got sick, to when Phil moved away and left Justin in charge. I have the paperwork from the estate he set up for Christine and Justin, but that doesn't necessarily mean Phil left town right away."

Laura pulled out a pad and made notes. Like cops, reporters knew how to write in the dark, one word per page. He'd seen her do it before.

"What I'd love to do is interview Hannah and her son, the one who went to school with Justin, and Chelsea, Christine's caregiver. Get each of them to tell me Christine's story as they know it. Stacey is a few years older than Justin, so she probably remembers more than she thinks about the onset of Christine's illness and how the family managed early on. I could tell them I'm writing an article, and do everything from home so it's not so obvious."

Oh, it might be obvious. It was a brilliant idea all the same.

Chapter Thirty-one

Laura
Philadelphia, December 2016

Halftime, and Damian's team was down only three points, but those enormous suburban high school boys were really putting the hurt on. How were those kids so muscular they made my fit 6-foot-2 son look skinny? Hours in the weight room?

The seat under me was shaking, and I clutched my phone protectively, to keep Drew from bouncing both it and me off the riser. Another ten minutes until the second half started, then fifteen minutes on the game clock plus the usual foul calls and other whistles by the referee that drag play out. I was running on about three hours' sleep. Whenever I felt myself nodding off, Drew stuck his face in mine, to make sure I didn't.

"Mom, Mom, do you think Damian will start at forward again? Where's Nick? He's gonna miss everything. Isn't he coming?"

I had texted him as the game was starting. No reply. "He must be tied up, sweetie. Detectives don't work regular hours."

"So he works all the time like you do, because you both have two jobs now? You work at the newspaper and do book stuff, and Nick is a policeman and guards you too?"

"Pretty much."

My baby had figured out the madness taking over my life. Not a good thing.

"Does somebody want to hurt you because of your book?" Drew stopped jumping and landed hard on the bleacher. He tucked in close and put his arms around my waist, sweet little guy.

"I hope not, but it's best to be as careful as we can, just in case. Somebody was killed a few weeks ago, and we think it's because that man knew something no one else did about the fire in my book."

Drew hugged me tighter. "That was when you were in college, a really long time ago. Nick was a regular policeman, right? But now me, Daddy and Damian can protect you."

I kissed his worried face. "I'm so lucky to have you guys."

My boys loved me; I *was* lucky. Maybe even the big one, I couldn't tell anymore. David had been oddly quiet this morning—no interrogation about Maine, no snippy remarks about Nick. Was Karla enough of a chaperone to make Mr. Infidelity feel guilty? No, mustn't go there, not after what Nick and I did at Jane's house, and all the things I kept wishing we could do again.

"Whip those Dogs! Whip those Dogs!" the crowd around me chanted as the teams jogged onto the gym floor to warm up. The Main Line school hosting the holiday tournament quaked. Drew clambered onto the riser behind me, holding my shoulders as he jumped and shouted, drowning out all those other voices in my head.

My phone vibrated in my hand. My editor texting, he'd seen my email. "Love this idea, Cunningham. Mitchell Aldridge's hometown and the bloody stain he's left on it. Doable by midweek?"

Was it? Good question. "By New Year's Day, maybe," I replied. "Not certain about earlier."

The whistle blew for the tipoff, and the ref tossed the ball. The Dogs whipped it away.

"Dad, Dad, you made it! Look, Damian's starting in the second half too."

"I see," David said. "Did he score in the first?"

I twisted just enough to see Brightman Father and Son, the shorter one spinning on the bleacher. "Two shots from really far out, but not three-pointers."

A large hand settled on my shoulder. A kiss brushed my right cheek. "You must be wiped out. Mom said you didn't sleep much." David stepped down a row. "She headed back home to Chadds Ford to get Christmas presents wrapped. That will actually give us a whole day alone tomorrow, just you and me and the boys."

"What have you done with my husband? He barely said a dozen words to me earlier, then he disappeared."

David draped an arm around me.

"I went to the bookstore near the mall to do some work. I was afraid if I hung around the house, we'd end up fighting. That's what usually happens."

He lifted my right hand and kissed it. "This business about Mitchell Aldridge being alive and suspected of killing John Poole, it's scary. I'm glad Nick went to Maine with you."
I squirmed away, uncomfortable. Public displays of affection, even small ones, were never David's thing.

"I'm no damsel in distress. If that takes the luster off what I've accomplished with *Bloodstrains*, sorry."

"I know you and Nick are on to something big. I also know you've chosen not to tell me what that is. Steve hinted, not so subtly, that if I love you at all, now would be a good time to start showing it and stop acting like a sulky teenager. This is me doing that, Laura."

Cheers rose to a deafening pitch around us as my older son stepped to the free-throw line. "Mom, they can go ahead if

Damian sinks this!" Drew flung his arms around my neck as he stomped on the metal bench.

Damian made the first shot, so he got to take a second.

"Nothing but net!" David yelled, pumping the air.

I blinked back tears at the simple joy of this moment, of just watching my kid's basketball game. I was exhausted. I needed a break from being frightened for Kate, for Nick, for myself. Peace of mind, I gave up on a long time ago. Family peace was enough right now.

The underdogs snarled their way to the win, sending the pups from Chester County home whimpering. We went out for victory pizza then watched goofy Christmas specials on TV. And after getting my sons settled down for the night but before seeing how sincere David really was, I shut down my work phone, shoved it into the bag with my laptop, and stashed them both in the hall closet for a little while.

See ya later, outside world.

Monday morning, the day after Christmas, another twenty-four hours I'd hoped to devote to my boys, my overactive brain woke me several hours before dawn. The alarm clock's display glowed red, like the sinister eyes of a sleep thief. David shifted next to me, disturbing our elderly cat, who rolled over onto my midsection.

"Sorry, Shadow," I whispered. I eased out from under the cat and slipped free of the bedcovers, wrapping myself in a shawl Grandmother Cunningham brought over from Galway. From the basket of unfolded laundry I had carried upstairs to the bench between the boys' bedrooms, I stole a pair of Damian's socks and put them on my freezing feet. Only slightly warmer, I padded downstairs, fetched my laptop bag, and put the kettle on for tea.

On my work phone, I found a couple dozen unread emails. Among them was a voicemail transcription from a number with an 860 area code. Connecticut, a quick search confirmed. I listened to the message.

"Do you have TTY?" a vaguely familiar female voice asked, then left a different phone number, which I scribbled on my hand. The caller was passing along a line that could type out a conversation. Only one person I knew might want that.

I flipped through my newspaper's app to find our Circulation Department's TTY line. I ran upstairs and dressed silently.

The sun peeked between the downtown towers as I drove a lonely stretch of Sixth Street past the Liberty Bell and cut over to the parking deck. I bought a cup of coffee at the corner doughnut place and walked a few blocks to the newspaper office.

Back in Circulation, a whole row of desks sat unoccupied, which worried me. Then I remembered that because Christmas was on a Sunday, Monday was the official company holiday. I walked into the phone room, relieved to find a handful of folks with headsets, a full coffee pot, and an assortment of goodies. All eyes turned my way.

"Uh, hi! Happy holidays? I'm Laura Cunningham, one of the reporters. I need to borrow your TTY phone, though I have no idea how it works."

A woman roughly my age pointed to what looked like a fax machine and the laminated sheet posted on the wall behind it. "All yours. The instructions are right there. It's pretty easy."

She passed me a plate of brownies. "Thanks, I skipped breakfast. What time do you guys shut down, in case of trouble?"

"We're here until 10:30. We'll walk you through it if you get in a jam, so don't worry."

On my way out, I helped myself to a sugar cookie too, and topped off my coffee cup. "I'll be back in about an hour then. I need to pull a few notes together."

I threaded my way through deserted departments to my desk in the newsroom, feeling utterly inadequate. What I knew about ALS could fit into a contact lens. How advanced was Kate's condition? What kind of computer did she ordinarily use? If it hadn't been bashed to hell, how well could she have communicated with us?

I replayed the voicemail message. *That voice, whose was it?*

After several more repeats, it clicked: Chelsea. It was after 8 a.m. now. With a small child and a sick woman to tend to, she'd be awake.

The small child was sobbing when Chelsea answered the phone.

"Hi, this is Laura Cunningham. We met at the emergency room a few weeks back, when I was sitting with Miss Chris. I just got your message. I hope you had a nice Christmas."

The crying subsided, and Laura heard sucking. "Works every time—Cassidy stops hollering the minute she sees the pacifier," Chelsea said. "She's almost two years old, though, so I have to get her off it."

Shuffling noises and a man's voice suggested the little girl had been handed off. "That's better, now I can actually talk. How come you're calling *me,* Miss Cunningham? Don't you want to talk to Miss Chris? Want me to let her know you'll be calling soon on the TTY line?"

No. Before that I needed some sense of what was going on up in Aldridge.

"Can I talk to you for a while first? I'm working on an article about your town and its history because the police now think Mitchell Aldridge is still alive and maybe killed somebody here in Pennsylvania who's connected to my book."

A cabinet door banged. "Amazing, isn't it? He fooled people into believing he was dead all those years. I hear the police think he *wanted* them to know he killed John Poole. I had no idea this place had such a violent past! And I grew up here."

"How old are you? Too young to remember when Mitchell Aldridge killed his ex-wife, for sure. Maybe too young to remember when Miss Chris got sick?"

Chelsea laughed. "I'm twenty, and I do remember when Miss Chris first got sick. I was in middle school. She started to drop stuff, which people notice real quick in a diner, and she got weaker until she couldn't walk without help. Then she couldn't stand, so they got her the motorized wheelchair. About three years ago, when she couldn't talk anymore, they hooked her up to the eye-activated computer. She reads a lot and goes online, but it's not much of a life. I don't think even the doctors know how long she can go on this way."

It was all I could do not to scream and cry like Chelsea's toddler, demanding that somebody make me feel better. I closed my eyes and summoned my meditation techniques, all those strategies for accepting the now and letting go of the past. Except I wanted the past back, I wanted to be in college again, having fun with Jane and Kate. Before the fire, long before Kate became Christine.

There was no turning back, though, just stepping up to meet the future.

"Tell you what, Chelsea, can I call you back later this week? I want to know more about growing up in Aldridge, but the people I work with who can teach me how to use the TTY will be going home soon."

"Sure. I'll get Miss Chris all set up. We have hearing carryover, but it'll take a few minutes for me to contact the relay service, and then they have to arrange for someone to get on the call."

"Hearing carryover?"

"Yeah, that just means Miss Chris can hear you talking and what she wants to say goes through the TTY to a relay person, who reads it to you. It's more like a regular phone call, but it's a lot of hurry-up-and-wait because you have to get the signal that it's okay for you talk again."

"I hope to interview Miss Chris too. Does she have email? Would that be easier?" Or would a digital paper trail come back to bite us in ways worse than a third party listening in? I would have to watch what I said either way.

"Miss Chris insisted that I send you the TTY number so she could hear your voice and answer in real time."

And, no doubt, verify that I recognized her.

"Then we'll do it her way." I supplied the newspaper's TTY number. Chelsea agreed to text me in five minutes, to be sure all was ready on my end.

"One more thing: Miss Chris wanted you to know she'll be alone when she's on the phone with you, so she isn't distracted by me and my husband, or by Justin if he stops by. Better for her mental focus, she said."

Better to keep secrets that way too.

"Hello, this is Laura Cunningham."

A stop. A prompt from the relay service.

"Good Christmas with your boys? Two?"

Kate, or rather Christine, was setting the tone for this conversation.

A stop. A prompt.

"Two boys, yes." I sounded nervous. I *was* nervous. "Damian is fifteen. Drew is eight. You met Damian's dad up there in Aldridge, Nick Fabrizzio."

"Crash Man."

"My ex-husband," I reminded her, grinning at her funny comeback.

"Doesn't act like an ex, acts like a still."

God, she really was Kate. I started to cry and took a deep breath, telling myself to stay in the present, in the moment.

"I'm babysitting right now. Cassidy wanted to stay with me."

"They live with you, Chelsea and Cassidy and her daddy?"

"Yes. Cassidy can say Miss Chris. She sits on my footrests. Smaller computer again, better chair balance."

"How long have you needed the wheelchair?" I reached for the tissues on a neighboring desk, a hedge against more tears.

"Almost seven years. Philip took charge for a while. Judge Endicott helped after he left."

What was it Philip Anderson supposedly said to the judge about moving to Aldridge? That Christine didn't get to decide? Was his taking charge another example of that?

"What is your life like?"

"On the highway, I think, *please hit me.* But no one wants to, not on purpose."

Had Kate hoped Nick would kill her? I coughed, unable to find my voice.

"I was young for ALS. The medicine worked. Many people die in five years. I'm still here."

"I have so many questions, I don't know where to start."

"Philip will rearrange our lives again. Could lie about my troubles. Why bother anymore? My soul's free."

A prompt: Call ended.

"You can hang up," the relay said.

When Christine Anderson first encountered us, she fed Nick, then me, all sorts of clues with her single-syllable bursts. Christine counted on my recognizing that she was Kate. Today, her comments were guarded, but she was passing along information—if only I could decode it.

"Philip will rearrange our lives again." Kate's life and her son's, but her son with whom? Justin was born in November 1992, but did she carry him to term or was the baby born early? By November, Barry Poole had been dead for eight months, though he and Kate had dated for a few months before the fire. He could be Justin's father, but it didn't mean he was. Did Aidan Anderson, the man Justin told us was his father, pass along the distinctive birthmark? Was Philip Anderson just a controlling father-in-law? What else was there to know about him?

"Could lie about my troubles. Why bother anymore?" When did the lies begin? Did I waste too much time asking what happened to Kate the day of The Challenge fire instead of what occurred in the days that followed?

"My soul's free." Free despite the illness destroying her body? Free because of it? Newly free, now that Nick and I had found her?

I replayed every comment in my head, and tried to remember how Kate would have spoken it.

An AP news bulletin beamed onto my computer screen, breaking my focus. Behind me, I heard Drew and wondered whether I was hallucinating from lack of sleep. I turned to see him bound into the newsroom and high-five one of the morning web producers.

The place was sparsely populated on this quasi-holiday, but still busy enough that handshakes and hellos stymied David's forward progress. He'd been gone less than a year, with the understanding he would be welcomed back if the job at the Oh So Fabulous Magazine in the Big Apple didn't live up to expectations. As if that would happen.

"The hometown hero returns." Damian flopped into my cubicle mate's chair. "It's not like he's famous. Jeez."

Everything was relative. "In here, he's famous. Two Pulitzer Prizes will do that."

Nick's son rolled his eyes, unimpressed. "You have a Pulitzer too. Do two make David twice the reporter you are?"

David thought so, that much was clear. Confidence like that helped get you where you wanted to be in journalism. In life, too, especially if you were a handsome, talented white guy from old Philadelphia money. I fell for him, didn't I?

Eventually, the hero and his young offspring widened the circle of chairs around me. "You texted you'd be home before lunchtime, Mom. We knew better. Surprise!"

"Quiet, Drewser, people are trying to work. It may be Mom's day off, but not everybody's."

So subtle, my husband.

"I'm almost done, but I'm dying of thirst. Can you guys go get me a diet soda?" I waved a credit card in front of Damian, whose eyes lit up. "Whoa, I mean at the vending machines. Bring this right back, and if I see more than four drinks in your hands, I won't be happy. No candy, not with all the Christmas goodies we have at home."

"Curses, foiled again!" Drew bolted from his seat.

"*I* have the plastic, dummy," Damian shouted, holding the card over his head. At least he wasn't advertising that fact outside, in the middle of Market Street. I turned back to the news bulletin.

"Look at this. It's an age-progression image the state police are circulating for Mitchell Aldridge." The authorities had also juxtaposed the new image with a photo of Aldridge taken when he was arrested for killing Elizabeth Poole.

David rolled his chair as close to my screen as possible. "Diabolically brilliant, passing off a half-decayed corpse about his height as his dead self."

"All Aldridge had to do was dress the body in his prison orange, complete with his name stitched right there on the front. Nobody gave further identification a second thought."

David stared at the images. "So, let's see: Old Mitch gets miles away from the prison he slipped out of during a riot some inmates started, then somehow frees himself from his shackles and manages to survive several weeks outdoors undetected. Odds are slim he finds a conveniently dead body."

"Excellent point. Odds are much better he kills someone about his size, lets the body ferment for a while, then hauls it out and positions it where it will be found." From beneath a pile of mail on my desk, I unearthed a copy of *Bloodstrains* and paged to the photos at the center. Specifically, to the driver's license pictures of Andrew Michaels and Michael Andress.

"See any resemblance to Aldridge?"

David retrieved his reading glasses from his pocket and peered at the book. "Not really, should I?"

"The evidence Michaels died in The Challenge fire was sketchy: a body that could be his, in a place you might expect to find a body. What if Aldridge, knowing the trick worked once, tried it again?"

"Interesting theory." David didn't sound convinced. I wasn't sure I was either.

"There's the initials thing, too: A.M. for the possibly unexpired Andrew Michaels, and also possibly reversed at some point in Ohio for Michael Andress, but also applying to the definitely-not-dead Mitchell Aldridge. And another A, Philip Anderson, Christine's father-in-law, whom I met in Connecticut and thought I saw again in Maine last week. Did I tell you that? There was this eerie vibe that night. I can't explain it."

Giggling near the elevators signaled the boys were nearby. David let fly the whistle he used to round up stray children. Drew came running and delivered my diet cola. I twisted off the top and took a big gulp.

"Ah, caffeine. I needed that. Okay, give me a few minutes to shut everything down, and then the Big Guy here can buy us something to eat. Let me hit the ladies' room first."

"Comb your hair, Mom. You never can tell who you'll run into," Damian mocked. I was grateful he didn't mimic my nagging verbatim and ask whether I was wearing clean underwear. I grabbed my purse, knocking my personal cellphone to the floor, screen up. No texts from Connecticut, none from Nick.

About halfway to the restroom, I reversed course, back to my desk, where I printed out the two state police images of Mitchell Aldridge. *You never could tell who you'd run into.*

Chapter Thirty-two

Laura

Central Pennsylvania, December 2016

A gust of frigid air propelled me down the alley behind Trilby's, tossing trash cans into the path my phone struggled to illuminate. I slipped on the ice and fell into the door, thudding rather than knocking to announce my presence.

The window shade moved, and Jane scowled into the darkness, her expression softening only slightly as she recognized me. The bolt slid, and the storm door flew wide. A blast of warmth contrasted with Jane's greeting.

"What the hell? It's 3:30 in the morning!"

"No other ears, no other eyes, just us."

"Way to be cryptic, Cunningham."

Jane let me in and pushed a counter stool my way, then turned to check the oven behind her. Sweet aromas, cinnamon and nutmeg, rose around us. On a rack, I spied miniature carrot cakes, four cupcake pans full of them.

"My pastry intern arrives in less than an hour, and we're already filling New Year's orders. You know I don't have time to socialize now."

"Kate's alive, Janie. Nick and I found her."

The oven door slammed.

"Oh, my God, Laura! How is she? *Where* is she?"

"In Connecticut. She's not the Kate she used to be, but she's alive. We always believed it, and it's true."

Metal legs scraped the kitchen floor as the other stool skidded out of Jane's way. She flung her arms around me. Her tears joined mine, soaking through my sweater and warming my neck. "Nothing else matters," she whispered as we cried.

A timer pinged. "Those do. Take care of them first."

Coffee was already brewed, so I poured us two cups and poked around for milk and sweetener. Jane set pans of warm cake on the counter in front of us to cool. I pushed a cup her way.

"Kate changed her name and has a grown son. And she's sick. She's had ALS for the last eight years, so she can't walk anymore and can't talk except through a computer. There's no knowing how much longer she'll live, and we have very little sense of her life during the last two decades."

"Then tell me what you can."

The when and how of our discovery, I shared in detail with Kate's other oldest friend. But I went annoyingly short on specifics about where she was now.

"That's all I get?" Jane protested. "No chance to talk to her the way you have. No seeing her."

"Not yet. John Poole was murdered because he knew something that drew Mitchell Aldridge out of hiding. Until we're sure what that was, we have to be cautious."

Jane popped some cupcakes onto a serving tray and added a bowl of buttercream frosting to the counter. She placed an icing spatula near them. "So that's it, we wait for Aldridge to make his next move?"

I stepped to the sink to wash my hands. "Do we have a choice? Kate's a sitting duck in that wheelchair."

"Unless she isn't the one he's afraid of." Jane handed me an orange, a cup, and a zester.

I scraped orange peel into the cup. "Aldridge could have killed John Poole years ago, but he didn't. He shot him after Nick visited John and after Nick first saw Kate, though Nick had no idea it was her."

The back door opened, startling me. Jane rescued the zester before it hit the floor. "It's okay, it's just Tamara. She has a key."

I let out the breath I was holding. "I'll move to a table out front so you can work." I patted my laptop bag. "I have a couple things I can take care of. I'll be gone when the sun rises, promise. We'll talk more soon."

Dawn was still a few hours away, so I settled into a spot just outside the kitchen door and sketched out interview questions for Justin Anderson, if he'd agree to talk about his childhood, when his mom was still healthy. He was my best source, potentially. I could ask Chelsea only so much. Stacey could fill in some of the blanks. Maybe Scott Wozniak, her fellow Connecticut state trooper, and Scott's mom, Hannah, the cashier who worked at the diner with Justin, could be persuaded to do the same, though I'd need to watch my words with all of them. I played around with possible questions for each and the right order to schedule the interviews. I'd put my editor off once already, telling him I'd just started to scratch the surface of Aldridge, Connecticut, and the people who lived there. That was true enough.

Equally true was that with Mitchell Aldridge in the wind, I'd have to do the interviews from Philadelphia rather than heading north again.

By 6 o'clock, Jane was bustling in and out of the kitchen and all around me, replenishing small bowls with sweetener packets, carrying out trays of the baked goods she and Tamara had created, and filling the display cases with cupcakes and scones and croissants. As Jane flipped Trilby's sign from "closed" to "open" at 7 o'clock, the spicy aroma of oatmeal raisin cookies stole out of the kitchen to greet the first customers of the day.

The coffeehouse was filling up quickly, despite the university's holiday break. Time for me to move along. I packed up my gear, zipped my coat, and squeezed past the growing line.

"Hey, Cunningham, don't say goodbye or anything!"

Of course, what was I thinking?

As I turned to blow Jane a kiss, a bullet whizzed past my head before I heard the shot. I dropped to the floor. A geyser of blood rose behind the counter. Jane sank out of sight.

A second bullet, then a third and a fourth took a straight course along the counter. Panicked customers screamed and pounded on their phones as they dived for cover.

The kitchen door swung open. "Stay where you are!" I shouted. The door swung back just enough for me to see a dark red stain bloom across Tamara's chest as she collapsed.

On my hands and knees, I pushed my way through the horrified crowd, batting away bullet-riddled napkins and avoiding broken display-case glass. When I finally made it behind the counter, I found Jane under a mound of takeout cups and lids. I pulled her onto my lap and coiled my scarf around the wound in her throat. I worked my arms out of my sleeves and spread my coat over her. In her eyes, I saw terror and tears, hers and the reflection of mine. "I'm here. I won't leave you, Janie. Don't leave me."

A dozen new shots knocked out the pendant lamps overhead, laying down a sulfurous-smelling shadow. Vintage metal signs clattered to the linoleum. Porcelain coffee cups and saucers fell from shelves along the walls and shattered.

Light blasted from the kitchen as an explosion sent the doors flying into the coffeehouse. Jane shuddered. I fumbled for a pulse. Faint, but there.

The smell of burnt cookies mixed with the stench of scorched leatherette and laminate as flames seared a path toward the front entrance.

As I prayed, I gagged, then vomited onto the blood-slick floor.

Drenched in Jane's blood, I watched from the ambulance as EMTs lowered the stretcher carrying her and wheeled it into the emergency room. A hospital worker helped me down, then hustled me out of the way as the doors of another university medical center ambulance disgorged the blanket-shrouded body of Jane's intern.

"Do we know who she is?" someone shouted.

"Tamara. I don't know her last name," I told someone circulating with a clipboard as police cars deposited more of the injured. He wrote down the name.

I started coughing, and someone maneuvered me into a wheelchair, but not before I spotted my brother-in-law standing apart from the cluster of Trilby's customers waiting, like I was, for someone to rewind the tape on the last agonizing hour of our lives. Steve sprinted past a cordon of medical personnel, trying to follow Jane's stretcher and the paramedics into the ER proper.

A guy in scrubs blocked his way. "Family only."

"This is a college town, no one has family here!" Steve's raised voice carried over the whine of more sirens. "That woman, Jane Baker, is my friend. So *we're* Jane's family, okay? That person with Jane's blood all over her, and me." He pointed my way.

Scrubs Guy didn't budge. "Someone will come out to see you as soon as we have news."

Steve retreated through the Trilby's customers and dropped into a crouch next to my wheelchair. "How bad is it?"

Looking down, all I saw was the ugly stain that had seeped into the wool of my coat, collar to hem. I felt it on my skin too, neck to hip—or was I just imagining that?

"Her throat. Blood kept spurting out."

"What about you, were you shot?"

I choked on my words, barely holding back a sob. "The bullet missed me. ..."

Missed me and wounded Jane so terribly.

Steve grabbed my hand and studied our entwined fingers; his were damp. I couldn't tell where Jane's blood ended and our tears began.

"David called me in a panic as soon as he got a bulletin about a shooting here. I didn't know, Laura ..."

So cold, I huddled into the blanket an EMT had folded around me after I let them take Jane from me.

"Laura Cunningham?" a woman at the sign-in desk called. Steve signaled her, and an orderly moved in our direction.

"Did you bring anything with you in the ambulance? A purse?" the orderly asked.

"Nothing." I had dropped it and my laptop bag when the shooting started. The orderly disengaged the wheelchair's brakes.

"Steve, please call David, and Nick too, he has Damian. Let them know I'm okay."

I was alive. Beyond that, I wasn't sure.

Past the intake area, in a room curtained in beige and pink, a nurse helped me out of my clothes, her gloves quickly turning red. A police officer took my coat and placed it and everything else—shirt, jeans, boots, bra, the now-bloody blanket—directly into one of several bags she'd brought into the space. The nurse arranged two hospital gowns so they covered me front and back, placed slipper socks on my feet, tucked two clean blankets around me, then left. A second nurse replaced her and inserted an intravenous line into my arm. He hung a bag with clear liquid from a pole.

"What's that?"

"Electrolytes, to keep you from dehydrating."

"I'm freezing."

The nurse layered on a third, warmed blanket. "Maybe this will help. You're in shock right now."

Because I just felt the life drain out of my friend. My head ached at the memory, and I closed my eyes.

"Let me dim these lights a little," he said, then tapped the call button against my wrist. "Let us know if you need anything else."

What I needed, I wouldn't find here.

The nurse wrapped a blood pressure cuff around my right arm and took my pulse. A doctor came in and shined a flashlight beam at me, pressed a stethoscope against my chest.

"You weren't wounded, is that right, Laura?"

"I wasn't. I told the EMTs that."

"Did you hit your head? Did anything fall on you?"

"I don't think so. My head hurts though."

"Are your ears ringing?" I nodded. "And it feels like the skin on my face is scraped off." The doctor felt along each jaw, across each cheek and up to each temple. I flinched as her fingers neared my left ear. She examined my hands and elbows, then my knees.

"These are bloody and cut."

"There was broken glass everywhere. I crawled to get to Jane."

"Clean those please," she instructed the nurse, "and let's get a tetanus shot into her."

"Don't say that."

The doctor looked puzzled. "Say what?"

"Shot."

The nurse swabbed something on my face, then on my arms and hands and legs. Then he ran an alcohol wipe over the muscle in my upper arm and plunged another needle in.

"How many are dead?"

"I don't know," the doctor replied, almost in a whisper.

The nurse didn't make eye contact.

"We'll keep you here a few days, Laura, two or three. You have a concussion, and lacerations all over, and powder burns on your face. Plus, you inhaled a lot of smoke. Bill here is going to give you a mild sedative and set you up with some oxygen. We'll take you up for a chest X-ray in a little bit." I gave the doctor a fake, feeble smile, and she left.

Bill added something to the IV line. "I don't want to sleep."

"For now, this will just help you relax." Bill disengaged the line from the pole and attached it to the bed. The orderly returned and pushed me out into the emergency room's main corridor.

"Tamara died. Did Jane Baker? You have to tell me," I insisted, even as I felt myself floating away.

Flames appear, the old dream, but it isn't Kate's face I see, it's Jane's. Blood flows from her throat, licks at the fire but doesn't

extinguish it. Smoke rises from my coat. Jane clutches at her neck; my scarf hangs from it, saturated red.

I hear screaming. My own.

I walk backward toward Trilby's front door, step into the path of the bullet, move left so it will stop at me, pierce my skin instead. Lean right so the next bullets stop with me too, so not a single one gets far enough to hit Tamara as she rushes through the swinging kitchen doors to see what's happening.

I reach over the counter and catch another bullet. This one won't slip through those doors, won't help spark the explosion and blow out the back of Jane's business, her pride and joy.

I do it all again, and again, and the blood still gushes and the fire still burns.

A sliver of sunlight blinded me. I turned my pounding head away from it.

There was Drew, asleep in a chair next to me, and Damian sprawled across the bottom of the bed, watching me, his eyes moist with tears. Standing near the door were my husbands, past and present.

"She's awake," Damian signaled his father and stepfather. He draped himself over my legs and hugged me. "I'm not letting you leave the house ever again, young lady." I tucked a finger through one of his dark curls, unsure which of us the gesture was meant to reassure.

David and Nick approached slowly, as if they had choreographed what they would do, what they would say.

"Just tell me," I whispered, the words thick on my tongue, the smoke still clogging my throat.

David sat on the bed. "The bullet tore an artery. Jane lost too much blood."

My hands still felt unwashed, my chest still wet. I was still behind that counter, pressing my blue scarf against the terrible hole the bullet made.

"One minute she was selling cupcakes, and the next …"

Sobs shook me, and I couldn't catch my breath. David gathered me into his arms. "They found a weapon in the park across from Trilby's. They'll get evidence."

Nick knelt by the side of the bed. I searched his face and knew there was more. "The gun?"

"Military-grade sniper's rifle." His eyes confirmed my worst fears.

"He came after me. I did this to Jane," I rasped, then started coughing as if I were about to lose a lung.

Drew jumped up, awake and scared. "Mommy? What's the matter?"

David took my face in his hands. "This isn't your fault."

I slapped him away. "Aldridge followed me and killed Jane. How am I *not* to blame?"

"David's right, Laura, listen to him." Nick stood and moved toward the door. "I'm going to the police station to see how I can help."

"And I'm supposed to lie here and do nothing?" I yelled, remembering Jane's outrage.

"For now, I'm afraid so," Nick said, and stepped into the corridor.

Forty-eight to seventy-two hours at least—they wouldn't release me any earlier, doctor's orders. I needed respiratory therapy and rest, every nurse I questioned told me. I had been through a lot, they said, spouting the same script.

"No more sedation," I commanded each nurse. "I need my head to be clear, so I can talk to the police."

Someone finally removed the IV. The latest nurse had left a pill, but I doubted it would be any better at chasing off my dream demons. I tried to breathe deeply and meditate, to embrace this moment and every one that spared me a replay of the shooting. Instead, I lapsed into another fit of coughing.

"Anybody home?"

I squinted and saw Steve outside my room.

"Jailed here until at least tomorrow," I gasped between coughs. "There's this, and they think I'm traumatized." I stuck the oxygen thing into my nose and took a hit.

Steve pulled a chair closer. "Traumatized? Yeah, I should think." By the looks of him, he hadn't slept. "Trilby's is destroyed. Jane would be devastated to see her baby that way."

The mess belonged to me now. Jane prepared a will a few years back leaving everything to me, plus generous bequests for Damian and Drew, whom she loved as if she were their aunt. She was. She was my sister.

Steve unlocked his phone and placed it in my hand, open to an email from his former student, the AP reporter in Harrisburg. All the unsealed depositions about The Challenge fire were being made publicly available—finally.

"In light of recent events, the university dropped its objections to a wider release, beyond the DA's office," Steve said. "The school has everything to lose now, Laura, and nothing to gain."

I traded the oxygen for the controller that raised the bed, so I could sit up more comfortably. "Have you seen anything yet?"

"Sifted through the first batch today. She'll share the whole document dump as it comes through. She worked at Trilby's when she was a student; she loved Jane, too."

From his pocket, Steve pulled a roll of papers bound with a rubber band, a look of vengeful triumph on his face. "Since you have some free time now, give these a read and tell me what you think. I'll forward this particular deposition in its entirety when you get your phone back—or do you have it already?"

"The police are supposed to return everything when they interview me, maybe this afternoon." I opened the bundle and scanned the first pages. "This is from an expert hired by the university to support the conclusion that the fire was intentionally set. Was the idea that he'd show neglect of The Challenge building wasn't an issue?"

"If it was, he did just the opposite. Apparently, the university's insurance carrier required it to maintain a rigorous inspection schedule even for structures no longer used for academic purposes. Filed with this deposition were reports showing The Challenge building passed every inspection from January 1991 through February 1992, despite the fire investigators' conclusion that electrical systems had been jury-rigged in every room, and that circuits on the main floor and in the basement were intentionally overloaded shortly before the fire. Seems the building had two electric meters, and the one for the lower floors showed dangerous surges."

Included with the deposition were an electrical inspection contract and a photocopy of the inspector's certification.

The name on the contract was A. Michaels.

"Explains why the university wanted this deposition permanently sealed, doesn't it?" Steve said.

Exactly what I was thinking.

"Also explains why Andrew Michaels might have wanted people to think he was dead. I always knew he was behind the fire. I just couldn't prove it."

I hugged Steve until we both cried.

Chapter Thirty-three

Nick

Central Pennsylvania, January 2017

In the small-town police station where his career had begun, Nick faced off against twin whiteboards, artifacts of a time before sophisticated DNA analyses, crowdsourced public-records searches, and social-media mining became tools of the detective's trade. Like Nick gave a damn if someone considered him a dinosaur.

On the left board, he'd scrawled "Unsealed Depositions Reveal" and listed the high points of the stories Steve Brightman's former student had written for the Associated Press:

1. Andrew Michaels had persuaded the university to allow him to renovate a former commercial dairy barn at the edge of the campus at his own expense in exchange for its indefinite use free of rent and other fees as The Challenge residential counseling center.
2. For The Challenge's services, Michaels had charged each student two hundred seventy-five dollars per month, or close to three thousand dollars per ten-month academic year. The facility's bank records suggested that The Challenge routinely housed twenty fulltime residents, though legal occupancy of the building's dormitory was fifteen.
3. Several former residents of The Challenge had described Michaels as abusive and said their

personal counseling sessions often included being coerced into performing sexual acts.

4. Neither university administrators nor their legal advisers had asked Michaels to produce formal proof of the credentials to renovate the structure and operate a counseling center that he purported to have.
5. Michaels' agreement with the university gave him tacit responsibility for hiring contractors as needed to inspect the electrical, water, and mechanical systems of the building to bring them up to code and maintain them.
6. According to a forensic expert examining the charred ruins, someone had tampered with the wiring, causing the spark that set The Challenge building ablaze and killing the ten students, one employee (Stacey Endicott), and Michaels in the process.

On the right board, Nick had drawn three overlapping circles. Inside each, he'd taped an enlarged, somewhat blurry photo, and layered in about a dozen sticky notes in neon colors. The photos were the driver's license headshot found in Andrew Michaels' wallet at the fire scene, a newspaper shot of Mitchell Aldridge taken at the time of his arrest on murder charges several decades ago in Connecticut, and the Maine driver's license headshot of Philip Anderson.

He pondered yet again the obvious connections: Michaels' link to The Challenge fire, in which Barry Poole, adoptive son of John Poole, died; Mitchell Aldridge's link to Barry Poole, his biological son, and Barry's mother, John Poole's wife, Elizabeth, whom Aldridge killed; and Anderson's possible family link to Aldridge, Connecticut, where John Poole and

Mitchell Aldridge also had ancestral roots and where Anderson had relocated a reluctant Kate McDonald and her son, who was purported to be Anderson's grandson.

Andrew Michaels had been declared dead in The Challenge fire. Mitchell Aldridge, once declared dead, had recently proved to be very much alive. Philip Anderson was present and accounted for, but Nick had found only a thin paper trail for a man his age. That raised certain red flags beyond Kate's comments to Laura and Laura's unease about the man she saw at her book event in Maine. No birth certificate or passport could be located for Anderson; no recent records of payroll deductions made by him or benefits paid to him, though he had a Social Security number; no Selective Service or military records; only a smattering of old tax records; few known financial transactions aside from his cash purchase of the diner decades ago; no voter registration in Connecticut, where he was known to have lived, or in Maine, where he currently resided.

Nick kicked the tripod, upending this whiteboard, scattering the puzzle pieces. No loss—so far, the evidence he had amounted to zip.

In his pocket, his phone vibrated.

"Need to talk now," Laura texted. "On my way to Connecticut."

Nick grabbed his coat and sprinted to the Jeep as another message came through from Laura.

"Kate texted me: 'He did it all! Chasing the story.' WTF?"

Now he was chasing them both. Nick ignored Laura's calls until he cleared campus traffic and was heading for the highway.

"What don't you understand about the words *talk now*?" Laura shrieked. "I'm on I-95, dodging construction in Northeast

Philly. I have to get up there." She was out of breath, as if she were running between the Jersey barriers on the road.

"What if the text wasn't from Kate? What if it was someone using Christine Anderson's phone to lure you there?"

"I'll take that chance. I know Kate."

Sounded like the old Kate McDonald, Nick had to admit. He took the northbound ramp, toward I-81, and called his Connecticut State Police contact.

"Shit's hitting the fan here, Fabrizzio, I can't talk," Stacey Poole Endicott shouted. "The Anderson cabin's on fire."

Chapter Thirty-four

Nick
January 2017

"He did it all!" suddenly sounded more ominous. Nick stomped on the accelerator. There was a whole lot of distance to cover before he'd catch up to Laura.

When his bosses approached him with the Pennsylvania State Police request that he sign on as lead investigator for a joint task force with the Connecticut authorities, Nick didn't hesitate. For the last week and change, he had been beating his head against those damn whiteboards in that musty old cop shop. A few walls had been knocked through since he last worked there in the early 1990s, some ceiling fans and better lighting had been installed, but the wood floors were no less scuffed and the steam radiators no less noisy.

Same crappy coffee, too, but without the alternative down the block. Trilby's was gone, nothing left but wreckage and a few spent casings the crime-scene folks hadn't swept up. All his old police compadres missed the coffeehouse and its owner. Nick did too—he had known Jane Baker as long as he'd known Laura.

Between the attack at Trilby's and John Poole's murder, Nick's focus had shifted away from Connecticut, but he and Laura had been waiting for Mitchell Aldridge to strike again. Was this it, this fire at the cabin?

Hours of pedal-to-the-floor driving, his light bar ready on the Jeep's dash in case a fellow officer took issue with his speed, and Nick was well into upstate New York by the time Laura called again.

"I pulled over to check my news feeds. The AP in Hartford is reporting one dead, one injured in an Aldridge, Connecticut, fire. Know anything?"

Nick switched on the light bar. "Fire was at the Anderson cabin, unless there were two in Aldridge today."

"Holy shit! I'm almost there."

"Do not, repeat, *do not* drive into that town by yourself, Elsie. Check into the motel. Wait for me."

"Where are you? How far?"

He looked at his GPS. "Not far," he lied.

Laura was pacing outside the motel office when he arrived. Nick reached over to open the passenger door. She barely got it closed before he peeled out of the parking lot and back onto the road.

"No more detail about the fire online. Too small to keep updating, I guess." Laura tucked her hands under her thighs.

Nick cranked up the heat. "I've called Stacey every ten minutes, but it goes to voicemail."

"What if Kate is the one dead, Nick? We just found her."

He couldn't imagine what that would do to Laura. Not after Jane.

"We may not be able to get anywhere near the fire scene." Even hours after a fatal blaze, investigators would still be there past sunset, floodlights trained from every possible angle. Unless Stacey was on site, Nick rated their chance of access as slim.

Laura blinked back tears, from the stress of rushing here or the anticipation of more bad news, he wasn't sure. "The hospital then, to see who survived and who didn't? If Kate's dead, will anything else matter?"

It might not.

Nick followed his gut and instead took the hard left that led to the Anderson cabin.

He flashed his Philly PD shield and Pennsylvania State Police credentials at the first barricade. Nick left Laura in the running Jeep with heat and walked over to Scott Wozniak, one of the two men stationed at the second. Wozniak recognized Nick and escorted him past.

"What's the story here, Trooper? One dead, one injured?"

Wozniak blew on ungloved fingers. "Dead guy worked for a security company. Central station dispatched him when the front door triggered a silent alert. I didn't know Justin and his mom had this place alarmed. Apparently, neither did Philip Anderson—he was the one who opened the door."

A whistle reminded Nick of Laura's presence at the barricade.

"Who's the victim?" she shouted.

"Security guard, and Philip Anderson's injured," Nick yelled back.

Wozniak gave his partner a thumbs-up to let Laura pass. She ran through in full-on reporter mode.

"Security guard?"

"A security system had been installed here, recently it seems," Wozniak said. "Philip Anderson triggered it very early this morning. The company sent the guard to check on the place."

"What about the fire? How did it start?"

"Still looking at the surveillance footage." Wozniak pointed to cameras mounted on tall evergreens at several locations between where they stood and the house.

"Any idea why Justin had these installed?" Nick asked, pretty sure he knew the answer. Their unannounced visit around Thanksgiving had angered Kate's son, but it didn't explain why Kate's father-in-law didn't know about the new security set-up.

Wozniak shook his head. "My mom says Miss Chris has been wanting to come out to the cabin. Maybe Justin thought it would be safer out here for her? I hear Miss Chris was real upset when she heard about the fire. She got out to the highway and was heading this way when Justin caught up with her. She loved this place."

Nick looked at Laura, certain they were thinking the same thing: *"He did it all. Chasing the story."*

"Is Trooper Endicott around?" Laura stamped her feet against the cold mud, a soup of water and firefighting foam eddying around them.

"She left a little while ago for the security company, to watch that footage." Wozniak showed Nick the address Stacey had texted him.

Laura checked her watch. "You go off shift soon, Scott? Want to join us at the diner?"

Wozniak shrugged. "I'm stuck here for another few hours, but thanks."

As they picked their way back to the Jeep, Laura plucked a thought right out of Nick's brain.

"Scott grew up with Justin Anderson. Is it me, or was it odd that he didn't mention how badly injured Justin's grandfather was? The only person he thought to mention was Christine."

They found Stacey staring at a bank of monitors.

Six of ten showed dawn breaking, as recorded by closed-circuit cameras. Thin January sunlight shone amid evergreens and the branches of leaf-bare trees. A red pickup truck approached the front door of the weathered cabin. A red-haired man got out, carrying a knapsack and a plastic gasoline container as he limped toward the porch. He opened the front door with a key. Four more monitors lit up as four interior cameras activated.

Not every motion was easy to interpret, a combination of low light and no audio. Then the man turned on a lamp, aimed a flashlight at the top of a bookcase and stepped closer, studying the titles. After three minutes, the man threw the flashlight across the room—they all knew the word he was silently shouting. He moved into a bedroom, searched a closet and a nightstand, then seized a stuffed bear by the neck. He twisted a knob on the container and doused the bed, the bedding and the rug with liquid. He moved into the bathroom and doused its contents.

Stepping into the kitchen, he turned knobs on the stove, and doused the curtains and a towel hanging from a hook near the refrigerator. He tossed liquid onto the stovetop. Flames climbed the fabric at the window and the wall. In the main cabin space, the man poured the liquid onto the wood in the fireplace grate and set a match to it. He soaked the books and lit several more matches. The couch, then the chair, then the rug ignited.

A man in uniform appeared in the doorway, shouted, and pulled his phone from his pocket. The red-haired man threw liquid onto the other man's clothing. New flames coursed up and down his body, and the man in uniform retreated, screaming.

Still holding the container, the red-haired man emerged from the smoke, pushed the man in uniform to the ground and kicked his head repeatedly, until the man in uniform lay motionless. Then the red-haired man poured liquid on his own hands, and splashed it at his waist and at the tops of his thighs.

From the porch, he tossed the container into the cabin. He dropped and rolled toward his truck. A plume of fire rocketed toward him before he reached it.

Smoke obscured views of the fire's progress inside, then those cameras went dark. Exterior cameras recorded the arrival of Connecticut State Police vehicles, followed by fire first responders, and documented their efforts to extinguish and extricate.

Two firefighters made their way forward and found a person on the driveway. They wrapped him in quilted blankets to smother the flames consuming the man's clothing. Others retrieved what no longer looked like a human being.

Several hours into the morning, the roof of the cabin collapsed in a blizzard of firefighting foam. Like frenzied fireflies, sparks hovered above the pickup truck and security vehicle as investigators in hazmat suits searched both.

"That's Philip Anderson's pickup. I recognized it as it first approached the cabin, and I ran the plates to verify," Stacey said. She signaled a security company tech that they were finished, and the monitors went dark. "But it's hard to tell if the guy we saw was Phil. Last I saw him, his hair wasn't red."

"I've only ever seen him wearing a hat, and he had a full white beard then," Laura said.

"When he gave Laura a ride a few weeks ago, Anderson was favoring one leg. This red-haired guy was limping too," Nick said. "Anything could account for that—the cold or a cramp from sitting in one position for too long—but I wanted to throw it out there."

Stacey stood and stretched. "It's been a real long day for everybody at my barracks, and at the local fire companies. If we want to find out who our fire starter is, the hospital is our best bet. No one's been able to question him yet, but you know everyone's eager to have a crack at him."

If the red-haired man, presumably Philip Anderson, survived his injuries, he would need a good lawyer. Nick didn't see a way out of premeditated arson and murder charges.

Law enforcement officers had been posted at the exits and nurses' stations, Stacey said, and an armed police officer was stationed at the door of the intensive care unit. Anyone who knew about the cabin's security cameras would have thought twice about leaving his wallet in a truck outside—that's where her colleagues found Philip Anderson's identification and vehicle registration.

In the hospital lobby, Justin paced while speaking on his cell.

"When I reported the fire earlier today, I told you the property owner, Philip Anderson, my grandfather, was injured in it. Now, you're telling me that he has twenty-four hours to start the claim process under the homeowners' insurance policy. He can't do that because of his injuries. I'm named as a secondary party on the policy, which you know because *you* just called *me*. I'll hold as long as I have to, just let me do whatever you need done."

Christine Anderson was sitting in a corner so far from the entrance that Nick didn't see her until Laura ran over to the wheelchair.

"Miss Chris, it's so good to see you." Laura hugged her new old friend so tightly she almost tipped the chair.

"Pennsylvania's too far," replied a loud, computer-synthesized voice identical to the one Nick remembered as Kate's.

A chorus of "Shh!" rose from the front desk.

"Your mother can talk?" Nick figured Justin could use a distraction while he was on hold. *Who better than an annoying out-of-town cop?*

"I can't keep her from tearing down the highway, and she won't sit still, so I gave her a souped-up computer for Christmas. It's a really thin notebook, and the weight doesn't throw her chair off balance as much as the other one."

Justin held the phone away from his ear, treating Nick and Stacey to the irritating instrumental disco hit the insurance company offered its on-hold clients.

"While we were choosing the options, Mom let me know she wanted a speech-simulation program. Turns out she had banked her voice, starting back when she first got sick, recording words and phrases and storing them so she'd have them to use someday," he said. "She's still getting used to the new software. Sometimes words come in bursts, sometimes more like full sentences. And it's really slow—it's faster for her to write what she wants to communicate than say it. But it's amazing to be able to hear *her* again."

"Your mom resisted that kind of program for years," Stacey said. "What suddenly changed?"

Anguish etched Justin's face. "She feels more trapped than ever in her body. And when I think about how she planned for the day her voice would be lost ... I can hear her reading to me when I was little, book after book." His eyes filled with tears and he walked away, still holding the phone away from his ear. Stacey rushed after him.

Nick understood why Kate might have balked at replicated versions of her voice. Being thought of as silenced had to be safer. So why do all that preparation, and why change her mind now, unless she had also planned for the day someone would recognize her.

In the corner, that someone was kneeling next to Kate's wheelchair, whispering, telling her Jane had been murdered. Nick waited to approach until he saw Laura lean her head against Kate's leg, her shoulders shaking as she cried.

"We bring nothing but trouble, Miss Chris," he said, and covered one of Kate's hands with one of his.

"Friends," Kate said, much more softly. "Sad, but together."

Nick watched as Laura quickly dabbed tears away from her own eyes and cheeks. It would be perfectly normal for Christine Anderson to cry about the fire that destroyed her cabin and injured her father-in-law. Not so normal for some random woman from Philadelphia to shed tears over Philip and the security guard who'd shown up at the cabin at absolutely the wrong moment. After a while, he dragged himself away to give them some privacy, treating himself to a view of the hospital parking lot.

When Stacey returned to the lobby, Justin was not with her. She pointed, and Nick joined her as she walked over to the women.

"I left Justin talking to one of Phil's doctors outside the ICU," she told them. "We'll know something soon."

Nick hoped the son of a bitch would live a long, miserable life behind bars.

"Philip did this," Kate said. "Poor security guard."

"Miss Chris, we know Phil had his own key to that cabin. I watched the surveillance video, and I'd say there's little doubt he set it on fire intentionally. I don't see the insurance company honoring a homeowners claim for whatever was lost."

"I lost nothing," Kate replied. "Cabin was going to be Justin's someday."

Her son appeared over Stacey's shoulder. Nick helped Laura to her feet so Justin could get closer to the wheelchair.

"I filed the claim anyway on the old man's behalf, a formality so they can reject it, I suppose. Just talked to the doctor, too. Gramps is in critical condition, with third-degree burns on his hands, torso, and thighs, and breathing issues because of the smoke, but he's stabilizing. As soon as possible, he'll need skin grafts."

Connecticut's prison system would be footing the bill for those grafts one of these days, Nick guessed.

Justin sank onto his haunches. "Gramps has no health insurance—seems he never signed up for Medicare. So I have to hang around here to sign paperwork the hospital needs to get his treatment covered. But, Mom, you should go home, you need to be fed and take your meds. Maybe Stacey can drive the van."

Nick couldn't pass up the opportunity. "I can drive it and leave you my Jeep," he offered. "We'll get Miss Chris home and wait for you there to swap the wheels."

Justin wasn't wild about the idea, Nick could see, but his mother represented one complication too many at the moment. "You're staying at the motel, right? Things go too long here, I'll ask Chelsea to lend you her car."

They exchanged keys. Laura pulled a notebook from her purse and wrote down their phone numbers.

"Don't worry," Miss Chris told her son. "I'm in good hands."

Chapter Thirty-five

Nick

Connecticut, January 2017

Nick pushed the wheelchair up the van's ramp and secured it to a docking system in the floor. Stacey inspected the chair's fittings and kissed its occupant on the cheek.

"It's way past time I checked in at the barracks, Miss Chris, but we'll talk soon. Watch out for these two, okay? They'll get your whole life story out of you."

They could hope, couldn't they? Nick craved a torrent of truth, but recognized they might get only a trickle. The day had already been upsetting, and Kate's health was precarious.

He settled into the driver's seat, adjusted the mirrors, and started the engine. "Where to, ladies?"

"East toward Waterbury. First rest area. Just far enough," Kate said.

She might be getting used to the speech program, but Kate knew her way around that new computer. She had mapped out their next moves. *Impressive.*

Laura buckled herself in next to Nick. He stepped on the gas and maneuvered the van out to the highway, taking liberties with the speed limit until he saw the rest area signs advertising the usual array of coffee and fast-food options.

They weren't there to eat so much as be eaten up by the crowd in the parking lot.

"Seats swivel toward me," Kate said after he cut the engine. "I'm like a dead campfire. Always cold."

Nick found the swivel mechanism and turned his seat. Laura watched, repositioned hers, and tucked her gloved hands under her thighs. Nick started the engine again, directing heat to their shoulders and feet.

"Not-so-dead campfire," Kate amended. "Thank you."

Laura flew out of the seat and embraced her friend. "I imagined our reunion so many times. But never this way, and never without Jane. How did it come to this?"

Nick knelt on the van floor and wrapped his arms around the women. "I could have killed you with my Jeep, McDonald. What were you thinking?"

"One good bounce off your bumper, goodbye Christine Anderson."

"Stop it!" Laura scolded. "We have only so much time before Chelsea gets worried that we haven't gotten you home safely. We need a plan to get you out of here."

"Out of Aldridge?" Nick and Kate asked simultaneously.

"Awfully complicated," he said, trying to envision how much medical equipment would be involved, plus the effort and expertise required to manage Kate's care each day.

"Not going anywhere," Kate said. "Phil's my problem. I'll solve it here."

With a glance, Laura beseeched Nick to make Kate listen to reason. What seemed reasonable to them might not seem reasonable to Kate, though—her illness had robbed her of a lot of options.

"Even if it's just the condensed version, Kate, Laura and I need to understand what happened when you escaped The Challenge fire."

"No time to rehash," she protested. "Phil killed the guard. They'll arrest him. They can't take him to prison."

"Oh, yes, they can, they'll send his homicidal hide to maximum security," Laura countered. "If we're lucky, they'll lose the key."

Barring a setback, in another three days at most, Nick estimated, Philip Anderson would be arrested. "He's heavily sedated now, for sure. The police will wait until Philip is lucid enough to understand the charges as they read them to him, and inform him of his rights, but not a minute longer."

"I'll stop them. They can't move him," Kate insisted.

"You think you can prevent that all by yourself, do you? Fine, but what about us?" Laura demanded. "Before you turn avenging angel, we don't get to know why Kate McDonald dropped off the face of the earth? We mourned for you. Jane mourned for you. You owe her, if no one else."

The van went quiet. Laura turned her back on them.

"You don't understand," Kate said. "Phil burned his hands, his groin, to scar identifying parts. He won't stick around."

Laura spun around to face her again. "You watched the security footage in real time, as Philip was lighting the match, didn't you? You're good with computers, Justin said. I bet you designed the surveillance setup. So tell us how all this fits together."

Kate's eyes moved quickly away from Laura to Nick. "Did you hack his pickup truck, or was it his phone?" he asked. "You tracked where Phil was going earlier today. Why?"

"You showed up here. Then Laura. Never dreamed he'd go after Jane. I had to act."

"Wait, you're saying Philip Anderson fired the shots that killed Jane?" In Kate's eyes, Nick saw all the confirmation he needed.

"Killed John Poole. Killed Jane," Kate quietly acknowledged. "Phil is Mitchell Aldridge. I let him silence me too long."

"More like you silenced yourself by refusing to talk!" Laura shouted. "Why did you let this happen?"

"To keep Justin safe. I'm always an accomplice. They should arrest me, too, for what Phil's done."

"How about me, should I be arrested?" Nick asked. "I bulled my way into town one afternoon and hit a deer with my car, then a woman in a wheelchair. I might as well have pointed the guns at Poole and Jane myself."

"And I wrote the damn book that brought Nick here." Laura pushed past him to the empty driver's seat. Once behind the steering wheel, she moved the seat closer, fastened the seatbelt, and started the engine.

"Take me home. Promise," Kate said.

Laura wasn't promising anything.

"We'll take you home," Nick promised for her. "But we'll wait only one more day to get the whole truth from you. Because you're right, Kate, he will try to get away. No matter what it takes, he always gets away."

From the floor in the back, Nick looked up into the rearview mirror and saw Laura staring at them, waiting for some sign Kate would agree to his terms.

Kate was slumped lower in her wheelchair. "So many lies," she said. "Not sure I'd recognize the truth. But I'll tell you everything I can."

Laura backed out of the parking space. "We'll continue this quote-unquote interview tomorrow, and I intend to bang at it for as long as it takes. I'm not leaving Connecticut until you tell us everything, *Miss Chris*."

Laura hadn't said a word on the drive to the Anderson house. Not a word as he and Chelsea maneuvered the wheelchair out of the van. Not a word when Chelsea offered coffee, which he declined for both of them. He wasn't sure how long he had before Laura lost it—screamed, cried, laughed as if she'd suffered a psychotic break. He simply knew he needed to get her out of there.

Away from Kate, ironically.

"I'm hungry," she finally said as they approached Chelsea's car.

"Diner's right here. We'll eat, we'll feel better, and we'll figure out what's next." He put his arm around her shoulder. "Buck up, Cunningham."

She elbowed him in the ribs. *Mission accomplished.*

The hostess-cashier was a new face. Nick was grateful not to have to chat with Hannah Wozniak, who would have gotten at least a partial report from her son on the cabin fire and Philip's involvement in it.

Laura waved off a menu. "Grilled cheese and a diet cola," she ordered. Bland and carbonated was her go-to stress diet.

"You need more than that," Nick said. "Did you eat anything before you embarked on this field trip?"

She ignored him. He ordered a cheeseburger and two servings of fries, one for her.

"You should talk," she said. "Keep eating like that, and you're going to have a heart attack."

"My cardiac health is none of your concern. You want to tell me why you're so pissed off?"

Laura sipped at the water the server brought, then leaned across the table. "Jane's dead because of us, because we came here and upset whatever truce existed between Philip and Christine," she whispered. "But Jane's also dead because Christine didn't talk. Simply decided not to, when she had a voice for the last however many years. I can't even guess what she was thinking."

None of it made any sense, Laura was right about that.

"We've asked her to tell us her story. We have to give her that chance, Elsie. We don't know what kind of bargain she made with the devil."

Laura practically spit, she was so mad. "At any moment since she recognized us, she could have told us something, but she didn't. She knew it was you on the highway, Nick, and look what happened to John Poole. She knew I had written *Bloodstrains*. She could have reached out anonymously."

"But she didn't. Those were the choices she made, for her reasons, not yours."

The server returned and set plates before them. She refilled their water glasses. Laura didn't look at Nick.

He bit into his burger and savored it for a little while. Over Laura's right shoulder, he saw the kitchen door swing open. Justin backed through it holding a plate with a sandwich and some potato chips. He put the dish down on their table and walked behind the counter to get himself a cup of coffee.

"Chelsea said you'd left, but I saw that her car was still here. Saves me a trip to the motel." Justin slid into the booth next to Laura.

She pounced. "Chelsea and her husband are living at your house. Where are you staying, here at the diner?"

"None of your business." Justin looked at her, then at Nick. "Why are you two back here in Aldridge anyway?"

"I'm interviewing your mother for my newspaper," Laura said innocently, completely changing her tone.

Justin rolled his eyes. "A newspaper article about my mother? She would never agree to that."

"About this town and its tragic legacy: the murder of Elizabeth Aldridge Poole and her son's subsequent death in The Challenge fire in Pennsylvania. I wrote my book about that fire, and this place is a critical part of that story."

"The Poole family connection is what drew me to Aldridge the day I hit your mother's wheelchair," Nick said. "Quite a coincidence that John Poole, Elizabeth Aldridge Poole's husband, was murdered hours after I left."

How much did Justin know? More to the point, how much would he admit knowing? Nick sat back in the booth and waited.

Justin bit into his roast beef and cheese on rye, and nibbled on a few chips. "We're not the ones from Aldridge. My father's family is."

Laura maintained her demure tone. "I'm glad we were with Christine today. Your mother was distraught about what happened at the cabin."

Close enough to the truth.

Laura gnawed on a french fry, then on a second. Nick gave her the advantage in this comfort-food chess match. So, it seemed, did Justin, who either decided to trust her or figured he didn't have much choice.

"We didn't move here until I was six. We lived in Pennsylvania, in the northwestern part of the state. I knew John Poole since I was a baby—he was my uncle, Mom said, my dad's relative. I remember him being nice to us, when he visited. He was the only family we had until my grandfather showed up one day."

Nick grabbed at the opening. "You didn't know Philip Anderson before that?"

Justin shook his head, walked behind the counter and returned with a half-filled coffee pot and two mugs. Nick nodded, doubting he'd sleep much tonight even without the caffeine. "No thanks," Laura said.

"Gramps just showed up one day, like I said. Mom was not happy to see him, I remember that. We were doing fine without him, she told him."

Laura went fishing. "I can see where he might be concerned about a young woman and a little boy on their own."

"We were doing fine," Justin repeated, having none of it. "Mom had a computer job at the Penn State campus in Erie. We lived in a trailer park about halfway between there and Bradford, where Uncle John lived. She had a long commute, so we spent a lot of time in the car. Before I was old enough for preschool, she hired college students to babysit while she worked. We ate in diners so often, I think that's why we ended up owning one. Mom suggested it when Gramps didn't want her involved with computers anymore."

That would have been the late nineties, Nick calculated. More people worked with computers and had them at home, and email made passing along information and exposing secrets possible with a few keystrokes. Kate must have wanted to remain public enough that someone might eventually recognize her, so she picked a diner, an old-school, low-tech strategy, and persuaded Philip to go along with it.

That was a telling little detail.

Nick went in for another: "Before the trailer park, where did you live? With your Uncle John?"

Justin peered into his coffee cup. "No, it was just me and Mom."

"Because your father died before you were born. What do you know about that?" Laura pressed.

Justin shrugged. "Mom told me he crashed his motorcycle, but she would never answer my questions about where it happened and when, so after a while I didn't believe it anymore. She said all the pictures of him were destroyed in a fire; I didn't believe that either. The way Gramps always talked, Mom belonged to *him*—she was his, and so was I. No one would have told me the truth, so I never asked what that meant."

Long past being subtle, Laura did. "Do you think Philip Anderson is your father?"

He stared at his food, pushed the plate away. "Do I want to know? Philip Anderson, Mitchell Aldridge, I can add two and two and get four, just like you can. Whatever name you choose to call him, whether he's my father or not, the man killed John the way he killed the security guard at our cabin today, in cold blood."

"We think he also killed my friend Jane Baker. Shot her and another woman in front of me." Laura closed her eyes; Nick wasn't sure she'd ever blot out the memory. "He was aiming at me because I'm a threat to him. Is your mother a threat too?"

Justin tossed the keys to Nick's Jeep on the table. "Dinner's on me. Give me Chelsea's keys and get out."

Nick clamped a hand onto Justin's wrist. "I'm not just here to chase a killer. Laura's not just writing a story as a follow-up to her book."

Justin shook free of the grip. "This is not your life, it's my mother's and mine." "Both of you, get the hell out *now*."

They drove for a while, first to the liquor store, then to the motel. Driving felt like all they did, he and Laura. Cut down on the possibility they'd actually talk about all the things they didn't want to face.

Laura entered her room and flopped onto the bed without switching on a lamp. Nick turned the lock on the knob and pulled her door shut. One room over, he groped for the light switch before closing his own door but leaving it unlocked. He poured two fingers of bourbon into a plastic cup and added an inch or so of tap water from the bathroom faucet. After a day like they'd had, he liked his alcohol warm and slightly chlorinated.

She knocked before he got more than a couple swallows down. He knew she would. Too exhausted to sleep, both of them, and too tired of the ghost they'd been chasing forever. One who, it now turned out, could be heard as well as seen.

"Buy a girl a drink?"

"Don't you have a husband and kids to call?"

She patted the phone in her pocket. "Texted David. He'll be ticked off, and I'm already angry, so no sense provoking something we'll both regret. Drew's probably asleep. If I called Damian, he wouldn't hear the phone over the video game he's playing instead of studying."

"As usual."

Laura took the cup Nick handed her and downed half its contents all at once. She choked and spit out what she wasn't strangling on. "I deserved that."

"Deserved it?"

She sat on his bed. Nick lowered himself to the questionable carpeting, his back hard against equally suspect wallpaper.

"Yes, for being a selfish, unsympathetic bitch, and for not recognizing Kate's fear that she's the only one separating the monster from everyone else."

He raised his cup. "Been there. So have you. Here's to us against the monster. We'll win, I promise."

She set the bourbon down at her feet. "And what's my prize in the end? What do I win by knowing that my best friend got away from the fire but at some point became ensnared by a man we now know is Mitchell Aldridge? That she became pregnant—by Aldridge, if Justin has it right—and settled down with her child for six years, living a life she designed, until Aldridge returned and snatched it away. The ALS was a huge insult, Nick, but was it the worst she's suffered? I think Kate will tell us it didn't come close."

"I agree. Seems as if her illness gave Kate back some of the freedom Aldridge stole. She got more control, though she won it in an unexpected fashion."

From her wheelchair, when she was connected to better functioning computers, Nick was sure Kate had monitored Aldridge, the way he must have stalked her. Yet Aldridge still wasn't behind bars.

Stretching his legs, Nick knocked over Laura's bourbon, disinfecting at least a small portion of the rug. "So what's next, Elsie?"

She pinched the bridge of her nose, but he was certain a sinus headache wasn't the problem. "Let's see, I've done anger and denial and bargaining and depression. Time to accept that the old Kate is gone, and that the new Kate makes choices I don't agree with. She's done what was necessary to protect herself and her boy, and now Justin is trying to do the same. So we help, that's what's next. How we help is up to Kate."

What she didn't say was most disheartening of all: that they couldn't change what happened. They couldn't find Kate sooner, or find her healthy. Laura picked up the toppled cup, handed it to Nick, and kissed him on the cheek. She was out the door before he could appreciate it.

Caffeine and anxiety conspired to keep him restless, but when he finally slept, he slept deeply. Sometime before dawn, the sound of a car engine startled him awake.

Through the window blinds, he saw Laura drive out of the motel's parking lot.

Chapter Thirty-six

Laura

Connecticut, January 2017

The sun was only a shimmer on the horizon when a single headlamp appeared, stark against the winter morning's darkness. It approached along the opposite shoulder of the highway then switched course, moving into and across the traffic lane. Brakes squealed, and a bread truck doing at least forty skidded, spinning horizontally to a stop at the center line to avoid the collision.

My heart hammered as I cut my steering wheel hard to miss broadsiding the truck. I swerved the Volvo and coasted onto the berm.

"Jesus, Miss Chris, give somebody else the honor of killing you today!" the truck driver yelled. "Not me, not that lady, okay?"

The headlamp flashed three times. Its wearer and her wheelchair crossed in front of the truck, weaving onto the shoulder and stopping ahead of me. I hit my emergency lights and got out.

"You really do have a death wish, don't you?"

Kate peered out from under a woolen hat. "Told Chelsea about our interview. I got tired of waiting," she complained, and set off in the direction she had come from, toward the diner.

"Damn it, McDonald." I scrambled back to my car.

Catching up proved easy. Driving slowly enough to maintain a safe distance behind my erratically moving friend was not so simple, especially once we were back on her turf and I had to dodge cars parked two and three deep for the breakfast rush and navigate around a nasty little curve just past the loading dock. In front of a supersized garage, Kate stopped the wheelchair and the overhead door opened. I rolled down my window for further instructions.

"Welcome to our Fortress of Solitude."

I parked and ventured inside. The décor was early 1970s patio furniture, plus a couple of lawn mowers, a leaf blower, and the Airstream trailer—where Justin now lived, I supposed. I eyed a space heater longingly but dubiously; it felt like the Arctic in there.

"It's electric. No carbon monoxide," Kate assured me in that voice that was hers yet not hers. "Sit."

The choices appeared universally uncomfortable. Shivering, I opted for the painted yellow glider closest to the heater, which glowed at the touch of a button.

Kate repositioned the wheelchair so she could face me and cozy up to the warmth. "I read *Bloodstrains*. Interesting. Lacking important details though."

"A recap of the obvious and the great whopping cover-up—when I started, that's all there was to work with. But I was desperate to tell the truth, not that fiction hatched by the university's lawyers. So I hit on the idea of telling *your* story and everything you knew and did leading up to the fire, then offering up a ton of speculation about what really might have happened that day. I wanted to force someone's hand. And I did, just in ways I could never have foreseen."

"Officially, I was not dead," Kate said. "Still true, for now."

Gears ground ominously, and, as if on cue, the garage door lowered. I searched for another exit. A side door that wouldn't accommodate the wheelchair only slightly lessened my claustrophobia.

"What else was true that day?" It was the question I'd spent twenty-four years asking people who couldn't possibly know.

"Long story," she warned. "I talk slowly, tire quickly. This will take hours."

"I have hours. I'm here to listen."

One of the lights above us flickered and hissed. We sat in shadow, appropriately.

"How did you get out of The Challenge as it burned?"

"Was never inside. Firefighters surrounded building. Trucks blocked dirt road. I left my car. Walked instead."

"The driver's door was open. The headlights were on."

"Went to scout some other way. Thought I'd be right back."

Birds honked above the garage, maybe the wild geese I'd been chasing. "The cops went over every inch of your car. Tore it apart looking for clues. Later, Nick bought the pieces and had them reassembled, on the outside chance he'd missed something."

I didn't tell her this: that Nick couldn't bear seeing the Firebird in pieces any more than I could. That's when I knew I loved him.

Tears spilled from Kate's eyes. "I followed an overgrown path we found. The day Barry moved into The Challenge, after Jim died."

"You went exploring there with Barry?"

"He wanted to find escape routes."

"Barry moved there voluntarily. Why was he thinking about escape?"

"Typing is faster than speech for me. Look at my screen now please." And then Kate turned the wheelchair so I could do so.

Words began to cascade, like a drizzle rather than a downpour. As each sentence appeared, I read it aloud to us both.

"Family was cursed. Barry was certain. Birth father murdered their mother and made Barry and Jim help.

"Rev Michaels said he could vanquish the curse at The Challenge. Barry had to surrender to hope.

"All I saw was hopelessness."

Little about Kate's expression ever changed. I wasn't sure whether she could smile or frown. But I could read her eyes, now that I knew to look there. I saw regret and guilt, like mine but deeper.

More of her story unfolded on the screen. This time, I waited to begin reading, until the words stopped.

"Someone came running toward me. His face was bloody. His coat was on fire.

"He was dragging another person whose coat also was burning. I rushed over to smother the flames.

"I shouted for the running man to drop and roll. He fell face first. Tooth dropped out.

"I pushed him to get him to roll. He grabbed hold of my ankle. Pulled me down.

"I ended up underneath him. Couldn't lift him. Thought I would suffocate and be found dead there."

Kate stopped and blinked repeatedly. "Do you know how many times I've wished I had?" her simulated voice asked.

I didn't. I couldn't imagine what that day must have been like for her. I reached for her hand. We sat there a few minutes, neither of us saying a word until I released it.

"What happened next, Kate? Help me understand."

Words began to appear. I tried to channel the twenty-two-year-old Kate who had lived those moments.

"Somehow, I wriggled free. Didn't run for help. Remembered Girl Scouts first-aid. Had to stop his bleeding.

"Was wearing your red scarf. Took it from your closet that morning. Wrapped it around his head.

"But his right ear was scorched. Hanging. He moaned, 'Cut it off, cut it off!'

"That's when I recognized the voice. It was Andrew Michaels.

"He handed me a knife. His ear was burning his face. So I did it.

"Blood squirted everywhere. Over us, over the other man. Michaels screamed, ripped off the last tissue.

"I couldn't watch. I knelt next to the other man. I checked for a pulse. Gone."

Kate stared ahead, as if trapped inside the memory. How long had we been in that garage? Already too long. I was sweating, I had to get some fresh air. I banged a wall switch until lights flashed on and off, and the door rose. Cold air whooshed past me as I ran outside.

The wheelchair followed me.

"Michaels put a knife in my hand," she said. "I could have put it into him, avenged Jason."

"But you would never have done that, you had to try to save Michaels. And you did. He survived the fire."

"Which he set."

"Nick and I know that now, Kate, but only just now."

She sighed behind me, or at least that's what it sounded like. I turned around and saw that she had resumed her story on the screen.

"He needed to see a doctor, before his face became infected. But I couldn't move them both.

"We needed to leave the dead man. The firefighters would discover him soon enough."

Investigators had presumed the badly burned body belonged to Michaels, whose blood was all over it and the ground around it. The ear, what they found of it, was a DNA match with the blood. The dead man was roughly the same weight and height as Michaels, and Michaels' wallet was found nearby. *Did he plant it there?*

What Kate had said about being an accomplice started to make sense. I gulped frigid air into my lungs.

"My original question stands, Kate, though for a different reason. How did you get out of there?"

I squatted next to the wheelchair, so we were face-to-face again. "I can't even guess how hard this must be for you. We don't have to do this now."

"We must," she said. "If not now, when?"

Letters flashed onto the screen. I stood and stretched, then stooped beside Kate again.

"No way I could get Michaels to my car. So I asked where his was.

"'Highway,' he gasped. I guessed he meant the access road from that side of the property.

"I half-carried him to it. Found keys in one of his pockets. Pushed Michaels into the backseat.

"Got behind wheel. Drove toward campus and hospital. Halfway there, he pressed a gun into my neck.

"Ordered me to stop where he said. Came to a half-built subdivision. Some houses had lights on.

"I drove to the end farthest from the highway, where there was another road leading out.

"Before we left the car, he forced me to tie the bloody scarf around my mouth.

"He held the gun to my head.

"We staggered to a construction trailer. Inside, he hit me with the butt of the gun.

"Then shoved me into a tool shed and locked it."

Ice began to pelt us; it was sleeting. I wheeled Kate inside, hesitating at the door's control switch.

"Leave it open. I can take it," the simulated voice said. "That trailer held things much worse than cold and darkness."

This was excruciating. It had already taken so much out of Kate physically, yet we had barely begun. When I demanded the whole story, I never realized what I was demanding of her.

I put my arms around her shoulders. Moisture from her tears clung to the sleeves of my parka; moisture from mine fell onto her hair.

Minutes passed like that, silently. She didn't say or type anything for a while.

Then she couldn't stop.

"When the shed door opened, Michaels was feverish. Side of his face had turned black.

"He pulled rope from a bag. Tied my hands in front. Shoved a syringe at me.

"Turned and lowered his pants. Said it was penicillin. Told me to inject his rear end.

"Didn't have much reach. I could barely see. Don't know how I got the needle in.

"He left me water and a bucket, then locked me in again.

"Didn't see him for maybe another day. He made me give him another injection and disappeared again.

"Next time, he brought a sandwich. He untied me, but not to eat. To feed him.

"Then he handed me alcohol wipes and the same knife I'd used to cut off his ear.

"Made me slice open the place where the ear had been, to let it drain.

"Foul pus and brown blood came out. He gave me antiseptic to put on it.

"All that disgusting stuff was on my hands when he tied them again and left."

I had to squint to see the words now. The light was dimming as the storm outside intensified. My reading glasses were in my bag in the Volvo, but I didn't want to leave Kate alone. I followed along the best I could.

"Not long after, Michaels returned. Held rag to his head with one hand. Gun in the other.

"Said bleeding wouldn't stop. Demanded I stitch his face. I didn't know how to sew, I said.

"He put the gun to my temple and told me it was time to learn.

"He untied me. And with a thin needle and thread, I poked and poked.

"The skin finally broke. And broke again. And broke again.

"So many little holes.

"I left a horrible crosshatch. Like Frankenstein.

"Gave him another penicillin shot, then he bound my hands.

"But pain must have distracted him, he forgot the knife. I saw it near a tarp.

"When he came back, he was furious about what I had done to his face.

"He hit me. Pushed me to the floor.

"Smashed my face into it and pinned me there.

"Pulled my jeans down. Raped me from behind.

"Slapped and punched me until he finished.

"I must have passed out.

"Don't know how long I lay there on the trailer floor.

"I prayed he wouldn't reappear, but he did.

"Ground my face to the floor again, punched me in the kidneys.

"I couldn't breathe, couldn't move.

"Raped me again, until I bled.

"Said he should turn me over, carve my face with the knife.

"Said I wasn't worth the trouble."

"When he was done, he didn't lock me in the shed or tie my hands.

"He just laughed at me. I was defeated. He had won."

Kate's eyes darted back and forth, as if she were frantic to get away from the recollected horror, but her computer uttered nothing. Tears streamed down her face. I felt suspended in time, with no way to relieve her anguish and no way to avoid compelling her to relive it.

"Let's stop."

"NO!!!!" the computer typed. *"I have to get through this!"*

But she couldn't, not yet. I could read the despair in her eyes. She needed to recover what reserve of strength might still be available to her.

I nodded and stamped my feet, to force feeling back into them. I powered up the space heater again, a small compromise between my phobia and the chill I wasn't sure either of us could overcome.

I walked to the Airstream and tested the door. It was unlocked. I spotted a blanket and yanked it from a banquette near the entrance. I wrapped it around Kate's shoulders.

"I have to finish."

The letters inched across her computer screen. Was she too exhausted to activate the voice software even briefly? Was she going into shock?

"In a minute, Kate. Just a minute to catch our breath."

I had to think. I looked around. I lowered the garage door

and moved the space heater closer to the Airstream, then I hauled myself up its steps and located a light switch inside. The illumination extended a few feet beyond the entry.

No more cold. No more dark. I could spare Kate that one reminder of the construction trailer torture.

I wheeled her chair over, backing it up as close as possible to the Airstream, so I could sit on the fold-down steps and stay close enough to touch her. If Kate needed to type what remained of the story, I could read it over her shoulder.

If she could speak it, I would turn her around.

More terrible details were yet to come, one way or the other.

"I'm ready when you are, Kate. But I can wait."

"I can't."

I rearranged the wheelchair slightly, so I could see her face, and I placed my hands on hers. They were warmer, I had achieved that much. Then I positioned the chair so I could read the words that continued to describe her nightmare.

"I swore he would never touch me again. I'd kill him first or die trying.

"When I could move again, I crawled to the knife. Hid it in one hand.

"The next time he came near me, he cocked the gun. Ordered me to check his ear.

"When he lowered his head, I stabbed him where I had stitched him.

"Twisted the knife in so deep, he dropped the gun. I kicked it away and ran.

"The car was still outside. Unlocked, key in the ignition.

"I drove with my hands tied for about fifty miles before it felt far enough away.

"Far enough to stop and breathe and figure out what to do.

"In the glove box, I found $400 and a Swiss Army knife. I cut one hand loose.

"Drove past Altoona. Ate for the first time in days. Found clothes, shoes at a secondhand shop.

"At a drugstore, I bought some makeup to cover my bruises, and some hair color.

"I got a motel room, dyed my hair red, and slept for hours.

"Next day, I abandoned the car.

"Walked to the bus station and bought a ticket to Erie.

"There, I called John Poole. Barry made me memorize his father's number, in case of emergency.

"John drove to Erie to meet me."

Kate called John Poole, the father of the guy she had been dating. Not the police, or her family, or her best friend. I studied her eyes, but they gave nothing back this time.

"Poole didn't ask questions or contact the police?" I asked. "He simply came when you called him? He didn't even know you, Kate."

She paused, as if she couldn't articulate the moment she knew she was truly safe.

"I knew Barry," she said. "He told me to call his dad. That was enough for John."

Soon, the screen lit up, and as the words materialized, I saw how Kate's new life took form.

"By then, John knew about the fire. Guessed or maybe knew Barry was dead.

"I told him I'd been kidnapped by Andrew Michaels. But I couldn't tell him everything. John understood.

"When it was clear I was pregnant, he cared for me as if I were his daughter.

"My child was mine alone, as far as John was concerned. As far as I was concerned.

"When Justin arrived, I saw the birthmark. It was like one Barry had."

John Poole saw it too. He must have been aware of its significance.

"And what about the fact that Barry's biological father also had the birthmark?"

"John neglected to mention that," she said.

Was Kate slumped lower in the wheelchair? Or was it only the sparse light and my worry that I was doing her more harm than good? As she went deeper into the story, it seemed as if her body recognized how urgently she wanted to tell it herself, with no chance of misinterpretation. It seemed to be fighting on *my* behalf.

I didn't know how much time we had before she'd need to get to her house, to Chelsea, to be fed and given her medicine. Was Chelsea already searching for her? No doubt Kate had been away hours longer than expected. But tomorrow wasn't guaranteed, and I couldn't delay posing the rest of my questions.

"What did John tell you about Andrew Michaels? Did John know who he really was?"

Kate didn't reply right away, as if how she worded this answer was key to my understanding the decisions she and John had made.

"In the beginning, we didn't talk about him. Other things took priority.

"I needed ID and a way to support myself. John provided the first.

"That's when I became Christine Lawrence Anderson. The name came with my new driver's license.

"Once I had that, I answered an ad for someone with computer skills. No college degree necessary.

"Tech dropouts were cool. I only needed to show I knew about programs and writing code.

"The job was with a systems contractor for Penn State's campus in Erie.

"Good place to hide, among students who looked more or less like me."

I stopped her there. "Okay, you became Christine fairly quickly. Why take a pregnancy test miles from Erie under the name Catherine Earnshaw?"

Kate's eyes seemed brighter when she answered.

"Wanted the most accurate test possible. Went where nobody recognized me.

"Didn't want to give my new fake name. I can't believe you discovered Catherine Earnshaw."

I shrugged. "But it was twenty-four years too late."

I was frozen to the bone, despite the space heater. The Airstream steps seemed welded to my bottom, and the closed garage was giving me the creeps again.

"Where were we?"

"Learning more about the devil I knew. And the one I was about to meet," the computer tapped out.

"If John ever doubted Andrew Michaels was Mitchell Aldridge, I provided the final proof he was."

"Yet John kept quiet," I said. "That, I don't understand."

"Aldridge was dead. The state of Connecticut said so.

"Michaels was dead. Killed in The Challenge fire, there was evidence.

"How could John say it was the same person, still alive? The two didn't even look alike.

"Who would believe John? And I couldn't confirm it. He would hunt us down.

"I had saved the devil's life, Laura. What kind of devil did that make me?"

The tears returned. Kate wanted this over with. I wanted this over with, this glacial march through her worst memories.

"Did John ever tell you about the day Mitchell Aldridge killed his wife? And did he tell you what he found?"

"All of it, eventually. How he moved the boys every few years.

"That he suspected Aldridge tracked Jim to the university and exploited his torment over his mother's death.

"John knew Jim's behavior got more erratic after he moved into The Challenge.

"He worried what might happen when Barry moved there.

"And then it was too late."

"For them, Kate, but not for you. John Poole watched over you for seven years, based on what Justin has told Nick and me."

Until the day came when John couldn't protect them anymore.

"Aldridge stalked John, and John led him to me.

"Bastard changed his appearance again. But all the plastic surgery in the world couldn't change those eyes.

"We recognized him immediately. John knew if he tried to intervene, Justin and I might be killed.

"So the lunatic threw everything we owned into the Airstream. Threw us in bodily. Because he could.

"We didn't stop until we got to the Connecticut state line. Aldridge became Philip Anderson.

"He warned Justin he'd kill me if anyone found out Gramps used to have a different name."

And so Justin kept quiet too.

"One last question: When did you learn Mitchell Aldridge had the birthmark? Am I right that you didn't see it in the construction trailer—"

Kate rotated the wheelchair until she faced the door once more. I turned to see what she was seeing. Just a blank expanse of stained green wood. Nothing that revealed anything.

"Sometimes," she said, "I really miss being able to scream. I miss being able to shake with fury and thunder with rage."

Kate had quite a temper. She could thunder with the best of them, I recalled.

"Judge Endicott told me about the birthmark. Or rather, about Stacey and Justin's adventure in heavy petting.

"The judge reminded me: Stacey's mother, her daughter, and Stacey's father, Reverend Michaels, died in a fire.

"That was all she had to say."

"Wait a minute, Judge Endicott knew Michaels was really Mitchell Aldridge? Did she know he was Phil?"

"She must have. She stayed out of his way mostly. Smoothed his way when he demanded help.

"Like me, she had a child to protect. I'm sure she knew he was an unpredictable maniac.

"If I had known that the day of the fire, I would have let him die.

"And I would have danced on his corpse."

For Jane and John Poole and everyone The Challenge fire killed, I wished to God she had.

The garage door sailed upward. Kate powered away.

Chapter Thirty-seven

Laura

Connecticut, January 2017

The diner was quiet mid-afternoon. The lunch crowd had dispersed, and the truckers and locals hadn't arrived yet for dinner. I drank the coffee Hannah poured into my cup. A sandwich appeared before me. I didn't like pork roll, but I ate it anyway.

I was too preoccupied to notice what I was eating. Too stunned by the horror story Kate had just told me. Too filled with the fear that there were so many questions Nick and I had failed to ask the right way, from 1992 up until today.

Weighing most heavily at the moment was this one: Why were those "Remember Connecticut" letters sent to the *Informed Student*? Did we focus on trying to identify who sent them at the expense of learning the reason behind them? Could we have uncovered the fire's secrets sooner if we had known?

Did Judge Endicott send them in the hope her daughter would heed the warning and run from The Challenge? No, that didn't sound right, based on what Kate had just told me. She clearly believed the judge had become an unwilling accomplice like she had, an accessory after so many deadly facts.

Whoever sent those letters was a provocateur, someone who intended to bring pain. That certainly sounded like Andrew Michaels, and his alter egos, as Kate had insisted from the start. Was he trying to lure Barry back into his orbit, as he had Jim? Was he trying to torment Jim into ending his romance with Judy Wright and marrying Judge Endicott's daughter to solidify his control over both of them?

The judge must have known Mitchell Aldridge—everybody knew everybody in this town. But we had not asked that question either. Nick had asked Stacey whether her grandmother grew up with Philip Anderson. It was certainly possible, as Stacey told me, that Judge Endicott didn't actually meet him until he showed up in the Airstream with his family. But accuracy didn't always equal truth. How many years did the judge help Aldridge cover his tracks, first to protect her daughter, then her granddaughter?

My phone vibrated on the counter, spinning itself around until I pulled myself back to the present.

"U ever coming home?" Damian texted. It was 2 o'clock. He should still be in biology class dissecting a frog, not messaging me.

"Maybe late tonight. Should know soon."

"David's volcanic. 17 on a scale of 10," Damian replied. "Drew's just sad without u. Me 2."

Angry husband, lonely kids. I missed my babies. I texted X's and O's. It was time to leave Aldridge, Connecticut.

"Thought I ordered you to get the hell out." Justin sat hard on the stool next to mine.

"Didn't realize I was permanently banished."

"You've been sitting here more than ninety minutes, Hannah tells me. Much longer and you'll have to pay to sponsor this space."

He pushed a chocolate walnut brownie in front of me. "My mother says you'll like this. Family recipe. Take it to go."

I tore off the plastic wrap and bit into it. "A McDonald family recipe, you mean."

Justin banged his hand down on the counter. "I'm done with all the bullshit, Laura. I read *Bloodstrains* after you shoved that old yearbook at me. *She* won't explain anything, and suddenly *you're* always here, you and Fabrizzio."

Where was Nick anyway? Not a single text complaining I left this morning without him.

"Detective Fabrizzio first came here on a hunch. Too many things pointed us to this place, and then John Poole was murdered, and I had to see for myself. We had no idea who we'd find here. And when we did find her, we didn't recognize her. But she left breadcrumbs for us to follow. You know that, don't you?"

He pinched off a piece of the brownie and popped it into his mouth. "When I was little, Mom would crush the walnuts and fold the cocoa into the batter and tell me how much her best friend loved her mother's brownies. I'd ask her about that friend and about my grandma, and she'd try to hide her tears. 'Sometimes, people you love are far away,' she'd say. 'That doesn't mean you don't still love them. Doesn't mean they don't still love you.'"

We did still love Kate, her family, and Jane, and I; Nick, too, in his way. "I knew Kate wasn't dead. I would have sensed when she left this life, I was sure of it."

"That's why you wrote the book."

I snatched the last piece of the brownie and savored it. "I should have written it sooner."

Justin backed off the stool. "Wouldn't have prevented the ALS, or changed what that old bastard did to her. Now, she's determined to watch him every minute, even if she has to sit in that hospital for days. You can't stop Christine Anderson when she's put a plan in motion, trust me."

What plan? I spent six hours with her earlier. I followed her as she headed off to see Chelsea and the visiting nurse less than two hours ago.

"You took your mother to the hospital? Isn't your grandfather still unconscious?"

"They transferred him from the ICU to a critical care unit. He was still out of it when I dropped Mom off at his room. The state police want him alert as soon as possible, so they can charge him and move him to a hospital with more security. Alert or not, the doctors want him stronger before he's moved."

Strong enough to escape from a transport van? He always got away. Kate knew that.

"Thank Hannah for lunch." I tossed a ten-dollar bill onto the counter, grabbed my coat, and ran to my car.

I dictated a text to Nick as I left for the hospital.

"Where are you? Still in Aldridge?"

"Still here, working with the locals, laying out all the reasons in two states why Anderson should be transported to a prison hospital without delay," he replied. "A judge wants to review our case ASAP. See you when I see you."

That wouldn't do. I needed to speak to him now. I dialed his cellphone number as I pulled away from the diner.

"I can't talk."

"Two minutes, that's all I need."

Nick sighed. I tried to articulate my doubts.

"Those 'Remember Connecticut' letters are part of the Jason Goldstein cold case file, correct?"

"Elsie, you know they are. It's in your book."

"But they were *officially* excluded from The Challenge fire investigation. Why?"

Kate had written stories about the connection between Jason's murder and the letters. Nick and I knew she was convinced Andrew Michaels was responsible.

"We ran prints on the letters the *Informed Student* got, but not a single one was a match for a fire victim—not Andrew

Michaels, not Judy Wright or Barry Poole, who we knew were aware of them. Also, there was no match for any of the Challenge residents who weren't home at the time of the fire," he said. "We knew how the fire started, and Michaels had been declared dead, so the letters were beside the point. We shoved them back into the Goldstein murder book and left them there."

"You don't think John Poole sent them. Kate doesn't think Judge Endicott did, though she just told me she believes the judge knew what Michaels was up to at The Challenge."

"Think about it, Laura. There's a bus station near the university. Why wouldn't Michaels just hop a Greyhound and get himself to Groton, Connecticut? Dump the letters in a mailbox, dump the gloves he wore when he wrote and mailed them, and head right back to the Challenge. His motives might have been twisted, and the trips might have been time-consuming, but it wasn't hard to pull that off."

Easy enough. Nick was right.

"So give the letters up as a loose end we might never be able to tie up?"

"They're one more reminder how quickly this investigation went off the rails. Good motivation to do better now. Gotta run."

So did I.

I parked in a ten-minutes-only lot outside the emergency room. After lying my way through a gauntlet of state troopers bent on keeping me away from Philip's room, I found Kate in her wheelchair, blocking its doorway—a strange last link in the chain of custody.

Trooper Wozniak was officially standing guard. "Not sure why she's so far away from him. You would think she'd want to be closer, in case he wakes up. But she's been in that spot the whole time, sort of like his shadow."

It was likely Kate had used her more sophisticated computer to hack into a video surveillance system. *Shadow* was a good way to describe her. I pushed the wheelchair farther into the room.

"Go away," she protested.

"Don't want me here? Too bad. Justin sent me."

"No, he didn't."

Wozniak rapped on the doorjamb. "I need to use the facilities. My mid-shift relief isn't due for a few more minutes."

"Phil's unconscious, Scott. I'm paralyzed," Kate said. "Unless you're expecting somebody to bust him out, Laura has it covered."

Once he left, opportunity knocked for me. I squeezed past the wheelchair and stooped until Kate and I were eye to eye. "What are you up to?"

Kate steered around me, clipping my left knee as she moved closer to the monitors and the IV pole connected to the man everyone thought was her father-in-law. She accelerated and snagged the IV line, pulling the pole down into the few feet separating us. A bag suspended from the pole spewed clear liquid onto the floor. Kate reversed, dislodging a second bag. I pounced on the call button wrapped around the side rails of the bed.

The wheelchair jerked forward again, ripping off a sensor. Buzzers beeped and bells clanged. Nurses and aides raced into the room, Scott Wozniak right behind them.

"Get these women out of here!" an older nurse shouted at Scott. He pushed past them, practically lifting the wheelchair to get it away from the patient.

"What the hell just happened? Miss Chris, are you all right?"

I couldn't see Kate's face as I took over the chair from Scott. "A mechanical glitch with the wheelchair controls, I bet. Miss Chris beats it up pretty hard, doesn't she? I'll take her someplace quieter, so she can call Justin about a repair."

Suddenly, doctors and more nurses were running toward us, dodging the chair and steering a defibrillator into Philip's room.

A crash team. He must have coded.

"Are you happy?" I whispered into Kate's ear.

"If he's dead, supremely," she said. "But he isn't."

I resisted the urge to scream. "His heart just stopped, what are you talking about?"

Within minutes, the crash team was dispersing, headed back to their stations. "My father-in-law, is he alive?" Kate asked.

A nurse turned, startled by something in the simulated voice. "Just a problem with the monitors, but we gave Mr. Anderson a shot of epinephrine anyway. Seems that as soon as he's fully conscious, Trooper Wozniak will be arresting him."

I watched Kate's hands, half expecting to see two thumbs up.

The attending physician argued yet again, to maybe the fifth person in the police chain of command above Scott, that Christine Anderson, the next of kin, was present and was witnessing his strong objection to any attempt to move Philip to the more secure prison hospital in Middletown.

"Mr. Anderson needs to stay in *this* hospital until his condition stabilizes further," the doctor shouted into Scott's cellphone. "With third-degree burns on both hands and his abdomen and groin area, he needs extensive skin grafting soon to prevent infection. More immediately, he's in considerable pain even with medication."

Scott took his phone and stepped back, which allowed me to wheel Kate around the frustrated doctor and closer to her supposed father-in-law. "Pain isn't usually a problem, is it, Phil? Ask him, doctor."

I pictured the old Kate's sweetest insincere smile.

"Get this bitch out of here! Where's my grandson?" Philip roared. "And who is this other woman? Why is she here in my room?"

My own insincere smile shined brightly. "Mr. Anderson, you remember me, I'm Laura Cunningham. We met a few weeks ago. You gave me a lift in your truck to spare me from walking down the highway in a storm."

"Phil, you don't want me stranded here alone when the police take you away." As poor-little-me performances via assistive computer went, Kate's was utterly believable.

Except Philip knew this act. "Since when can the bitch talk? She hasn't talked in years."

He looked and sounded like a confused old man. I wasn't entirely sure he was acting. "Maybe Christine is more eager to talk because she has someone who wants to hear her story, Mr. Anderson. I'm very interested in hearing *and* telling it."

EMTs arrived with a gurney and a representative of the county Sheriff's Department, displacing hospital staff.

"Hear me out," the doctor said. "His blood pressure is dangerously high. The stress of his injuries and the pain are taxing his heart. Moving a patient with burns like his is against all medical advice. Moving a man his age with those burns is absolutely unacceptable."

A local TV news reporter, and the cameraman behind her, jammed into the room's doorway. "Doctor, are you saying the authorities are jeopardizing their own case if they move Philip Anderson today?"

The doctor waved his arms like a runway attendant. "Away, all of you! Trooper Wozniak, help me here."

The wheelchair slid away from my hands. "You're not in pain, Philip. Tell the doctor," Kate urged.

"Ask him, Doctor," I jumped in. "Given the circumstances, you want to make an informed decision."

"Sell popcorn while you're at it, and make a million, Doc," Philip snarled. "And no, I'm not in pain, so you can send this witch away happy."

"I'm happy if you're happy," Kate said.

Philip's motives, I understood: Being moved was his best hope for escape. Kate's weren't as clear.

The Sheriff's Department rep handed the doctor a clipboard with a form to sign. Scott unfastened the shackles holding Philip's legs to the bed, and the two EMTs negotiated his transfer to the gurney. Scott replaced the shackles and encircled Phil's chest with a strap.

"You will burn in hell for this, all of you!" Philip shouted, his head raised as far as he could manage. "Jesus will see to my protection and wreak his vengeance on my enemies!"

His eyes locked on Kate and me. "Find a real way to run this time, bitches. When I catch you, I'll deal with you harshly, I assure you."

An EMT pushed him flat and whisked the gurney past us, toward the elevator.

"I look forward to seeing you try," Kate said, when I was the only one left to hear.

Chapter Thirty-eight

Laura

Connecticut, January 2017

I pulled the hood of my parka low on my face, and casually walked around the press pack that had pinned police and prosecutors tight to the hospital's front doors. Fat, wet snowflakes fell on them all: the team with the guns, the team with the briefcases, and the team with the notebooks and microphones desperate to get the story, get it filed, and get out of the damn weather fast. Getting away, period, was what I needed to do, before someone recognized me.

The flashing lights of the prison ambulance were just clearing the hospital grounds. Ahead of it, I saw the taillights of two Connecticut State Police cruisers, behind it were two more. Scooting along the edge of the parking lot was Kate, faster than I moved on foot. No one noticed her now that Justin was there to sound off to the reporters.

"Without his attorney present, they have no right to move my grandfather. None," Justin shouted for at least the third time. "My mother may not have realized her words were being construed as consent to move him."

That was crap, and Justin knew it. Kate had provoked Philip, daring him to make a run for it. He might be crazy enough to try—he had succeeded twice before.

My phone buzzed. "Trapped here with state cops and lawyers," Nick texted. "Can't see the wheelchair anymore. Don't let her get away."

I spotted Nick in the second row. I was on my own.

I sprinted after the wheelchair then stopped, so cold I could barely breathe. I was closer to my car than to Kate, so I jogged to the emergency room parking lot, got behind the wheel, and hit the gas hard. I caught up to her on the access road to the highway and pulled onto the shoulder in front of her. She banged into my rear bumper.

"Good thing Volvos are sturdy."

I jumped out of the car. "What's your plan, McDonald? I know you have one."

She backed up the chair, angling it to get around me. "Go home. Write an epilogue. A whole new book. Christine Anderson dies in the end."

"Protecting me won't bring him to justice, and you can't do it alone."

"We'll see." She swung the wheelchair out onto the road, headed for the interstate. I held my breath until she was back on the shoulder again.

"Wait!" I ran behind her. "Give me time to get the keys to your van from Justin. I'll drive you to the prison hospital, so you can see Philip didn't get away. God damn it, stop!"

She ignored me and motored on. Ankle deep in slush, I slipped twice before I reached my car again. Short of a truck flattening Kate, I might be the only thing that could come between her and Philip Anderson.

I waited forever for a break in the traffic. The Volvo fishtailed as I got back onto the road, and as soon as I maneuvered into the passing lane, I floored it until I was doing sixty. The prison ambulance had about a twenty-minute head start—no way Kate would get to it before I did.

Unless that was part of her plan, for me to be able to say truthfully that I didn't know what she was thinking. Was Chelsea in the van somewhere, waiting for Kate? Was Justin's protest at the hospital an intentional distraction?

An overhead sign flashed, "REDUCE SPEED." I eased into the right lane again, eased up on the accelerator, and rode the brake as everybody in front of me slowed to a crawl. In the rearview mirror, I saw the wheelchair bump along. Kate passed me and kept moving.

All at once, my face smacked the steering wheel. Something slashed my left cheek as the airbag inflated. I flattened myself against the seat.

It was dark in the car; the airbag blocked the dashboard lights. I fumbled for the button on the side of the driver's seat and, digging my heels into the floormat, slid back as far as I could. Something wet, probably blood, dripped onto the airbag and onto my hand as I pressed gently along my throbbing cheek and forehead. I tested the skin around my left eye. Jesus, that hurt.

I stretched to my right, searching for the rearview mirror, but the airbag had twisted it away. I was rear-ended, but by what? And my car must have rear-ended someone else. Sirens screamed all around, but I couldn't see; my front view was obstructed, my back view unavailable. I slipped my head under the shoulder harness and freed myself from the seatbelt. I tried the door and got it open halfway. Cold air and snow blasted my aching head. I tucked my chin, angled one shoulder out, then the other, and wiggled free.

My phone and purse were buried under the airbag, as was the ignition key. I had no idea what time it was or how long I might have been unconscious. Headlights blurred the road behind my car; taillights and brake lights shone ahead. No traffic moved in the opposite direction. Was the highway shut down? When my eyes adjusted more, I twisted again to look around me.

I made out the silhouette of an SUV crisscrossed on the road. Did it swerve to avoid my car?

A fresh layer of ice coating the highway slush mocked the tread of my boots. I gripped the side of my car until I reached the place where the front bumper was embedded into the rear end of a station wagon. I inched along to that driver's door. I pulled on it, and the cabin light revealed splashes of blood and a woman slumped behind the airbag. There was a gash across her forehead, but her eyes were open. I spotted a purse near the brake pedal. Inside it, I found no phone, but there was a tissue. I pressed it into her bleeding hand.

"Can you breathe? Is the airbag pressing down on your chest?" The woman shook her head. "Can you move your legs?" The woman nodded.

A loud bang startled us both, the shock of something slamming into the SUV that maybe had managed not to hit my car or hers. "You'll be okay if I walk up a little farther? I want to see what's going on and find help."

"Go," she whispered. "Be careful."

"I'll do my best."

My face felt like it was on fire, and pain jolted through my left leg. But I moved.

Past a sedan with a crying toddler strapped in the backseat, her crying mother equally bereft, shrieking into her cellphone; neither seemed injured. Past a half-dozen SUVs and pickups and a refrigerated truck illustrated with dancing pints of ice cream. Flashing emergency lights came into view.

Ambulances raced up the open traffic lane. People shambled along the road, drenched like I was, zombies covered in blood and snow and snot. All of us trying to get closer to the front of the chain of wrecks, to see what had happened.

The nearest emergency vehicle idled at least four cars in front of me, its rotating red light glinting off metal at the shoulder's edge. Closer to me, two young people pointed down the slope. The young man shouted into his cellphone. The woman moved her phone's flashlight back and forth.

"We think we see someone, but whoever it is isn't moving," he said into the phone.

"Hello! Can you hear me down there?" she called out.

I squeezed between cars to get to them and followed the flashlight beam. Kate's wheelchair was tipped over onto its side, empty.

"That's my friend! That's her wheelchair," I hollered, waving at them. "She can't move, but she has a computer that helps her communicate."

"If she's conscious, or even alive," the woman said, handing me her phone. "If the computer wasn't crushed on the way down."

The flashlight illuminated snow-covered brush and rocks and who knew what else. I tucked the phone into my boot, sat in the snow, and inched forward. Not a sheer drop by the looks of it, but a very slick, bumpy slope.

"Come back before you kill yourself," the man shouted. "They're sending a ski rescue team that's used to these hills."

"There are people in the cars behind us who are hurt, too, tell them that," I yelled back. "But let them know that it's Miss Chris down here. Everybody knows her."

How long would it take a rescue team to navigate the highway crush? Too many banged-up wrecks, too many first responders trying to get through the only free driving lane.

I blinked away tears, made the sign of the cross, and dug my frozen fingers into frigid earth.

A few pushes, a few more, and then the pile of whatever it was I was sitting on shifted and I plunged through the darkness. My parka snagged on something. I pulled the coat free, checked my boot for the phone, and pushed farther down. I slammed my beat-up left leg into something hard and pitched forward onto a sharp point. The edge of Kate's laptop.

Then I saw Kate.

I had to think, not panic. Deep breaths, deep breaths, I watched them turn to mist as I exhaled. I saw nothing that looked like mist where Kate lay, a yard or so away. I nudged the laptop and inched along on my belly behind it, hoping to move the computer near Kate rather than push it past her head, or worse, out of reach.

Slowly, slowly.

She watched me as, at last, I stretched flat next to her. With one hand, I lifted Kate's head; with the other, I tugged on the plastic coil that had tethered the computer to the wheelchair, so the cracked screen faced her. It activated.

"Thank U," the computer typed.

"Help is coming."

"Love. Justin. Love. U."

Her cheek was so cold beneath my fingers. "Love you too, Kate. Always."

Her eyes closed. I felt for a pulse, but she was gone.

"One dead. Caucasian female in her mid-forties identified as Christine Anderson, known to be ALS-disabled," the EMT sitting next to me shouted into his radio over the wailing siren. "One injured. Mid-forties Caucasian female, identified as Laura Cunningham. Probable hypothermia, frostbite, concussion, laceration on left cheek, contusions. Probable strained left knee, probable fracture of the left orbital, the eye near it swollen half shut. Requesting an ophthalmologist at the emergency room."

With my good eye, I stared at Kate's body, covered with a dark green blanket. I sobbed and shivered and clutched her computer to my chest. The EMT wrapped an identical blanket around me. "Should be any minute now," he again assured me, but the ambulance didn't move. I had no idea where we were, but it couldn't be very far from where they found us. I tried to stand, and almost fell.

"Please sit, Ms. Cunningham. Ambulances with more seriously injured people have to get through before us. Then we'll be on our way."

"What happened to Philip Anderson?" I demanded.

"Who's that? It was just you and Christine Anderson on that slope." He gently clasped my shoulders to lower me back onto the stretcher.

"Did the prison convoy get to Middletown?"

"I don't know, but I can ask." The EMT radioed someone and listened long enough to worry me.

"Dispatch says the convoy's still up ahead. A tractor-trailer jackknifed, then its cab flipped on the ice and skidded into the lead car, and all the other vehicles plowed into one another. They've gotten the fatalities and injured out. They just need to tow a few more of the vehicles so the rest of us can get through."

"Fatalities. How many dead?"

The EMT asked and held up four fingers.

I tried to focus: How many came out of Philip's room with him after they kicked Kate and me out? Four state troopers, two EMTs, two prison guards, and Philip, was that right? Nine people, four dead, but maybe the driver of the tractor-trailer died too.

I didn't like those odds.

"What do you think you're doing?"

"Leaving against medical advice." I pushed open the ambulance door and jumped down, pain stabbing through my knee as I landed.

I followed taillights and passed ambulances idling in a row along what had to be the center line of the highway. I climbed onto, then over, the trunk of a hatchback, seeking what I presumed was the safer side of the road since I was half-lame and half-blind and it was darker than anything and twice as cold as before.

I limped through, leaning on cars for support, four different ones before a flashlight blinded my functioning eye.

"Laura, what the hell?" The voice called back to someone, "She's here, I see her!"

Stacey Poole Endicott, Connecticut State Police, had fingered me.

"Don't try to stop me. I have to find Philip Anderson."

Stacey tugged me past a recreational vehicle. "Come on, come with me."

I shook her off. "I am not going to sit in some ambulance. I'll kill him myself, I swear."

Handcuffs clapped onto my wrists. "You're coming with me, Cunningham. Argue and see how fast I charge you with intent to assault. Not one word or I'll do it, *I swear*."

She led me from the automotive tangle to the police barrier cordoning off the southbound lane of the roadway. The tractor-trailer lay partly on its side there. A police cruiser was wheels-up nearby. Another cruiser sat silently, welded to the prison ambulance's front bumper by ice and firefighting foam.

"Scott Wozniak is dead. So are the driver of that rig and his partner in the passenger seat."

"That's three. Four died. Who's the fourth?"

Stacey opened the rear door of the ambulance, helped me up, and lifted a blanket. Strapped to the gurney he left the hospital on was Philip Anderson.

"The doctor was right: The old man's heart stopped within minutes of leaving the hospital. He was dead before the truck hit the convoy."

She didn't know she was looking at her father's body. Didn't know Justin could be her brother.

I sank to the cold ambulance floor, knocking my bad leg with Kate's laptop. Tears stung both eyes, the good one and the broken one.

Chapter Thirty-nine

Laura

Connecticut, January 2017

David gently woke me. I heard his voice, felt his hand around mine, but Nick's face was the first I saw. Déjà vu, but not quite: Drew slept at my feet; Damian was in a chair, snoring the way he did when his sinuses acted up.

"The joint investigative task force formed by law enforcement in Pennsylvania and Connecticut has determined, through physical and forensic evidence, that Philip Anderson, who formerly lived in both states but whose last address was in Maine, is actually Mitchell Aldridge," Nick said from the TV mounted on the wall across from my bed. "In the seventies, Aldridge was convicted in Connecticut of murdering his ex-wife, but was believed to have died several years later after escaping from prison. In Pennsylvania, Aldridge is believed to have been responsible for setting the fire at The Challenge in 1992 that killed eleven people."

The television showed reporters aiming tape recorders and mics and video cameras in Nick's direction. "More recently, last fall," he continued, "Mitchell Aldridge was charged in absentia in connection with the murder of John Poole at Poole's Bradford, Pennsylvania, home. Earlier this year, he is believed to have ambushed the owner and patrons of a coffeehouse in the university town where The Challenge had been located, fatally shooting two women and injuring thirteen. Here in Connecticut, police had Aldridge in custody in connection with a cabin fire and the death of a private security guard.

"Aldridge, who was seventy-five years old, died in a prison transport ambulance yesterday of an apparent heart attack. I should add here, however, that police are investigating the possibility that telemetry equipment at the hospital where he was being treated for third-degree burns may have been hacked."

David muted the TV. "Do you want to hear more?"

I shook my head and immediately regretted it. I shot a hand up to my left eye. A plastic shield covered everything from my eyebrow to my jaw.

"How long have I been out?"

David leaned a little more to my right, so I could see him better. "Six hours? Probably not long enough." He yawned, looking more exhausted than I could remember. "You were awake but dopey by the time we got here last night, laughing about your bad eye and your bad leg, which was good because Drew was pretty frightened. Nick had called the house to explain why you rushed out of Philly the way you did, and then hours later he called again to say you'd been injured and that Kate was dead. I didn't even know you'd found her. Nick told me to ask Steve."

He was hurt I hadn't shared the information with him. "I didn't tell Steve, Nick did. He thought someone else should know, David, just in case something happened."

"Like barreling down a snowy hill on your rear end to get to Kate? Amazing you didn't hit a tree."

Exactly like that, but more.

"After what happened to John Poole, I had to make myself more visible. I didn't want the killer coming after you and the boys."

"Explains Nick as bodyguard for the book tour in Maine."

I asked David to raise the bed so I could sit upright, inviting the pain in my head to duel the pain in my leg for supremacy. He upped the volume on the television.

Gathered at the microphones with Nick were Dixon Bott from the Pennsylvania State Police, some Connecticut state troopers, and the same prosecutors from the news briefing that followed Philip's arrest yesterday. But they weren't standing in front of the hospital in Aldridge.

"Where are we?"

"Hartford," David said. "They brought the less seriously injured people here—I asked, because this hospital is pretty far from the crash scene. The more severely injured went to Middletown. The fatalities too, I believe."

Damian partially appeared over my beat-up left leg. "There were so many people at the ER, Mom, we thought we'd never find you." He stepped around to the other side of the bed so I could see him, hug him. I kissed the top of his head and imagined what Justin must be going through.

The TV camera panned again to the reporters. Among them was Steve's former student, the one whose articles were instrumental in getting the fire depositions unsealed. She wanted details about Christine Anderson's death after a fall from her wheelchair near the scene of the highway pileup involving Mitchell Aldridge's prison ambulance.

"Is it true," the reporter asked, "that Christine Anderson was actually Kate McDonald, who has been missing since the 1992 Challenge fire in Pennsylvania, and who was the subject of Laura Cunningham's recent book about the fire, *Bloodstrains*?"

Bott stepped to the center mic. "All evidence points to that, yes. Also to the abduction, rape, and decades-long terrorizing of Ms. McDonald by Mitchell Aldridge. We will be interviewing her son, Justin Anderson, soon to get the full picture of how the fire at The Challenge led to his mother's ordeal at Aldridge's hands and how that situation met its conclusion yesterday here in Connecticut."

It wouldn't be just an epilogue. It *would* be another book entirely. Kate was right about that.

Chapter Forty

Laura
Suburban Philadelphia, May 2017

Two funerals, two weeks apart. Two groups of mourners. Some grieving a woman they had seen for years but had never known completely. Others finally laying to rest the daughter they had lost a long time ago, only to find her now, after her death.

It wasn't fair to compare their farewells, but I couldn't help it.

The first, in Connecticut, was a celebration of life filled with warm tributes to Christine Anderson. If the citizens of Aldridge were shocked to learn she was not who she portrayed herself to be, they didn't let on to Nick or me. They loved Miss Chris, missed her terribly, and though they wished they had been able to help more, they understood the reasons behind her secret. She was their friend, period.

It was fitting that the memorial be at Christine's diner, which Justin had decided to sell once his mother's estate was settled. Saying that his memories were all the legacy he needed, Justin had offered half the sale proceeds as compensation to the wife and children of the security guard who was Mitchell Aldridge's final victim. That only seemed right, everyone agreed.

This second funeral, at a Catholic cemetery outside Philadelphia, was beyond joyless, as sterile as the labs that officially confirmed Christine Anderson's true identity as Kate McDonald. Time had dimmed the smiles that once came readily with memories of Kate. Too many tears had already been shed; too many years had passed without a single word from her. Her death, and what they now knew to be the truth about those intervening years, were too much for the McDonalds to take in all at once.

Holding a white rose and parroting the priest's recitation of the Lord's Prayer, I stood with Kate's relatives, and as far away as I could from the Bakers. Jane's family refused to discuss her violent death. Not with Steve Brightman, despite his and Jane's relationship, and certainly not with me. They blamed me for Jane's murder. They weren't wrong, and that fact floated, acknowledged, within the small space between us.

The graveside service that followed Kate's requiem Mass was short, thankfully. No more allusions to lost lambs, no more declarations that the Lord was my shepherd. Perhaps I should not want, but I wanted plenty.

Nick navigated the crowd at its edges, along with David and Steve and Steve's grad students Laird and Angel, whom Nick had brought onto the Mitchell Aldridge task force. He had wanted Stacey, too, but the recent revelations about her father's identity made that impossible.

Damian and Drew stood closer to me, close enough to hear the prayers while holding white carnations uncertainly. They tossed them onto Kate's casket when instructed.

So did Justin, sandwiched between the McDonalds and me. He was Kate's son and Barry Poole's, the DNA tests revealed when Justin insisted he needed to know for certain which man had fathered him. But he was also my son now, a child of my blood in so many ways. He didn't resist my need to mother him. Maybe it was his way of steeling himself against whatever else lay ahead.

The multistate task force had shifted its investigative focus to the Maine refuge for troubled teens Philip Anderson started six years earlier, when he finally left Connecticut at Kate's insistence—his freedom in exchange for hers. Her ALS, and its prospects for silencing her, offered Philip a sense of security Kate had capitalized on as long as she could. Whatever additional evil he did in Maine, under who knew how many more aliases, was the investigators' worry now as they accounted for those years, as well as the years after Mitchell Aldridge's prison break and the ones that followed Kate's initial escape from him as Andrew Michaels at the construction trailer.

The world wanted to know who Aldridge was and what drove him to kill. Those questions were not my questions. I had found my answers.

How much I was lying to myself because of them, I hadn't figured out yet. My publisher was clamoring for me to send the material that would flesh out an expanded edition of *Bloodstrains*, including that predicted epilogue summarizing how Nick and I found Kate. Thus far, I had ignored all entreaties for a second book, so I could move past the chaos the first had unleashed.

Reluctantly, I added my flower to those already strewn atop Kate's casket, the last person to say goodbye. As we had arranged, Justin followed his newfound family to the funeral director's limousine. He would ride with them to the funeral luncheon. The rest of us would be along shortly. In my case, also reluctantly.

"Laura's decided to take a leave of absence and also cut back on the *Bloodstrains* appearances she's been doing," I heard David tell some of our newspaper colleagues lingering at the cemetery. "I'm not sure working wouldn't be the better way to go—it seemed to be a good distraction as her injuries were healing. But she says she wants to stay home with the boys for a while. Says she needs to sit and think."

"With Mom, thinking can be dangerous. *Not* thinking can too," Damian said, quite a bit louder than his stepfather. "No telling what kind of trouble she'll get into."

I limped toward the place where the group waited for me, my leg still aching from my ride down that treacherous roadside slope. I squeezed in close to my mouthy older son, hugged him, then bent to kiss his little brother's head.

"I've gotten into enough trouble to last a lifetime. I'll do my best to avoid it from now on."

Steve, Laird and Angel looked at me, then at Nick.

"What do you think?" I asked. "Is that possible, Detective?"

He glanced up from his phone and winked.

"For you to avoid trouble? They say people can change if they want to. Do you, Laura?"

Nick waved to our son and walked to his Jeep, skipping further memorial moments in favor of another long road trip to New England.

I didn't run after him.

I wanted to. Kate had brought us together a second time. That had to mean something.

Maybe something worth investigating.

Joanne McLaughlin
Bio

Joanne McLaughlin began telling stories in second grade, creating superhero fan fiction in the Philadelphia rowhouse where she grew up.

Since then, Joanne has worked in public media and newspapers in Philadelphia, upstate New York, and northeastern Ohio, involved in topics ranging from politics and public health to fashion and financial markets, as well as Pulitzer Prize-finalist architecture criticism and a Peabody Award-finalist podcast.

Her published works include the vampire trilogy *Never Before Noon, Never Until Now,* and *Never More Human.* A Penn State graduate, Joanne currently lives in Philadelphia, in a different rowhouse on the other side of town.

Joanne McLaughlin's

Vampires of the Court of Cruelty series

Never Before Noon (Book One):
Chloe Hart is lured back home by her legendary rock star parents, only to learn they are vampires. What does that make her?

Never Until Now (Book Two):
As the daughter of rock-and-roll legends, Chloe Hart can't escape their legacy. Nor can she ignore the horror her vampire father has unleashed.

Never More Human (Book Three)
Where does duty to family end? When her vampire mother stirs up an emotional storm, how much more can Chloe Hart take?

Other publications from Celestial Echo Press

TIME BLINKED

Just like Dorothy in the Wizard of Oz, college athlete Bobby spends his days with those he loves and stays close to home. But unlike Dorothy, when Bobby's "tornado" bushwhacks his world, it doesn't move him into a fantastical realm of color and delightful beasts. He is propelled into a complicated past, where his dreams come true through a somewhat mystifying, somewhat terrifying wrinkle.

DRACULAND

A New York City real estate developer decides to buy Dracula's Castle in Romania and turn it into a theme park. Not her best idea.

THE TWOFER COMPENDIUM

"Twins are said to share special bonds, understand each other's unspoken communication, speak their own languages, even possess powers of ESP. Their double-ness continues to fascinate the rest of us. Adored or abhorred, sheltered or shunned, twins have universally and perpetually aroused attention and curiosity. It was that fascination that inspired this collection of twin-themed stories. In them, you'll find all matter of twins: the good, the bad, the fantastic, the fearsome, the magical, the envious, the secretive, the devious, and more. Being a twin. Fun, right? Think about it. *What could go wrong?"*

--From the Foreword by Merry Jones

THE TRENCH COAT CHRONICLES

This murder mystery anthology is dedicated to Sam Spade, Hercule Poirot, and Dick Tracy, as well as to all the writers of hard-boiled detective stories of years past, many of whom formed the basis for the crime mysteries we read today. Enjoy this wide variety of storylines, each of which includes criminals, victims – and trench coats.

All Celestial Echo Press publications are available at Barnes & Noble and other fine bookshops, and online at amazon.com.